GALAXIES

THE
RUINS OF DANTOOINE

Other Titles by Voronica Whitney-Robinson

NOVELS
Spectre of the Black Rose *(with James Lowder)*
Halls of Stormweather
Sands of the Soul
Crimson Gold

GAME PRODUCTS
Kindred of the Ebony Kingdom *(contributing author)*
Ravenloft Gazetteer IV *(contributing author)*

STAR WARS
GALAXIES

THE
RUINS OF DANTOOINE

VORONICA
WHITNEY-ROBINSON
WITH HADEN BLACKMAN

BALLANTINE BOOKS • NEW YORK

Star Wars Galaxies: *The Ruins of Dantooine* is a work of fiction. Names, places, and incidents either are a product of the author's imagination or are used fictitiously.

A Del Rey® Book
Published by The Random House Publishing Group
Copyright © 2004 by Lucasfilm Ltd. & ® or ™ where indicated.
All rights reserved. Used under authorization.

All rights reserved under International and Pan-American Copyright Conventions. Published in the United States by The Random House Publishing Group, a division of Random House, Inc., New York, and simultaneously in Canada by Random House of Canada Limited, Toronto.

Del Rey is a registered trademark and the Del Rey colophon is a trademark of Random House, Inc.

www.starwars.com
www.delreydigital.com

ISBN 0-345-47066-4

Manufactured in the United States of America

First Edition: January 2004

OPM 10 9 8 7 6 5 4 3 2 1

For my mother, Inge M. Whitney, who in the summer of '77 said to me, "Have you heard about a movie called *Star Wars*? I think you're going to want to see it."

THE STAR WARS NOVELS TIMELINE

6.5-7.5 YEARS AFTER
STAR WARS: A New Hope

X-Wing:
Rogue Squadron
Wedge's Gamble
The Krytos Trap
The Bacta War
Wraith Squadron
Iron Fist
Solo Command

8 YEARS AFTER STAR WARS: A New Hope
The Courtship of Princess Leia
A Forest Apart
Tatooine Ghost

9 YEARS AFTER STAR WARS: A New Hope

The Thrawn Trilogy:
Heir to the Empire
Dark Force Rising
The Last Command

X-Wing: Isard's Revenge

11 YEARS AFTER STAR WARS: A New Hope
I, Jedi

The Jedi Academy Trilogy:
Jedi Search
Dark Apprentice
Champions of the Force

12-13 YEARS AFTER STAR WARS: A New Hope
Children of the Jedi
Darksaber
Planet of Twilight
X-Wing: Starfighters of Adumar

14 YEARS AFTER STAR WARS: A New Hope
The Crystal Star

16-17 YEARS AFTER STAR WARS: A New Hope

The Black Fleet Crisis Trilogy:
Before the Storm
Shield of Lies
Tyrant's Test

17 YEARS AFTER STAR WARS: A New Hope
The New Rebellion

18 YEARS AFTER STAR WARS: A New Hope

The Corellian Trilogy:
Ambush at Corellia
Assault at Selonia
Showdown at Centerpoint

19 YEARS AFTER STAR WARS: A New Hope

The Hand of Thrawn Duology:
Specter of the Past
Vision of the Future

22 YEARS AFTER STAR WARS: A New Hope

Junior Jedi Knights series
Survivor's Quest

23-24 YEARS AFTER STAR WARS: A New Hope

Young Jedi Knights series

25-30 YEARS AFTER
STAR WARS: A New Hope

The New Jedi Order:
Vector Prime
Dark Tide I: Onslaught
Dark Tide II: Ruin
Agents of Chaos I: Hero's Trial
Agents of Chaos II: Jedi Eclipse
Balance Point
Recovery
Edge of Victory I: Conquest
Edge of Victory II: Rebirth
Star by Star
Dark Journey
Enemy Lines I: Rebel Dream
Enemy Lines II: Rebel Stand
Traitor
Destiny's Way
Ylesia
Force Heretic I: Remnant
Force Heretic II: Refugee
Force Heretic III: Reunion
The Final Prophecy
The Unifying Force

ACKNOWLEDGMENTS

ACKNOWLEDGMENTS

I would like to thank Eban Trey, my favorite Rodian, for showing me around the galaxy, and my husband, Roderic, my favorite test player. And a special thank-you to Sue Rostoni and Haden Blackman for all their information and guidance. Finally, to Shelly Shapiro for steering me through the whole project.

PROLOGUE

A light rain misted the hillside. Other than that slight patter, the only sound disturbing the evening was the sudden cry of the peko peko. The large, blue-skinned reptavian's pitiful squawk carried across the still lake before stopping as suddenly as it had begun.

"The tusk-cats must be hunting," Inquisitor Loam Redge said quietly to himself, smiling at the idea of the sleek, fawn-colored beasts circling the Retreat. Peko pekos weren't the only thing that the large predators could kill; simply the opening course.

The cloaked human stood alone on the stone balcony overlooking the placid lake and the hills beyond. For the last few moments, he had watched the final glow of the setting sun turn the world a brief, shimmering pink. As soon as the molten ball had disappeared, though, the sky had turned several shades of gray, from dirty white to steel. The colors layered themselves one on top of the other, so it was impossible to discern where one began and another ended. And then the rains had come.

1

With a parting glance toward the twinkling lights of Moenia off to the east, the Inquisitor returned inside, where he brushed at his cloaks furiously, as though their exposure to the abrupt shower had somehow sullied them. He smoothed back his rich brown hair and stood with his spine at ramrod attention.

No one knew how old the Inquisitor was, and Redge preferred it remain that way. There were precious few secrets in the Empire, and he liked to keep as many as he could.

Inquisitor Loam Redge was one of those rare individuals who derived great pleasure from his work. Finding those sensitive to the Force, torturing them, and destroying them were his topmost priorities, and they also gave him the greatest joy. He was very good at his vocation, and he always looked as though he was enjoying a private joke when he was at his busiest. This twisted happiness had, over time, etched its mark on his face in the form of the faintest crinkles near the outer edges of his dirt-colored eyes. Other than that, his face was mostly unlined. He might have been thirty, he might have been fifty.

When he was satisfied that he looked properly groomed, Inquisitor Redge moved out into the hallway. He padded silently across the plush, gold-trimmed maroon carpeting that lined the walkway. It was so thick, he barely heard the MSE-6 that almost scurried past his feet. The tiny, black, rectangular droids littered the Emperor's Retreat, as they did so many of the Imperial starships and ground installations throughout the galaxy. When the struggling company Rebaxan Columni had found itself facing imminent bankruptcy, it had offered the Empire a cut-rate deal on millions of them. Because the navy was extremely short on droids, it accepted. Now the Empire was crawling with the little automatons.

The small droid stopped a few feet beyond the Inquisitor and extended its heavy manipulator arm, clutching a rag. It scrubbed feverishly at some unseen smudge on the tan marble wall. Redge studied the droid for a moment as it buffed the already highly polished surface before slightly raising his cloaks up and moving past it. He found that the mechanism reminded him vaguely of a type of small vermin, and it disturbed him slightly.

There was no one else in the corridor, and he continued to revel in the quiet luxury of Emperor Palpatine's Retreat on Naboo. The Emperor's homeworld was calmly green, with areas of dense swamps broken up by rolling plains and verdant hills. Redge found the view soothing and knew that Emperor Palpatine had chosen the location for just that effect, not because of any maudlin sense of homeworld loyalty. While he had traveled to Theed, Moenia, Kaadara, Dee'ja Peak, and most of the smaller cities on the relatively peaceful planet, Inquisitor Redge had not yet ventured into the streams and canals that honeycombed the interior core of the planet. He had heard from a reliable source that it was possible for one to travel throughout the whole of

Naboo and never once stick a head above ground. At some point, he would have to explore the passageways himself, or send a trusted associate in his place. There was no way of knowing just what or who might be hiding down there. Naboo might be a haven not just for artists and architects, but for other, less desirable sorts as well.

Since establishing the Retreat, the Emperor had had little trouble planetside and seen no sign of the Rebellion, as far as Redge was aware. And Redge made it his business to know. Queen Kylantha had pledged and proven her loyalty many times over to Palpatine. But it irked the Inquisitor that she had not bothered to dissolve the Naboo Royal Advisory Council or to impose any real changes on the democratic structure of the government. If she were truly that loyal, then why hadn't she made the simple and overt gesture of disbanding the mock administration? Was it simply for her vanity, so that she could retain her empty title, or was there more to it? These questions nagged at the Inquisitor during the darkest hours of the night.

Rounding a corner, Redge arrived at the entrance of a cavernous, domed antechamber, large enough to hold several garrisons comfortably. Like the hallway that led up to it, the chamber was composed entirely of mottled pink-and-tan marble. Hanging along the walls and from the curved ceiling were banners of maroon and gold, like the rugs that carpeted the myriad hallways in the Retreat. Cylindrical gold lamps hung down, casting shining puddles of light on the polished floor. Along the far wall, two of the Emperor's personal guards, draped entirely in crimson, stood as sentries by the door the Inquisitor knew led to the Emperor's inner sanctum. Like avenging spirits, the guards remained steadfast in their duty, not moving a muscle. However, the vast chamber was not entirely devoid of movement.

Along the curved wall, near a small computer terminal, two stormtroopers stood. Unlike Redge, these troopers were relaxed in their stance. One leaned casually against the wall—no easy feat, given the fact that he was clad from head to toe in sparkling white armor. His colleague held only a slightly more militaristic pose. Neither man faced Redge, so both were unaware of his presence. Gliding over slightly, the Inquisitor could just hear their clipped conversation.

"I tell you," the one against the wall squawked to the other, "if they haven't started building a new one yet, they're not going to."

"It's only been about a year," the other replied with more static in his response, his transmitter clearly in need of some attention. "Equipment that awesome takes time to repair."

"I'm telling you," the first argued, "that if they haven't repaired or replaced the Death Star by now, they won't. And that should tell you something."

"What do you mean?" his comrade responded, and even Redge could hear the unease in the man's mechanized voice.

The first stormtrooper shifted his stance slightly. "I've heard rumors that the Rebellion is growing, becoming more powerful. If they could take out a weapon as great as the Death Star, there's no telling just how strong they really are. I think the Emperor is hiding that from us." His voice had dropped surprisingly low, considering he had to speak through a transmitter. "I think he's hiding many things."

"Talk like that will get you killed," his friend warned him.

"Or worse," Redge added in a gentle, melodic voice.

Both troopers turned suddenly, clearly caught off guard. That was the technique that Redge enjoyed the most: knock an opponent off balance and strike while he was teetering.

"Sir, I-I didn't know you were here," the first stammered.

"Obviously," Redge replied easily, enjoying the man's apparent discomfort. He decided to let him squirm a moment longer and so remained silent, forcing the trooper to try to dig his way out of his shallow grave.

"I'm sorry, sir, I meant no disservice. I was just explaining my concerns to—"

"Don't bother trying to explain anything to me, soldier," Redge interrupted coldly. "I know exactly what you were trying to explain to your 'friend' here." He nodded to the other man. "You feel our Emperor is keeping things from you, keeping you in the dark, so to speak?"

"It's just that—"

"It's just nothing," Redge warned him darkly, his facade of pleasantness a memory. "You know all that you need to know and nothing more or less, like the rest of us. To serve the Emperor is to trust in him completely and question nothing."

The stormtroopers remained silent, and the Inquisitor knew they were both too frightened to speak. That fear warmed his cold heart. The corners of his thin lips twitched in growing pleasure. He relaxed his stance ever so slightly.

"But," he graciously allowed, "you do make a good point in your own simplistic fashion."

"Sir?" the second soldier asked, and Redge knew they were fishing for anything to redeem themselves.

"The war is far from over," he admitted. "We do have the strength and the power to crush the Rebels; that much is obvious. However, the Rebels are devious, and like fanned rawls they have hidden themselves well and fashioned nests and lairs at the highest levels of power. Only when we drive them out and exterminate those hidden in our midst will victory truly be ours," Redge explained, momentarily caught up in his own fervor.

But before he could pursue the discussion further, he felt an almost imperceptible change in the air pressure of the chamber. The wiry hairs on his arms rose, and Redge knew the Emperor's door had slid open.

He turned his back on the two stormtroopers, their presence completely inconsequential now, and watched as a black figure separated himself from the impenetrable shadows of the doorway. As the stark figure moved forward, Redge felt his stomach turn and experienced a moment of vertigo. Sensitive as he was to the Force, the Inquisitor was nearly overwhelmed by the power of the man moving toward him.

The giant figure was covered from head to toe in obsidian armor. On his chest plate, a series of devices blinked blue and red, in time with his breathing and his heartbeat. His face was covered by a grotesque, helmeted breath mask that resembled the skull of some dark god. He moved swiftly yet deliberately toward the Inquisitor, his black cape billowing behind him. He looked like nothing so much as a winged bird of prey.

Redge vaguely saw, from the corner of his eyes, that the troopers snapped even straighter at the ominous presence than they had for him. He didn't notice much more as he sank gracefully to one knee in a deep, obsequious bow.

"My Lord Vader," he whispered with just the right amount of reverence.

"Rise, Inquisitor," Lord Vader ordered in a deep, rich voice, his orders punctuated by his unmistakable mechanized breathing. "Rise and walk with me."

Redge rose as gracefully as he had knelt and resisted the urge to shake out his cloaks yet again, refusing to appear foppish before a Dark Lord of the Sith. He stretched his back even straighter, but still had to look up at the Sith Lord who stood two meters tall. Before he moved with Vader, however, he turned to face the two soldiers.

"Since you both have so much free time on your hands to reflect, I will see about relocating you to a post that you will undoubtedly find more . . . challenging," he told them. "Perhaps something in the Hoth system," he mused. "I don't believe we have sent many satellites out there yet. Report to your garrison commander for new orders. Your tour of duty here is now over." With that, he turned and marched alongside Lord Vader, briefly contemplating what hellish location they would eventually be dispatched to.

After a few moments of silence that were distinctly uncomfortable for Redge, he addressed the dark shadow. "Yes, my lord?"

"The Emperor wishes to know how you are progressing," Lord Vader demanded.

Redge struggled to keep his equilibrium. The dark power of the Force rolled off Vader in crashing waves.

"Inquisitor?" the distorted voice demanded, and Redge knew he would not ask the question a second time.

"My lord," he began, "I understand the seriousness surrounding the nature of the mission."

"Do you? I am honored that you agree with me," Vader replied. Redge thought he could almost hear the sarcasm in the Sith Lord's voice.

"I only meant, Lord Vader, that I fully comprehend my role in this."

"Do you, Inquisitor?" Vader asked him, stopping just before both men reached another hallway. Only Vader's mechanized breathing could be heard echoing in the antechamber. Redge was momentarily at a loss for how to proceed. Darth Vader was the only creature that ever inspired this effect in the Inquisitor.

"Do you truly know what it will mean," the Sith Lord eventually continued, "if the holocron should return to the Rebels' hands?"

Redge swallowed hard. "Yes, my lord, I think I can appreciate what should happen. If the Rebels manage to retrieve that device—with, among other things, its list of high-level Rebel sympathizers—and activate those spies, the Empire could very well crumble from within."

Vader regarded him stonily before he raised a gauntleted finger to point accusingly at the Inquisitor. "What are you doing about it?" he demanded.

"Lord Vader, I have my best operative on the trail of this item even as we speak. I have trained this agent for many years, and I believe there is no one better suited for the mission. We will not fail," he promised, barely hiding the quaver in his voice.

Vader stared a moment longer and then turned to walk down the hallway, his heavy footfalls muffled by the thick pile of the carpets. The Inquisitor hastened his step to keep up.

"The Death Star incident will never occur again," Vader told Redge. The Inquisitor knew the Sith Lord was not really sharing a confidence with him as much as he was simply thinking aloud. However, he did nothing to interrupt Vader, awed as he was in the moment.

"The fact that those plans slipped through our fingers and reached the cursed Rebels . . ." Vader's voice trailed away and he tightened the fingers of his left hand.

As he did so, Redge felt a pressure build up around his heart. His breathing grew more rapid, and black spots began to dance around the corners of his vision. He slowed his pace and vaguely saw that Vader was continuing on, unaware that he had lost his stricken companion. Redge placed a hand against his chest. He felt as if a fambaa were settled atop it. His head swam. Then, as abruptly as the pressure began, it disappeared. He rested one hand against the marble wall and tried to catch his breath before trotting weakly after Vader, who had not paused in his march.

"Inquisitor?" Vader demanded.

"Y-yes, my lord?" Redge stammered, barely recovered from Vader's unconscious assault.

"Your best agent, you say?"

"Yes, Lord Vader," Redge said, his voice growing stronger with every passing moment. "This agent will not fail."

Darth Vader turned and stared at Redge once more. "Inquisitor, you should know full well that that there is no such thing as failure within the Empire. I suggest you remember that." He raised a finger and shook it once, ominously, toward the Inquisitor and then turned and left. The hiss of his automated breathing faded as he marched down the length of the passageway. Only when Redge was no longer in the presence of the Sith Lord did he realize that he had been holding his own breath. He let it out slowly.

Redge turned from the hallway and walked over to an alcove with a view of the Emperor's personal shuttle, an AT-ST standing guard nearby. He leaned his head against the cool marble wall and sighed. His thoughts drifted from the holocron to his operative and back to Vader's barely concealed death threat. He understood only too well how much was riding on the success of this mission. Redge sighed and continued to stare out into the night. The rain fell harder.

The young woman gazed out into the clear night sky. She sat on the forest floor with her arms wrapped around her drawn-up knees, her hair hanging down in thick braids. There was nothing extraordinary about her at first glance. In her loose shirt and trousers the dappled color of the forest, she could have been nothing more than a young woman doing a little stargazing at the end of a long day. It was only when her face came into view that anyone would have recognized the self-possessed manner in which she held herself, even while sitting on the ground. And the ancient look in her eyes.

Senator of a now dissolved government and Princess of an obliterated world, Leia Organa had not lost her faith or her purpose, though her titles carried no meaning. Her will was forged of the hardest metal, and that will had so far carried her through the many dark times the Alliance had faced. Though only in her twenties, she was wise beyond her years. She wore her mantle of responsibility with a strength that defied reason. The many troops and commanders who followed her wondered at the woman who never showed fear to anyone. And Leia maintained that confidence in front of everyone. She knew she couldn't afford not to. Still, there were times, mostly in the dead of night, when she doubted and worried. At those moments, if it was possible, she would sneak out from wherever she was and breathe in real air, not the manufactured atmosphere of a hidden base or starship, touch the soil and look to the stars. That simple act grounded her and always brought her peace. It reminded her that she was a part of a greater whole and that there was an order to things that had to be followed. Knowing that she was a part of this order renewed her and gave her the strength to carry on. She had always done this alone, since she was a child. But this had changed recently.

Leia heard the faint rustle behind her but didn't reach for her pistol. She suddenly ducked her head, closed her eyes, and smiled. She knew who it was.

The blond youth dropped down to squat next to her. He was dressed in much the same fashion as she was. In the starlight, Leia could see he also wore an easy smile. But his blue eyes weren't quite as innocent as they had been when she had first met him so many months ago. There was a touch of faded sadness to them and something else, as well. Something that Leia could see was growing. She knew that with each passing day, Luke Skywalker was learning more and more about the mystical ways of the Jedi. And that path of knowledge was changing him.

"It's late," he told her, and she noticed he didn't bother to ask why she was outside the hidden Rebel shelter. Over the last few months, Leia had discovered that he shared the same need that she did to feel the worlds they were on, even for a little while. What had surprised Leia was that she didn't begrudge his presence as an intrusion, but welcomed his company. They sometimes sat for hours in companionable silence. The closeness she felt to him was something new for the Princess.

"I know," she whispered back in a husky voice.

"What's troubling you tonight, Leia?" he asked.

Leia sighed. She didn't resent his question. She *had* been more preoccupied of late. And there was perhaps only one other person she might have shared her fears with, but he was on a mission far from their temporary base on Corellia. And, when she was honest with herself, Leia had to admit sometimes she was nervous around the smuggler-turned-Rebel, as though there were an uncertain current that passed between them. With Luke, she simply felt at home.

"We have so far to go," she eventually replied, trying to mask the weariness in her voice.

"But we've come so far," he told her gently. "The destruction of the Death Star alone was a huge victory."

"I know," she agreed. "It was a momentous success and a great rallying point for the Alliance. It crystallized the hopes of so many who were undecided or afraid. But it was only one victory, and it cost us so many lives," she confessed tiredly.

"You're right on all counts," he agreed. "But the Empire will fail because they put their faith in technology rather than people. They don't recognize that all the lives they're trying to crush actually make a difference and will determine the outcome of this war."

Leia studied him more closely. For a moment, he had the same enthusiasm and naïveté as when they had first met, when she knew he felt like he could conquer the Empire single-handedly. She smiled and felt her mood begin to lighten.

"I know that, too, Luke," she said. "I think that's why this latest mission weighs on me so heavily."

"The holocron?" Luke asked, already knowing the answer.

"Yes. The names stored there could turn the tide for us," Leia admitted. "As you said, our greatest strength lies in those who work toward the same goal as us. If that list should fall into Imperial hands, not only would it mean certain death for those sympathizers but it could spell the end for us, as well. Just as we needed help from within the Empire to defeat the Death Star, we need these people and the glimpses inside the Empire they can offer us now even more."

Luke moved closer to her. "You've sent one of your best agents to retrieve it, haven't you?"

"Yes," Leia replied and didn't bother to hide the weariness in her voice now. "Yes, I've sent another one out into the void, perhaps to death again. One more . . ." She lowered her head on her knees and squeezed her eyes shut. And not even Luke's comforting arm across her shoulders was able to ease the burden the Princess of Alderaan had to bear alone.

ONE

"Where do I go?" Dusque Mistflier shouted to her colleague. She turned to look up at him, barely able to hear herself over the noise of the crowd.

"I believe we have seats farther to the left," he replied.

Several members of the rowdy assembly turned at the sound of Tendau Nandon's unusual voice, despite the raucous atmosphere. It was a rather difficult sound to make out, and it had taken Dusque many months to understand the unusual harmonics of his speech.

Nandon was an Ithorian, a species some referred to as "Hammerheads." Standing nearly two meters tall, he had a domed head that rested atop a long, curving neck. What lent his speech such a curious tone was that along the top of his neck, he had not one, but two mouths. So whenever he spoke, there was an unusual stereo effect; some found it disconcerting when he used Basic and impossible to understand when he communicated in his native tongue.

Dusque nodded to him and turned to face the direction he had indicated. She brushed her nearly waist-length, sandy-brown hair out of her eyes and cursed herself again for not tying it back away from her face. But Dusque hated fussing with herself, considering it too feminine a trait. Being feminine, she was learning, was not the most ideal situation within the Empire, so she made a concerted effort to appear as unfeminine as possible. She even thought about cutting her hair short. In her heart, she was certain her gender was why she was being held back and not utilized to the best of her abilities. Her current assignment, she felt, was proof enough of that.

Of course, she told herself, *I've only been assigned to the Imperial corps of bioengineers for a few months now, but that still should afford me a measure of respect I have yet to see.*

Instead, she found herself on the relatively peaceful and beautiful planet of Naboo at an animal handler and trainer event, sponsored by a casino, of all things. Not exactly a dream assignment, and Dusque suspected she had been given the task of collecting genetic tissue samples and recording trained animal behavior simply because most of her other colleagues, who were senior to her, felt the assignment beneath them. Granted, there was always something of value to learn from captive behaviors, and Dusque would have been the first to argue that fact to anyone else, but she wondered for the umpteenth time just what could be learned from this debacle.

The Aerie was a new casino that had opened very recently near the city of Moenia and was already touting itself as one of the premier gambling facilities in the galaxy. And as Dusque surveyed the throng of Bothans, Rodians, humans, Corellian animal traders, and others in attendance, she couldn't deny that it had drawn a very large crowd, adding credence to its claims. A special arena with chairs had been set up near the casino, and impromptu betting tables had been hastily erected for the event. Hundreds of people had shown up. Dusque saw that nearly every seat was taken and that scores of other observers were hanging around behind the official viewing area. As Imperial scientists, Dusque and the Ithorian had ringside seating.

Dusque spotted two empty seats up front, and she picked her way over to them very carefully. She knew that Nandon was not comfortable walking planetside, and she adjusted her stride accordingly without drawing his attention to the fact. She didn't want him to think that she was patronizing him, but she knew his struggles. Ithorians in general spent most of their time in floating cities above Ithor, never setting foot on their beautiful homeworld, so most were comfortable only on ships or other artificial constructs. Some of the more adventurous of the peaceful species had made their way into the stars, though. Tendau Nandon was one of those pioneers. But that didn't change his discomfort.

Dusque was still learning about his species, but she understood how much they revered nature. In fact, they worshiped the very nature of their planet and referred to it as Mother Jungle. Considering how highly they regarded the natural ecology, it was no wonder that many of the Ithorians actually came to be biologists and bioengineers, fascinated by all forms of life. And Nandon was one of the best biologists Dusque had ever known. The only reason her current assignment was at all bearable was because he had requested to go with her when no one else would.

Dusque was unaware what a sight they presented even in the eclectic gathering at the arena. Standing a full human head shorter than Nandon, Dusque was a slim woman, but she expertly hid her wiry form under loose trousers and an oversized top. Nandon had clicked in disapproval of her attire. Even he had recognized the false importance of the evening and had dressed accordingly, donning a special wrap he reserved for solemn occasions. He had urged her to wear something more formal, and Dusque had chuckled at his surprise when she informed him that she didn't own any dresses.

"What would be the use?" she had asked him, her gray eyes twinkling. "You can't run or climb with any amount of ease in the blasted things, so why have them?"

"That's not what they are meant for," he had countered.

"I don't see you wearing one, although that wrap does set off your silver skin very nicely," she said, and they had both shared a laugh. Once again, she was glad she had an ally among her stoic colleagues. Despite her growing friendship with the Ithorian, however, Dusque still felt like an outsider in the sterile labs of her workplace.

"Here we are," she said and seated herself, trying not to sound too discouraged.

"It could be worse," Nandon told her in his lyrical voice.

"How so?" Dusque sighed.

"It could still be raining," he pointed out, and that brought a crooked smile to Dusque's face. She sighed, realizing that he would always point out something on the positive side. And he was right. It had rained heavily the previous night, and there was still a decidedly slurping sound as they had maneuvered through the spectators, but their chairs didn't sink too far into the ground as they made themselves comfortable for what was undoubtedly going to be a long night.

Tendau's right, she told herself. *We're bioengineers and this is our job.* Resigned to her assignment, Dusque pulled out a datapad and a stylus, ready to make notes on her observations. But her heart wasn't in it. Not for the first time, she wondered where the choices in her young life had taken her.

From a large family, Dusque had been the youngest. And she had been the only daughter her parents conceived. Growing up on Talus, she had alternately been the baby and the pet, always under the watchful eyes of her four brothers. She had followed them around on their childhood adventures, eventually growing strong enough to keep up with their running and climbing and building makeshift camps. Their tricks and pranks had made her tougher than most, because Dusque felt she had to take their teasing with a stiff upper lip. There had been no such thing as tears when she was little. Her brothers didn't cry, so she didn't, either.

Her father had toiled diligently for a small company manufacturing starship components. Not as prestigious as those companies located above Corellia, but it had been good work. And he had been a hard worker. Her mother kept the house and bandaged up the children when they had their cuts and scrapes. It had been a simple but good life. Unfortunately, it didn't last.

Even though she had been little more than a child at the time, Dusque remembered when the Imperials started to make their presence known to those who worked on Talus. And she recalled how her father would come home at night, exhausted and worried, wondering just what the ships he helped construct were being used for. Many times he and her mother had talked late into the night about it, and Dusque remembered sneaking out of bed to listen in on them once in a while. There had always been tears and accusations when they spoke on the matter. But most of all, there had been fear. Even she had sensed that her parents were frightened. Tensions grew in their modest home. And then there was the day her father didn't come home.

Her mother received word that he had collapsed

in the manufacturing facility and that by the time his coworkers had carried him to the medic, it had been too late. His heart had simply given out. Everything changed for Dusque at that point. Without her father to hold the family together, it frayed at the edges and eventually collapsed. Her mother never really recovered from the loss of her husband and became more of a shadow than ever. She catered to her sons and moved about like a ghost, as though she had lost her substance and ceased to exist. It was at this point that Dusque swore an oath: she would never let herself become like that, no matter the cost. And she would never again care about anything as she had for her family, because the price of loss was too steep.

Her two oldest brothers quit their studies and took up their father's crafting profession. Dusque saw how it aged them prematurely, so she buried her nose deeper into her schoolwork, determined not to take that path. And when her studies were done for the evening and her home too somber, she would sneak out of their small compound and hide out in the forest where she and her brothers used to camp in happier times. She became more withdrawn from people and spent hours and hours studying the creatures native to her town. She began to prefer their company to that of other people, finding their cues and habits easier to read than those of humans. Her youngest brother joined the ranks of the Imperial forces, determined to become a pilot and soar through the stars, as resolute as

Dusque was to leave their small home behind. A few months after joining, he died in a training accident. And for the first time since the death of her father, Dusque saw her mother display an anger and a fire she hadn't known the woman possessed.

For one moment, her mother was like a raging animal, and Dusque glimpsed just how deep her hatred for the Empire ran. She blamed them for her young son's death as well as that of her husband. But her rage burned out quickly and once again she was only a shell of the woman she had formerly been. That was the year Dusque graduated with high honors and chose to pursue a path of bioengineering. In her eyes, this career combined her two greatest desires: it let her continue to study and track animals, and it got her off her homeworld. But because it was a profession that answered to and was governed by the Empire, Dusque was never really certain how much her decision might have broken what was left of her mother's heart.

For the next few years, she completed the advanced studies required to proceed to bioengineering. The only effort she needed to make during her course work was mastering a medic's knowledge of organic chemistry. That turned out to be the one she had to struggle with, because it wasn't intuitive to her. The scouting aspect of her career choice came as second nature. Survival skills, as well as trapping, hunting, and exploration, were instinctive to her, and she excelled among her fellow students, finishing second in her class. Her high ranking caught the attention of several prominent scientists of the Imperial party, along with garnering a stellar recommendation from her trainer, and she was awarded a position as a bioengineer.

Dusque, however, soon found it frustrating to distinguish herself from her male colleagues when she was no longer competing for scores and marks on exams. She answered to an older supervisor named Willel, who never seemed to trust her with any project of worth no matter what she did. Boring assignment after boring assignment came in, each of which she dutifully completed. She even found ways to make the assignments more exciting for herself, although her superiors never knew of her extra excursions. Still, she continued to receive the most simplistic studies, and the only thing she could conclude was that she was trapped in a male world. Most of the others she worked with had held their positions for decades, and there appeared to be no room for advancement within the ranks. She had traded what she felt was a dead-end life with her family for what looked like a dead-end career with the Empire. And her current whereabouts just affirmed her certainty.

"I think it's going to begin," Tendau told her, interrupting her depressive reverie. Dusque returned to the present and looked in the direction the Ithorian had indicated.

A slight, humanoid figure in a garish robe was entering the arena from the side and making his way into the center. His green skin, antennae, and flexible snout told Dusque that he was a Rodian. She wasn't surprised to see one of his species taking center stage, so to speak. She knew of several clans who had escaped the watchful eye of the Grand Protector and left the devastated ecology of Rodia. Most became dramatists of the highest caliber, and Dusque had recently viewed an excellent performance by a traveling troupe. But there was always something she found shifty about them, with their multifaceted eyes that were nearly impossible to read. Dusque placed a great deal of value in what she saw in another's eyes.

The announcer cleared his throat before tapping a small transmitter attached to his cloak. "Let me extend a warm welcome to all of you this beautiful evening. My name is Eban Trey, and I will be your host for the tonight's festivities," he said with a great flourish.

"Let me be the first to welcome you to the finest gambling establishment of the Mid Rim: the Aerie Casino. To launch the official, grand opening of the casino, we have a night of extraordinary events for your entertainment. In a moment, I will turn this stage over to an incredible mix of exotic animals that the majority of you have never seen the likes of before or will ever see again in one venue.

"Coupled with their trainers and handlers, they will be pitted against one another until only the most skilled is left standing. But"—he added with a dramatic flair—"that will not signal the end. After the winner has been awarded his or her prize, we will officially open the doors to the casino, and the first one hundred through the entrance will be given one hundred credits."

At his pronouncement, the crowd went wild. The Rodian, clearly a master of timing, bowed deeply and dashed out of the arena. Dusque shifted in her seat and sighed disappointedly. The external lights that surrounded the makeshift arena dimmed dramatically, and the crowd grew silent. The only sounds were those that drifted over from the nearby swamps. When the lights came on again, they pulsed in a flashing pattern. From the eastern point of the arena, Dusque saw the first of the contestants enter the ring.

Leading the parade of creatures was a rare sight. A female, pale-blue-skinned Twi'lek sat atop a cu-pa and actually rode the bright pink-and-blue-furred beast into the arena. Cu-pas were native to Tatooine, Dusque knew; resembling tauntauns, they were very passive but not nearly as intelligent. The simple fact that the woman was able to mount and direct the creature was a fascinating spectacle. Dusque noted that the Twi'lek had her two head tentacles wrapped tightly around the cu-pa's neck, and she wondered if that aided her in directing the animal. She recorded her observations, reserving her conclusions for later, when she would, she hoped, have more information.

A Wookiee led in a small herd of floppy-eared squall, and quite a few snickers could be heard among the spectators. Even Dusque was hard pressed not to laugh at the sight. However, all laughter stopped as soon as the Wookiee threw back his head and roared his displeasure. The ferocious sound made even Dusque sit a little straighter in her seat.

After the Wookiee, a bevy of handlers and creatures made a single pass around the arena. Mon Calamari carried anglers in on their shoulders, their spearlike legs dangling, Trandoshans rode in on tusk-cats, humans followed behind flewt queens that strained against their tethers, and even stranger sights marched by. Dusque recorded it all, down to the minutest detail.

"I haven't seen this many creatures since we were at the Coruscant Livestock Exchange and Exhibition," Tendau whispered to her from his two mouths.

"You're right," she grudgingly agreed. "Now that you've reminded me, I wouldn't be surprised if we see some of those traders here, as well. There certainly is a large enough gathering."

The Ithorian nodded in agreement. "I suspect we will."

Most of the attendees looked like well-dressed tourists, no more and no less. Dusque saw that most were making frequent trips to the betting tables, and it was clear that the odds against the matches were in constant flux. As she craned her neck around, she was momentarily startled to see a pair of nearly black eyes regarding her steadily. She cocked her head sideways as she saw that the eyes matched the ebony hair of the human male who was watching her. She turned back abruptly toward the scene in front of her. As a trained bystander, Dusque was suddenly uncomfortable when she realized she was the one being studied.

Very flustered, she busied herself with her observations. A zucca boar was pitted against a womp rat. Both animals were native to Tatooine, and Dusque realized that for the opening rounds, only animals from the same planets were forced to fight one another.

"While the boar has weight on his side," she whispered to her colleague, "he doesn't stand a chance against those incisors."

"Care to place a bet on that?" came a snide remark from behind her. "My credits are on the zucca."

Dusque didn't even turn her head to acknowledge the speaker. "Then you're about to become very poor." She shook her head as he snorted in derision. He'd see soon enough.

As their handlers turned them loose, the two competitors charged each other. And as Dusque had suspected, although the boar had more muscle behind his attack, he didn't have the agility of the hopping womp rat. When the boar was nearly close enough to gore his opponent, the smaller native of Tatooine hopped to the side. The zucca wasn't able to stop his rush in time to escape the wicked teeth of the womp rat. The boar's hide was tough, but not tough enough to withstand the repeated attacks of the competition. Every time the boar attempted to regroup and charge, the womp rat sidestepped him with a nimble hop. It was only a matter of time before the boar expired. The womp rat's handler emerged from the sidelines and called his creature to follow him. With only one backward glance, the womp rat fell in behind his handler and hopped out of the arena. A judge rushed out to check on the condition of the boar and, as the boar's handler struggled with the carcass, the womp rat was declared the winner and advanced to the next round. Dusque noted everything.

From behind her, she could hear the disgruntled gambler swear. He threw his handful of tickets to the ground and stomped off. Tendau leaned toward her once again.

"I'm impressed," he told her.

"It was obvious," Dusque replied, waving off the compliment. "That match was no contest."

"No," he corrected her, "I meant I was impressed because you didn't tell him *I told you so.*" She saw that he was smiling with the mouth that faced her. She smiled back.

The next few rounds went much the same, and there was very little that Dusque learned about behavior that she hadn't seen demonstrated on some other world before. Although she kept her facial expressions to a minimum, she was growing more nauseated as the evening wore on. She watched as one magnificent specimen after another was torn to shreds simply for the multitude's amusement and a handful of credits. The only conclusion she was drawing was that there was no end to what the Empire allowed to propagate.

Unable to stomach the slaughter, she found her eyes once again wandering from the staged events back toward the crowd. The more vicious the fights, the more frenzied the throng became. She saw that most were on their feet, tickets and chips clutched tightly in their hands. Many were shouting threats or words of encouragement to their favored choice, alternating indiscriminately between them. And, almost discreetly, a small garrison of Imperial stormtroopers patrolled the periphery of the arena, ostensibly to keep at bay anything that might be drawn from the swamps by the growing stench of blood. As always, the Empire was ever present. While Dusque continued to observe the mob, she discovered that same pair of obsidian eyes staring back at her again.

As he lifted a hand, Dusque unconsciously raised her hand to her throat. For a moment, she thought he was going to somehow signal to her, and she wondered what she would do. But he simply brushed some of his unruly black hair from his eyes and continued to regard her steadily. She turned away again, feeling suddenly foolish and at a loss.

"It's almost over," the Ithorian told her. "Only a few are still standing."

Dusque focused on her datapad, trying to busy herself with her notations. The last creatures left were a malkloc from Dathomir and a flit harasser from Lok. The malkloc had literally mowed over her competition. Larger than a tauntaun, malklocs had a heavy body and long neck. Dusque recalled from her studies that they were near the top of the food chain on Dathomir due to their sheer mass. Only an adult rancor bull had any hope of bringing down one of the giants. Luckily for the rest of the creature population, malklocs were herbivores, content to spend their waking hours chewing thousands of leaves every day, blissfully oblivious to their surroundings. This malkloc, however, had been trained to respond to her handler's commands, as had all the other specimens that performed in the arena. She had crushed every one of her opponents under her tremendous feet. But her feet would not help her against her final opponent.

On the other side of the arena, a Trandoshan female was bringing out her prized creature. It was one of the largest flit harassers Dusque had ever seen. Indigenous to Lok, the creatures had a tough, leathery hide, an incredibly sharp beak, and a wingspan that was usually greater than the height of a large Wookiee. Very few living things could face down one of these reptavians.

"The only chance the malkloc has," Tendau whispered to Dusque, "is the fact that the flit has a damaged wing from its tussle with the dire cat in the previous round." He pointed out the injury with his long silvery arm.

"And the fact that they normally hunt in swarms," Dusque added. She saw the Ithorian nod in agreement but look away as the signal was given for the animals to attack. She knew he was just as sickened as she was by the bloody scenario in front of her. Travesties such as this were not the reason either of them had become biologists.

The match ended fairly quickly. The malkloc made her charge and miscalculated. The moment she unsuccessfully thundered past the flit, the repta-vian swooped awkwardly around the massive beast and landed on the malkloc's back. It dug its claws into the tough hide of the herbivore and raised its beak high above. When it was certain it had a solid grip, the flit dropped its head and buried its beak deep into the malkloc's neck. And then it began to feed.

Dusque turned away, having no desire to watch the bloodsucker at work. Almost unconsciously, she looked back in the direction of the human male who had been watching her—and found that he was still watching her, just as he had been earlier. She met his gaze and held it for a few moments until he did something unexpected. He winked at her.

Dusque was at a loss. She knew she should have been offended, or should ignore him at the very least, but she didn't know how to respond. Almost against her will she could feel the color rise in her face. But before she could say or do anything, a sud-den thud shook the stands and she whirled back around to face the arena.

The malkloc had finally fallen to the ground. The flit's handler trotted out from the sidelines and tried to pull the bloody victor from its prize even as he accepted his credits as the evening's grand-prize winner.

When Dusque collected her thoughts, she turned back toward her admirer, but he was gone. She scanned the crowd quickly: he was nowhere to be seen. The Ithorian noticed she was distressed and placed a hand on her shoulder. Her flushed appearance couldn't be missed, either. He asked, "Are you all right?"

Dusque took a moment before she replied, "I'm not sure."

TWO

The moment the official winner was announced, a cry went up from the masses. Almost as one, the spectators turned and made for the casino entrance as quickly as they could, and Dusque was certain it was with the gleam of free credits dancing before their eyes. A few of the slower members of the throng squawked in surprise and pain as they were shoved aside and stepped on by the more assertive guests. But she saw that even the slow recovered and tried to push their way through.

Dusque collected her materials and picked up her small pack. She grabbed the railing and easily swung her legs over the side. She looked back over her shoulder and told the Ithorian, "I'm just going to collect a few samples. Won't be but a few moments." She knew Tendau would probably become ill if he had to walk through the blood-spattered arena. She wasn't thrilled by the prospect either, but she knew she wouldn't become physically sick from the contact like her colleague would.

Dusque walked off to the far side of the temporary stadium where she had seen most of the carcasses hastily dumped between rounds. There was only one handler who had remained behind, along with a few attendants who were already beginning the tedious task of breaking down the show grounds. She noticed the handler was still stroking the side of his fallen wrix. He paid no attention to her, but one of the attendants approached her.

"Dusque Mistflier," she identified herself and showed him her credentials. As always, the sight of her authorization left no room for questions, granting her immediate access to anything she required.

"Imperial bioengineer, hmm? Little out of the way for you here, isn't it?" he pointed out.

Dusque ignored his snickers and his implied insult and moved past him. Breathing through her mouth to avoid the smell, she pushed her hair back and removed her tools from her bag. She then began methodically drawing blood and tissue samples from the fallen creatures. When she had collected and stored all of the DNA, she cleaned her hands on a sterile wipe and started to walk back over to the Ithorian. But the wrix trainer called out to her and trotted after her. Dusque stopped and waited for him.

By his tattoos and vestigial horns, Dusque realized he was a Zabrak. And he was obviously distraught by the death of his creature.

"What can I do for you?" Dusque asked him politely.

"I saw you take samples of my wrix. I want to know how many credits you want to clone him," he demanded.

"I'm sorry," she replied, somewhat surprised by his request. "I don't have the proper equipment for that kind of procedure. And I don't believe in cloning," she added. "When things die, they should stay dead."

But the Zabrak didn't seem to appreciate her answer. "I know what you and your kind do," he spat, his anger obviously making him reckless. "You run around the galaxy, collecting your little bits and pieces of everything you find and scurrying back to your labs.

"You mix and match things at your whim, or the Emperor's, without batting an eye. Well"—he grabbed Dusque by her upper arm—"you'll clone him for me and you'll do it now."

Dusque twisted around sharply and freed her arm from his hard grip. But before anything else transpired, the two attendants rushed up to restrain him.

"Now, now," the attendant who had spoken to Dusque soothed. "You don't want to mess with her kind. You saw her rank. Touch her and we'll have to find a way to clone you," he joked nervously and Dusque saw him eyeing the patrolling troopers. The situation became more apparent to the Zabrak, and he angrily shoved off the attendants.

"You're right," he growled, "she's not worth it. None of her kind is. They're worse than the

abominations that they cook up in their labs."
And with that, he trudged back over to his fallen
creature.

Dusque turned and walked the rest of the way
back to Tendau without further incident. She could
see the Ithorian looked worried, so she pasted a
smile on her face and shook her head in mock disgust. But the Zabrak's words stuck with her. She
knew many of her superiors back at their labs did
exactly what the trainer had accused her of. They
experimented and tampered and went against the
natural order of things, all in the name of the Emperor. Dusque tried to convince herself she was just
a xenobiologist, taking samples for study and docu-
menting behaviors. Still, she had an inkling what
some of her samples were used for; she simply chose
not to recognize the truth.

"Are you well?" Tendau asked her when she
reached his side.

"Yes, yes," she reassured him. "I'm fine. He was
just distraught by the death of his pet. If he cared
about it that much, he should never have entered
the contest."

"The lure of credits can be very strong to some,"
Tendau said. "And sometimes people just make
mistakes."

Dusque looked up sharply at his last statement
and saw that he was regarding her steadily with his
deep brown eyes.

"Enough seriousness," he went on after a moment's silence. "It is still early. Now that all the

foolish have pushed and jostled their way into the casino, why don't we go and see what all the fuss is about, hmm?"

"It's a little late," Dusque began, trying to beg off, but she recognized the determined set to the Ithorian's face.

"It's barely past sundown," he corrected her. He thrust out the crook of his long arm and said, "Why don't we try our luck tonight?"

Dusque shook her head with a smile. "You never give up, do you?" And she slipped her arm through his.

Dusque raised a hand to her eyes and found that she needed to squint against the flashing lights. The casino was a hive of activity, sights, and smells. As soon as she and the Ithorian had rounded the corner after the entrance, their senses had been assailed by the noise and lights.

The main room was huge and filled beyond capacity with eager gamblers. Along one of the far walls, row after row of lugjack machines beeped and chirped. And almost every one of the devices was in use. Dusque watched for a few moments and saw that far more credits were pouring into the machines than were coming out. But every once in a while, a patron would jump up and down as her machine screeched a winning alarm and a few credit chips came shooting out.

Off to her right, Dusque saw at least three spinnerpits in operation. A dozen or more players were crammed around each of the tables, piling their chips on their favorite numbers. Dusque noticed that some discreetly consulted small datapads; she wasn't sure if they were trying to play a system or simply wanted to see how many credits remained in their bank accounts. She couldn't even begin to guess how much the casino was raking in for its grand-opening extravaganza.

"My dear," Tendau told her, "why don't you try your hand at a few of the games?"

"That's all right," she told the Ithorian as she patted his hand. "I wouldn't want to throw away any credits."

"I've seen you staring at a few of the tables; you know you want to try. Go ahead," he urged her, "and have a little fun." He leaned down close to her right ear and whispered, "I'm sure we can find a way to claim any losses as necessary expense."

She was momentarily shocked, but a smile spread across her face in spite of herself. It wouldn't be the first time she and the Ithorian had bent the rules just a little bit.

"All right," she finally agreed. "What about you? Not going to leave me holding the bag, are you?"

"Don't be foolish, child. I think I saw Mastivo, the Coruscanti trader, here and I would like to exchange a few words with him," he said.

"Tell him hello for me, would you?"

"Of course. Now have some fun." And with that, the Ithorian shuffled off into the noisy mass.

The only thing he hadn't done, she thought, was

pat her on the head and hand her a few credits, but Dusque knew he meant well.

She went over to one of the spinnerpits and threw out a credit chip onto a number at random, more to humor the Ithorian than anything else. When the wheel stopped turning, she was delighted to find out she had won. She smiled broadly and scooped up her winnings. Without her colleague acting as escort, though, Dusque soon realized that more than a few of the human males around the table were sizing her up, despite her drab attire. She moved to a different one and tried again. She surprised herself by winning yet again. Even Dusque couldn't deny the tiny thrill of beating the odds.

With two pocketfuls of chips, she accepted a blue drink of indeterminate origin and sipped at it cautiously. She frowned at the taste. Whatever was in there was extremely intoxicating, and she set the beverage back down on the first empty seat she found. Dusque never allowed her judgment to become compromised, no matter the occasion, and she wasn't about to begin tonight. She wandered about the casino and realized that she had the beginnings of a headache. She noticed there were a few semiprivate rooms off toward the back that appeared to be fairly quiet, so she made her way over to them, hoping to find a place where she could collect herself.

When she got closer, however, she realized that each room was full of players seated at tables large enough to accommodate only five or so. Each of the players held a few chip-cards in his hands, and a dealer sat opposite them. Whatever the game was, she noticed they were all very serious about it, which explained why the rooms were so quiet compared to the rest of the casino. Dusque stood in the archway to the room and watched as the dealer pressed a special button on the table and the players then scrutinized their cards. Some proceeded to place one or more in the dealer's interface field, while others allowed the dealer to continue to press his button.

It must send out some kind of signal, she reasoned.

But it was what was heaped at the center of the table that puzzled Dusque. She knew that they must have been wagering, but she didn't recognize the markers they were using. They weren't the simple credit chips that everyone, including Dusque, used in the rest of the casino. She furrowed her brow in puzzlement, but could tell by the grim demeanor of the gamblers that no one would appreciate any questions from a nonplayer. She was so absorbed by the game itself that she wasn't aware of the man who came over to stand next to her.

"Well, hello there," he said after standing unnoticed by Dusque for several long moments.

Startled, Dusque turned and answered, "Hello."

"Allow me to introduce myself," the brown-skinned human said. "My name is Lando Calrissian. And you would be—?"

Dusque silently cursed Tendau for dragging her out when she could have been back in her quiet room going over documents alone. While there was no argument that the man was handsome and obviously charming, he was just a little too shiny and slick for her tastes. She had met his type before.

"My name is Dusque Mistflier," she replied with a smile and, after a beat, turned back to the game, hoping he would take it as a cue that she wasn't looking for company. The man was not deterred so easily, though.

"I couldn't help but notice that you were intrigued by the sabacc table. Care to play?" he invited suggestively.

Ignoring his innuendo, Dusque answered truthfully, "I think I understand the rudiments of the game, but I don't recognize the markers that they're playing with. Just what are the stakes?"

Lando smiled broadly, revealing even, white teeth. "They say if you have to ask, then you can't afford to play." He laughed deeply, but Dusque didn't sense any spite in his tone. She returned his smile.

"I guess you have your answer, then," she said and they both smiled again.

"Actually," he explained, using the opportunity to move a little closer, "the markers have different values. You see that blue one there?" He pointed out a chip on the table, and Dusque nodded.

"That one is for a spaceship," he said.

She sucked in her breath. "He's risking his ship?"

"Yes."

"That's ridiculous," she sputtered. "Who in their

right mind would gamble away a ship?" Dusque turned to her new companion for clarification, but he was silent for a moment. It was hard to tell, but she could almost swear Lando was blushing.

"Well," he started to explain, spreading his hands expansively, "sometimes the stakes are worth it, especially if he thinks he's drawn an 'idiot's array.' What are the odds of two players drawing that in a single round?" he mumbled, but Dusque wasn't paying attention.

One of the players, a Wookiee, revealed his hand, and Dusque watched the others throw their chipcards down in disgust. It was obvious he had won. The Wookiee wrapped his big, hairy arms around the pot and drew it toward himself, a self-satisfied grin plastered on his furry face.

Since the game seemed to be over, Dusque turned around to look back into the main room of the casino, and as she did, she caught sight of Tendau.

Her Ithorian friend was over in a corner, near some of the lugjack machines. She tried to discreetly wave to him, but he appeared to be so deep in conversation with a Bothan female that he didn't notice Dusque. She scrutinized the Bothan fairly closely and didn't recognize her from the arena. She was a bit puzzled as to who the woman was.

"Friend of yours?" Lando inquired solicitously.

Distracted, Dusque replied, "Yes, it is. I should go over and say hello. Thank you for the tutorial on sabacc," she added, seizing the opportunity to leave his company.

Lando picked up her hand and brought it slowly to his lips for a brief kiss. Dusque tolerated the gesture and smiled when he released her hand. "Until later, perhaps?" he asked.

"Perhaps," she answered and moved past him back into the main room, resisting the urge not to wipe her hand on her pants. However, when she looked back in the direction of her colleague, both he and the Bothan female had seemingly disappeared. Dusque was a little perplexed that she had lost track of him so quickly.

"This is probably his way of forcing me to mingle a little bit more," she told herself quietly. "Of course, here I am in a room full of people and I'm talking to myself." She chuckled.

"I could help you change that," a deep but gentle voice offered.

"Lando, you just don't know when to—" she started to say as she turned around. She caught her breath as she realized the voice hadn't come from the suave gambler. Instead she found herself staring into the black eyes of her admirer from earlier in the evening. "Oh," she said, immediately at a loss.

He was almost a head taller than she was, with thick eyebrows and ebony hair to match. His face was full of sharp angles, with a cleft chin and a strong jaw. Dusque couldn't see many lines on his face, but he still had a weathered look about him, and she would have bet all the credits in her trousers that he had spent some time outdoors. His clothes were nondescript, casual but practical like hers, not luxurious like Lando's.

He doesn't just push buttons inside some station, she thought. *He gets his hands dirty.*

When she glanced at his mouth, she realized he was still smiling at her and that she was still staring. Flustered, she dropped her gaze.

"Well," he continued easily, "this isn't good. You've gone from talking to yourself to not talking at all." He cocked his head and grinned crookedly. "Do you feel lucky?"

"What?" she blurted out and then tried to clear her throat, not certain of his question.

Without another word, he grabbed her hand and gently but firmly led her through the casino. Dusque was so stunned, she actually let herself be pulled around. She could feel how strong his hand was, and how rough. There were quite a few calluses on it, and she was comforted that at least one of her hunches was right.

"Wait a moment." She came to a stop. "Just where are you taking me?" she asked, no longer willing to be dragged around like a child's toy.

He turned around and looked at her. "This is a casino, isn't it? You did come here to have a little fun, didn't you?"

"Well, I'm really here to—" she began, but he simply turned away and started to tug her over to one of the spinnerpits, appearing to disregard anything she might have had to say that was contrary to his plans.

"If I have to steal you," he said, "so be it."

As they found a free space near the table, the Twi'lek attendant nodded to Dusque's abductor. "Back again?"

He grinned and held up Dusque's hand. "Now that I've found my lucky piece, there's no stopping me." He looked at Dusque and asked, "What's your favorite color?"

She was thrown so off balance by the question, she just said, "Red."

He winked at her and placed a handful of chips on the spot she had unknowingly selected for him.

"No further bets at this time," the attendant informed the group.

In spite of herself, Dusque became a little caught up in the excitement of the game. Ill at ease with the man next to her, she alternately hoped he would win or lose all his credits. Either way, she supposed, and he would eventually leave her alone. Yet there was a nagging voice in the back of her head that wasn't certain she wanted him to leave just yet. With an effort, she overrode the offending mental noise as she always did.

"Red it is," the attendant announced, and the man smiled at Dusque.

"See," he told her, "I knew you'd bring me luck." Dusque half expected him to kiss her hand with the same false gallantry Lando had shown, but he surprised her once more.

"Pick another for me?" he asked.

"Twenty-seven," she replied, nonplussed.

One side of his mouth curled up. He turned to the attendant and said, "Twenty-seven, please." And once again he won, much to Dusque's exasperation. In fact, he won the next seven colors and numbers that she chose.

Enough was enough. Determined that he should ultimately lose, Dusque told him, "Double zero." And she smiled wickedly when she saw his grin finally falter.

But he cocked his head sideways and told the dealer, "You heard the lady. Put it all on green."

"You do realize the odds, don't you, sir?" the dealer inquired. "And you do have a substantial amount on the table."

"If she says green, then green it is," her companion replied with a touch of bravado in his voice.

"No further bets," the attendant told the large group around the spinnerpit. Dusque vaguely noticed that the crowd had grown considerably since their lucky streak began. But even she was caught up in anticipation. She watched the ball bounce and hop its way across the jubilee wheel, and she held her breath.

"The wheel is slowing," the attendant informed everyone, although that much was obvious. Even he sounded a touch tense, though.

The ball landed on twenty-eight. Black.

Dusque was a little disappointed, but she flashed her unknown companion a smirk even as the others groaned in sympathy. The black-eyed man met her gaze with his own soft smile. Before either said any-

THE RUINS OF DANTOOINE 49

thing, there was a funny *pop* and the onlookers collectively gasped. Dusque broke away from his gaze and looked at the wheel. The ball was nestled in the slot marked DOUBLE ZERO. It was green. Against incredible odds, she had picked the winning number again.

"And the selector has popped the ball onto double zero," the astonished attendant announced. "We have one winner."

"Unbelievable," she whispered.

While Dusque stared in amazement at her companion, she noticed from the corner of her eye that one of the pit bosses had come over to talk to their attendant. The Gungan female was well dressed and stern faced. She leaned over to the attendant and whispered some instructions into the employee's ear. He nodded vigorously, and she stepped behind him.

"Sir," the attendant said to the black-eyed man, "considering the amount of your winnings, I'm going to have to cash you out tonight." He glanced back to his boss for support, and Dusque could see he was nervous. However, he didn't have to worry. Dusque's companion took the news without fuss and smiled easily.

"Cash me out," he told the attendant and made it sound as though it had been his idea. "My lady friend has had enough of the game anyway and wanted this to be the last spin. Didn't you?" he added and winked at her.

"Yes," Dusque answered truthfully, "I did want this to be the last round on the jubilee wheel."

"We'll go ahead and credit your account," the attendant offered.

"That will be fine," he agreed. "Shall we?" he asked Dusque and motioned to the entrance.

"I think I'm about done for tonight," she told him, trying to beg off.

He leaned toward her ear and whispered, "One last look at the stars for the evening? After all the luck we've shared?"

Dusque felt shivers along her back as he breathed against her ear. She knew better, and yet she was intrigued by the strange man who hadn't even introduced himself. She decided to take a chance. If he was like most, she knew she could handle herself. She understood she was considered attractive by most standards, and it wasn't the first time someone had tried to get her alone. It just frustrated her that she always seemed to be thought of as a woman first, and not a scientist. And a part of her hoped that he was exactly like all the other men she had met. Because, as it stood at the moment, she couldn't make him out at all, and she prided herself on her ability to read other creatures. He, however, was definitely a puzzle, and she was intrigued.

"Maybe just one glance," she quietly agreed. His smile grew wider.

I think I've got you pegged, she thought.

Lightly placing a hand on the small of her back, he expertly guided her through the busy casino.

Passing by the bar, Dusque noticed that a few of the patrons had become a bit rowdy. The free drinks had long since run out, but the serious folks had started tabs. As two disagreed on who owed how much, the very drunk Mon Calamari took a swing at his companion to punctuate his point. But he overcompensated for his inebriated state and completely missed his friend holding the bill. His swing brought him crashing toward Dusque. She started to flinch, but before she could make a move, her companion shot out a muscular arm and caught the drunk before he even touched her.

"What yer think yer doin'?" the Mon Calamari slurred.

"You should think very carefully about what you plan to do next, friend," her companion shot back in a deadly voice.

Dusque wasn't the only one who saw just how serious he was. The Mon Calamari's more sober friend, who had a slightly better grasp of the situation, grabbed his companion and started to pull him from the black-eyed man's grip.

"Sorry," he apologized. "Too much fun on the first night, I guess." And with that, he yanked his friend toward the far end of the bar.

"Are you all right?" the black-eyed man asked Dusque.

"Of course," she answered.

They walked out of the casino without further incident. Once outside, Dusque let her head fall back.

She breathed in deeply. She had forgotten her blossoming headache, and the cool air felt good. When she faced her protector, she realized that they weren't alone. A few of the other patrons had also escaped for some air, and they meandered around the marble walkway. One pair laughed in such a way that Dusque knew they wouldn't want to be disturbed, at least for a little while.

"It smells like rain," she told the stranger, slightly uncomfortable with the silence between them. "I don't think we'll see many stars tonight."

He stared at her hard and then said quietly, "I think I can still find something interesting to show you. Come on." And with that, he grabbed her hand and led her away from the other revelers, toward a fountain with a few discreet shrubs and alcoves. When they found an unused corner, he turned and faced her. He looked quickly from one side to the other.

Now is when he tries something, Dusque thought, prepared to stop him. "Look, whoever you are, I'm sorry if you thought—" she began, but he cut her off.

"I'm the one who should be sorry," he said, and Dusque noticed a change in his demeanor. He no longer appeared to be the sly suitor, but something very different.

"Let me explain," he said, further confusing Dusque. After another surreptitious glance at their surroundings, he continued, "My name is Finn Darktrin and I'm not what you think I am."

"Excuse me?" she asked.

"I'm taking a big chance talking to you like this. If anyone were to overhear us, I'd be dead," he explained without the bravado he had shown inside at the gaming tables. The lack of that cockiness made Dusque take notice.

"What are you talking about?"

He grabbed her upper arm and said flatly, "I'm part of the Rebel Alliance. I'm a spy."

If he hadn't been holding her, Dusque would have turned away. She couldn't believe what she had heard. But the gravity of the situation was carved on his face. She realized that this wasn't some sort of elaborate ruse to trick her into a clandestine, romantic liaison. He was serious. She was relieved but also a little disappointed.

"What?" she said again, feeling the beginnings of fear creep in. She found herself looking over her shoulder and overly aware of her surroundings, but they were alone.

"I wish I had more time," he told her, "to let you get used to the idea and for that, I am truly sorry. But time is the one thing neither of us has any longer."

"Then tell me what you want," she answered.

"You are absolutely vital to my current mission," he replied.

"How could that be? I don't even know you." But, just like at the jubilee wheel, Dusque could feel her pulse begin to quicken. *I'm vital to something,* she thought.

"Because of who you are. Look," he tried to

explain, and Dusque could hear the edge to his tone, "the mission I accepted is critical to the Alliance. It could even potentially turn the tide in the Galactic Civil War. And you are the one who can make it work."

"All right, tell me more," she said, lowering her voice and unconsciously taking a step closer to him.

"You are an Imperial bioengineer. One of the top-ranking scientists in your class. That alone gives you free rein when it comes to travel. You show your credentials and no one bats an eye, and they certainly clear out of your way. And," Finn added, "most important, it gives you access to any planet you desire. That's why I need you."

"Oh?" Dusque asked.

"I want to travel along with you as your assistant. I need to retrieve a device that contains the names of some vital personnel and I need to find it fast. The Empire knows of its existence and I'm sure they won't waste any time sending their agents after it. With you as my companion, no one will question me. I can be in and out before anyone could be the wiser," he finished.

"Oh," she said again, and she was hard pressed to hide the disappointment in her voice. *Of course,* she thought, *he only wants me for cover.*

Perhaps sensing that he was losing her, he loosened his grip on her arm and added, "And I knew you would be sympathetic."

Dusque yanked her arm free of his grip. "What

makes you think I would be a Rebel sympathizer?" she demanded, fear making her words harsh.

"I know about you," Finn told her, "and about your family."

"You don't know my family and you certainly don't know me," she replied, her anger on the rise. "You don't know me at all."

"That's where you have underestimated the Alliance. Do you think your name was chosen at random? Do you think I would ask this of just anyone within your class?" Finn's voice rose dangerously. "Please give me a little more credit than that."

Dusque folded her arms across her chest like a barrier against his words. But she didn't back down.

"Your father worked for the Empire," he recited to her, "and look what that job brought your family. It drove him to his death. He couldn't live with what he was doing."

Dusque lowered her arms slowly as though she were deflating, a shocked look on her face.

"Your mother basically died with him, no longer the woman she had been. Your younger brother died at an ill-equipped Imperial training facility, and that was the nail in your mother's living coffin, wasn't it? And your older brother—"

"Stop it," she hissed at him.

"All right," he agreed. "Then let's take a look at you. You study, you learn, and you take a job that turns out to be exactly what you didn't believe in."

"What are you taking about?" she asked through clenched teeth.

"Don't know what I mean? What about that mission on Tatooine?"

"What about it?"

"What happened to the genetic sample of the Sarlacc you were supposed to retrieve? Where did that disappear to?"

"It wasn't properly stored and didn't survive the transport," Dusque explained.

"Sounds plausible enough," Finn agreed. "Except you're better than that. I think that you had an attack of conscience. After all, if the Empire started playing around with the DNA, mixing and matching creatures with that kind of potential for destruction, how many innocents could they kill?"

"That's not my problem," she said, trying to dismiss his accusations.

"Ahh . . . but I think it is. I think it bothers you more than you admit to anyone. And then there were the snow slugs of Alzoc Three, the failed attempt to improve the combat arachnids of Carida, the clawing dinkos of Proxima Dibal, the—"

"That's enough," she interrupted.

"You're right," he agreed and glanced around. "It was more than enough reason for the Alliance to take notice of you. We did. And we need you now."

"For cover," she said, "and nothing more."

"Exactly."

She shook her head slightly, thinking that here again was someone who didn't realize her abilities. *He knew I had a sample from a Sarlacc,* she thought, *and didn't even recognize how difficult it must have been to collect.*

"So that's all I am to you people? You want me to risk bringing the displeasure of the Empire down on my head so that you can have a free ticket to go planet-hopping? I won't do it."

"Why not?"

"I'm surprised you even have to ask, after you laid it out so obviously before me," she countered, growing angry. She started to tick off items on her fingers. "The Empire destroyed my family. I won't lose anything more to them. I've got a good job and I'm safe," she added and started to walk away. Before she had taken two steps, though, Finn grabbed her and spun her around.

"Safe?" he nearly shouted at her, but remembered where he was and lowered his voice. "You think you're safe with your head buried in the sand? If we noticed the things you were doing, or rather not doing, it won't take your Imperial superiors much longer before they do—if they haven't already. And when they do," he added, "they will come for you. Make no mistake about that."

Dusque shook her head in refusal, but didn't say a word.

"Don't you see," Finn added, moving closer to her, "that there is no safety in not taking a stand. The Empire doesn't just kill exposed Rebels. Even if you choose to do nothing, you could still be choosing death."

Before Dusque could respond, Finn grabbed her

upper arms and pulled her to him in a deep kiss. Dusque was momentarily stunned. But even more startling was the fact that she found herself responding to him. For a moment, she forgot who and where she was. A flash of white and the clink of armor, however, brought her back to reality as a stormtrooper patrol passed by them a moment later.

Dusque pulled herself free of Finn's grip and dragged a hand roughly across her mouth. She looked at him disgustedly and said, "Was I just cover there, too?" In the subdued light, though, Finn didn't look so self-possessed. That observation off-balanced her more than the kiss, and she realized that she just didn't know what to make of the man. It frustrated her, but it confused her, as well.

"I've got to go," she said awkwardly.

Finn hadn't given up quite yet. He reached out and caught her hand once more. "What will it take?" he whispered to her.

Dusque shook her head and, without a backward glance, broke away. "I don't know," she answered, too quietly for anyone but herself to hear.

THREE

Tendau Nandon was slowly making his way around the casino. He hadn't seen Dusque for a while and suspected that she had managed to head back to her hotel room. He shook his head sadly and nearly banged it against a low-hanging lamp in the process. The casino was just not well equipped for his kind, although it did accommodate a variety of other species well, judging by the happy noises.

Or perhaps they are just too inebriated to notice, the Ithorian thought.

The place had become more crowded since the doors had opened for the evening. Scores surrounded the spinnerpits, and there were lines to the lugjack machines four deep. It seemed as if at least a quarter of the players were winning, but it might simply have been that they were drunk and found everything worth cheering about. And when the Ithorian thought it couldn't get any louder, he noticed an entertainer setting up behind a nalargon near the bar. As soon as he had tuned his instrument, though, he began to play a song that Tendau could almost recognize. As if on cue, a few Twi'lek dancers appeared from nowhere and began an impromptu show. Although the mood was festive, the Ithorian sensed an almost frantic pulse behind it.

Deciding to take one more look at the sky before retiring for bed, he stepped through the double doors, almost tripping over a body in his way. At first he thought someone had fallen and injured himself, but then he realized that some of the more raucous patrons had literally spilled out onto the walkway. A brief inspection told him they were no worse for the wear. Then, as he started to shuffle along, he saw Dusque walking back toward the casino. He smiled, but his two mouths gradually turned down as he got a better look at her.

She was walking with her head down, her eyes partially squeezed shut. With both hands, she was rhythmically rubbing her temples. She was so distracted that she nearly marched right past him. Tendau reached out with one long hand and brushed her shoulder. She twisted around with such a fearful look on her face, the Ithorian didn't know which of them was more startled.

"Are you well?" he asked her, concern echoing from both his mouths.

She didn't answer right away, and Tendau got an even closer look at her by the light of the casino sign. Her light brown hair was more askew than usual. Her face was flushed, and her eyes had the glassy quality of unshed tears. While Tendau knew that the human female was prone to fluctuations in hormone levels not seen in many other species, he had never known Dusque to fall victim to their cyclical nature. In fact, he could not recall ever seeing her so distraught.

When he had first met her months ago, he had been struck by how earnest she looked. He had not been in the service of the Emperor for very long, and his colleagues had still regarded him with mistrust. As the only Ithorian in the group, he was certain he would always be a bit of an outsider. So he readily sympathized with the newest arrival. Because she was the only female there, he knew she would have an uphill climb to mesh with the other bioengineers. She was diligent, hardworking, and, he discovered from his personal experience, immaculate in her collecting techniques. It didn't take him long to recognize that the woman didn't make mistakes; she was very intentional about every aspect of her profession. What had impressed him the most, though, was her affinity with other creatures.

Whether it was collecting DNA from anesthetized animals or sneaking into a lair or warren to investigate, he saw that Dusque moved as if she were a natural part of her surroundings. In those situations, she displayed a sense of balance that he rarely saw when she was with people. She appeared content when she was with animals, and at peace. She did not look that way now.

He reached a gentle hand toward her face and laid it briefly against her brow before brushing an errant strand of hair from her eyes. She lost some of her fearful look and closed her eyes at his touch.

"What's the matter?" he asked her again.

Dusque shrugged her thin shoulders and said tiredly, "Nothing is wrong, Tendau. I think the day has finally caught up with me. So I'm going to call it an evening, if you don't mind," she added and started to leave. But the Ithorian was not so easily avoided.

"As long as you are going back in, why don't you join me for something soothing to drink? You know it will help you relax," he reminded her, not willing to have her go before he could find out why she looked so troubled.

She smiled weakly up at him, and he knew her heart was not in it. But she agreed anyway. And he knew she did it for his sake alone.

"You never do take no for an answer, do you?" she quipped.

"Not where you are concerned."

Dusque shook her head and waved briefly. "It's nothing, really," she said, dismissing her obvious distress. "But maybe something to drink would be good before retiring."

Tendau nodded and motioned back to the casino doorway. He walked slightly behind her as they both sidestepped the drunken Trandoshan who was still lying on the ground. The doors slid open with an airless *whoosh,* and the sounds of the gamblers hit them like a wave. He saw that Dusque faltered a bit and seemed unsure of her footing. The Ithorian stepped alongside her and offered her the crook of his slender arm. She hesitantly accepted, and he led her toward the bar. He lowered his head enough so that one of his mouths was near her left ear.

"Just one drink, maybe a little something to eat, and we'll turn in. All right?"

"All right," she replied, and this time he saw that she smiled at him with some genuine warmth.

There were twenty or so customers lined up along the bar. As Tendau and his colleague walked the length of it in search of two free seats, he noticed that more than one male turned and stared at Dusque. It happened quite frequently, and Tendau was saddened that she should always be so distressed by the reactions of others. Like most Ithorians, he revered nature and saw the beauty in all creatures. It was not hard to see her beauty; it was just sad that so few managed to look past it and really see her. And he knew Dusque was aware of that, as well. No matter how she excelled at a very difficult job, her gender was always a stumbling block. And he had noticed that lately she had accepted more and more hazardous missions. He suspected it was in an effort to erase her gender in the eyes of their superiors. He feared that her growing desire to dive into risky situations was going to land her in some very hot water, and he wouldn't be there to help.

Toward the far end of the bar, he saw a small empty table. Tendau motioned to it, and Dusque nodded. When the waiter droid left with their order, Tendau tried again to find out what was wrong.

"Where did you get off to?" he asked her.

"I was just wandering around, taking in the sights," she replied evasively. "Isn't that what you were doing, too?"

"Did you try your hand at some of the games of chance?" he asked, sidestepping her question.

"Oh yes, I got a little more than I bargained for," she answered, and Tendau could discern a trace of bitterness in her voice. "What about you? Where did you end up?"

"Oh," he answered slowly, "I just walked around and made observations."

"Did you find Mastivo and pass along your regards?"

"No, I was unable to locate him. I'm afraid I saw no one we know, after all."

"Oh," she answered, "no one at all. Hmm . . ." She seemed to be fishing for some kind of answer, and the Ithorian wondered why. Normally, Dusque was one of the most straightforward beings he knew. Now she was coming across almost as devious in her approach with him.

The droid returned with their order, and Dusque grew silent. Tendau observed that while she picked at a bowl of melon, she was surreptitiously scanning the room. He wondered who she was looking for, or if she even knew herself. Starting to worry, the Ithorian tried a different approach.

"Our hosts have thought of everything tonight,"

he told her. "They even brought in a nalargon player. He is not bad."

"I can just hear him over the crowd," she replied. "I've actually been listening for the last few moments. Surprisingly, I think his playing is making my headache fade a bit."

"They are known to be very calming," Tendau agreed. The music and the food seemed to be relaxing her a bit. He tried again. "Will you tell me what happened tonight?"

Dusque looked at him sharply and seemed to be weighing something in her mind. She leaned slightly forward and he could see that she was chewing her lip. It was a behavior he had noticed she exhibited when something serious was bothering her. She seemed on the verge of speaking when she heard a piece of a conversation off to one side and shut down again.

"Not here," she said.

The Ithorian decided to let the matter rest for a while and they ate silently, the only ones in the casino who weren't talking. He concluded that she would tell him or not in her own time and fashion.

To their right, a few of the handlers from the arena had gathered. Tendau noticed that the ones who hadn't won had moved on from commiserating about their losses to discussing some of the latest gear that was available to them. The topics ranged from reinforced gloves to more specific tools used for training and animal enrichment. He was half paying attention to their discussions in case they had some interesting insights into their animals. He valued all perspectives, even those that were obviously skewed.

"It can't be done," one of the handlers said. "You can't tame those bats."

"Aw, you just haven't tried hard enough," her companion joked.

The Zabrak who had made the initial claim slowly pulled off her left glove. She slammed her elbow down on the table and waved her left hand in the air. Tendau could see she was missing two fingers.

"Believe me," she said, "I've tried."

Her companion lost some of his haughty air and lowered his eyes.

"Borgles are more than mean," she continued. "It's like they're evil right down to their core. Maybe because of all the time they spend in their caves, in the dark."

"Are they native to Rori?" her chastised friend asked, and Tendau saw that he was treating her with slightly more respect since she had revealed her compromised hand.

"Don't know," Fingers replied. "There's so much speculation about Naboo's moon in general, I don't know if anybody knows the straight answer."

"What do you mean?" he asked her.

"Well, I'm no historian," she began, "but I don't think folks can even agree on who colonized Rori, let alone what is and isn't indigenous to the place. As I understand it, some say the original human colonists of Naboo landed there first, hated it because it was too inhospitable, and then came here. Others say that a group of spice miners went there first in search of the mother lode. Nobody can agree."

"Actually," her friend said, "I heard that it was Gungans who first built a settlement there."

"See what I mean?" Fingers agreed. "No one has the same story."

"I heard it was the spice miner theory," Dusque whispered to Tendau. The Ithorian cast a surprised glance at her, unaware that she had been paying attention so closely. But when he saw the way she regarded Fingers, he realized Dusque was becoming intrigued by the thought of an animal that couldn't be trained.

"What someone should do," Fingers continued, unaware that her conversation was being so closely regarded, "is investigate a little more. I mean, there are so many unusual animals there. You'd think somebody would want to know."

"She's got a good point," Dusque told Tendau. He shifted uncomfortably in his seat, because he was afraid he knew where her interest was going to lead.

"If some of the animals could be sampled and it turned out that they were originally indigenous to another planet, it might help narrow down just who did colonize the place," she finished.

"It might," Tendau agreed tentatively. "But by

the same logic, it might increase the speculation, as well."

"Even conflicting data has value," Dusque argued.

Tendau was torn. He was glad she was starting to act more like her old self. Still, the gleam in her gray eyes was making him nervous. Although Tendau did not know the Zabrak handler, the woman looked capable enough. If she had lost two fingers trying to handle one, there was no telling what might happen to Dusque, with no experience tangling with borgle bats.

"All data is valuable," he said. "All right, just what do you have in mind?"

"Well," she began with an innocent tilt of her head, "as long as we're already here, I don't see why we couldn't look into this a little more ourselves."

Tendau sighed inwardly. It was as he expected. "The only issue, as I see it, is that we don't have the opportunity to get our superiors to approve it. This idea of yours doesn't have the sanctioning of the Empire."

He saw Dusque straighten her back almost imperceptibly at his concerns. She had resumed her wary stance, and he wondered again what had transpired this evening to cause her to become so distrustful of him.

"Since when do you care so much about Imperial endorsement?" she snapped, and folded her arms. "Are you afraid someone is watching us?" Her voice had dropped, and she cast a quick eye around the room.

"You know me better than that," he replied.

Dusque dropped her stern gaze as the Ithorian's words sank in.

"You're right," she admitted. "I guess I'm just surprised that you could walk away from a mission that has this potential for discovery. Doesn't seem like you."

"*Walk* is exactly the point, Dusque. You know how painful it can be for me to move around planetside," he explained. "Even here, where it is somewhat civilized, I have had some discomfort. Those two we were eavesdropping on mentioned that Rori was relatively inhospitable. I suspect that I will have some difficulty moving around there. I am afraid I would slow you down."

"I could go alone, " Dusque said. "I have to go," she added more intensely. "I have to get away from . . . all these people. I need—I don't know, some space to think, I guess." For a moment it seemed as if she were going to say more, but then she just clammed up. She looked unhappy.

"Even if I were to agree to this," Tendau said slowly, "we only have enough funds to pay for our lodging here and transport back to the labs."

Even as he threw up another excuse to dissuade Dusque, he watched as one corner of her mouth slowly curved upward. He knew that grin only too well. She always looked that way when she trumped one of their supervisors. She reached into her trouser pockets and pulled out handfuls of chips, which she promptly dumped onto the table. They lay there like a spotted rainbow.

"I think that'll cover it," she said gleefully.

Tendau tilted his curved neck and knew he had lost. She was determined to go, and if he didn't go with her, he was certain she would attempt it on her own. He shook his head at her, but found a small chuckle inside.

Dusque leaned back in her chair and slowly rolled her head from one side to the other. Even over the bar chatter, Tendau could hear the joints in her neck crack several times. He worried even more about what it was that was weighing on her so heavily. It looked to him as if the small trip would be the quickest way for him to find out.

"I just want to get out of here," she added quietly. "I feel like there are too many eyes on me. Just to have the ground under my feet and a sky overhead for even a little while . . ." She trailed off.

"All right," the Ithorian agreed.

Dusque straightened her head and focused her eyes on him. "Really?" she asked quietly, and there was a childlike delight in her voice.

Tendau nodded. "When do you want to go?"

"How about at first light?"

"Will that be enough time to gather appropriate equipment?" he asked her.

"I've got my pack and a few extra items," she replied, and Tendau watched as she perked up and grew more confident with each passing moment, now that she had something to focus on. "Anything else we might need we can probably get here. I think I noticed a crafting station near the spaceport. I'm sure that'll cover it." She shoved at some of her chips with a slim finger.

"There's a travel terminal near the spaceport. When we arrived the other night, I noticed there were at least a few shuttles to Rori on a daily basis. We shouldn't have any trouble purchasing tickets. We could be there and back in the matter of a day or so, no one the wiser." She looked at Tendau, and he could tell she was reining in some of her excitement. "Are you really sure you don't mind?"

"Anything for you, child," he told her. "And who knows what we might learn once we arrive there, hmm?"

"Exactly," Dusque agreed. "I'll find you at first light." She got up, and Tendau watched as she disappeared into the crowd.

"Who knows what we'll find," he repeated slowly to himself, "who knows?"

FOUR

"Where are you?" Dusque called, trying not to sound worried.

Waist deep in a marshy bog, Dusque was cold and miserable. She couldn't believe Tendau had disappeared. And when she got no response, fear set in.

She and the Ithorian had arrived on Rori a few hours earlier. There were only two cities on Naboo's moon, and they had chosen the one that bore the name of the man who had officially created the first colony: Narmle. However, what had started out as an outpost had grown into an almost respectably sized city, even boasting a hotel and a medcenter. Dusque had noted that the latter, tiny facility though it was, might come in handy, assuming one wasn't wounded too far away from it. A thick, reedy bog separated Narmle from the other city, Restuss. Other than that, there was just a vast expanse of jungles and swamps.

"I can see why Narmle eventually gave up on colonizing this place," she had told Tendau. "I haven't seen such an overgrown planet in a long time." The overcast skies added an ominous feel to the place.

Tendau had chuckled at her remarks. "First off, remember that this is a moon, not a planet," he'd corrected her. "And for one as young as you, nothing is really a *long time*." And then he had smiled at her.

The two had left the spaceport in search of more information prior to their search for the borgles. Before they had left Moenia, Dusque had questioned the fingerless Zabrak about the bats, but Fingers had grown hesitant to give out much information as soon as she had realized that Dusque was an Imperial biologist.

"Just why do you want to know?" she had asked.

"I overheard your conversation last night and I agreed with what you said," Dusque explained.

"You were eavesdropping?" Fingers asked, shocked. She got a wary look in her eye, and her answers became much more guarded. Dusque soon gave up, empathizing with how the woman felt about discovering her privacy had been violated. She was rapidly learning about that herself.

Upon their arrival on Rori, they tried to glean a little more information about the borgles and their habitat. The few who would talk to them, after a tankard or two at the cantina, spoke in low voices tinged with fear. The borgles, it seemed, as well as a few other creatures, had garnered quite a reputation around the area. And it was not good.

"I don't know anybody who's ever killed one

of them things," a drunken Rodian had slurred. "They're just evil," he added. No one else had been able to offer much more in the way of useful information except for the general direction in which they might find some caves that housed the creatures. They had to make do with that meager guidance.

Making sure she had emergency supplies in her pack, Dusque concluded that she was well equipped. Between her sampling tools and food rations for both her and the Ithorian, there wasn't much more she could think of. She hoisted her pack on her back, and strapped a small but effective Twi'lek dagger to her thigh. And in consideration of the terrain, she even tied back her waist-length hair. Then, certain she had everything, she had checked in with Tendau.

"Are you sure you want to come along?" she had asked him one more time. "You could stay here in Narmle and we could use comms to stay in touch."

"And what would be the point of my remaining behind?" he had asked. "I thought we were in this together. Besides, who would watch you if I weren't there?" He had smiled at that, but Dusque became uneasy.

"Why would anyone need to watch me?" she asked, on edge.

The Ithorian lost his easy smile. "I meant," he corrected himself, "who would make sure you stayed out of trouble?" The moment dragged out between them, filled with tension.

Finally Dusque broke the awkwardness. "Since

when do I ever get into trouble?" she asked, deciding she had to lighten up more around the Ithorian.

He raised his long hand and started to count off. "There was the time on Tatooine, Yavin Four—"

"All right!" She laughed with genuine warmth and threw her hands up in defeat. "You win. Watch away." And with that, she gathered up his gear, despite his protests, and placed the bulk of it in her backpack, to relieve him from some of the excess weight and pressure on his feet. She noticed one item that was out of the ordinary, however. Tendau had a CDEF blaster in his possession. She had never seen him carry any weapon before, other than a survival knife. She looked at him sharply.

"I have an uneasy feeling about this mission," he told her gravely. "And I did not want to go into it unprepared."

"Probably a good idea," Dusque agreed hesitantly, but she was still unnerved by the sight of the deadly weapon. Of course, she told herself, all weapons can be lethal with the right training. Still, there was something almost sinister about the black, shiny blaster lying there like an unspoken accusation.

And so they had left Narmle on foot and headed out into the wilds of the Rori backwoods. For a while, Dusque and Tendau did no more than follow the rough coordinates that they had received from the drunken Rodian, who had simply said to go southeast. Each seemed lost in his or her respective thoughts, and the wide plains were ideal for contemplation. The gray, overcast skies fit the mood. The farther in they proceeded, the more Dusque sensed herself relax.

With the fields under her feet and the lack of prying eyes, she felt as though a weight were lifting. The only thing that preyed on her mind was her colleague. The longer they traveled across the plains, the more Dusque realized that what was troubling her about Tendau was not his actions at all, but the fact that she somehow doubted him. That was what had set her off balance. She knew there was only one thing to do, and she stopped her light run dead.

"What is it?" Tendau asked, immediately on guard. "Did you see something?"

"Not exactly," she began. "But I thought this might be a good spot to do some foraging and surveying. We came here for samples, after all."

"Good idea," he agreed, but Dusque could see that at least part of the reason he was acquiescing so easily was because he was tired. She once again marveled at his fortitude in his work when he was so obviously in pain, and she wondered how she could have come to doubt him.

Whether it was the onset of shame or the fact that she just wanted to be honest with him, Dusque blurted out, "Are you an Imperial bioengineer?"

The Ithorian turned off his device, stopped surveying, and stood up. He had a perplexed look on his face, as though he was trying to figure out the joke in her absurd question. "You know what I am," he told her. "Why do you ask?"

The pile of rocks she had been surveying was abandoned. She lowered her pack to the ground and sat down with her back against it. The cold stones felt good on her shoulders. She motioned to Tendau with her hand, inviting him to sit with her.

As soon as the Ithorian had lowered his large frame to the ground, he asked her, "Is this about last night?"

Dusque smiled ruefully. "Right to the heart of it, as usual. Am I so transparent?"

"Child," Tendau started, "it's not because you are transparent that I know you, but because you are honest. And last night, you were not yourself. Something or some*one* frightened you. It pained me," he continued, laying a hand against his chest, "to see you so far removed from yourself. Will you tell me what has happened to cause you to question?"

Dusque turned away, once again consumed by doubt laced with fear. It was this unnamed fear that had changed everything for her. She shifted onto her knees and started to rummage through her pack. "If we're going to be here a while," she explained, "we might as well be comfortable." She found her small tool kit and in a matter of moments had a tiny but cheery fire burning. The damp was starting to seep into her bones and she knew that if she felt uncomfortable, the Ithorian felt worse, no matter how stoic he remained about it.

"As usual, you are a wonderful observer. Something did happen last night," she said and then faltered.

"Do you want to share this with me right now," he offered, "or would you rather we not speak of it?" Dusque knew he had made the offer because he sensed her unease. And with that simple act of kindness, she knew in her heart that if there was anyone she could or should trust, it was he.

"Thank you for that," she replied and he smiled at her, giving her the time she needed. "Does it ever bother you," she began, "to do the things we do?"

"Is that why you asked if I was an Imperial engineer?" he asked. Dusque nodded. The Ithorian stared into the fire a moment before he responded. "It is something I wrestle with," he admitted.

"I wanted so much," he went on, "to see all of Mother Jungle in her many incarnations. That need drove me from my herd ship to pursue the stars. And in the course of that pursuit, I was 'recruited,' if you will, into Imperial service.

"At the beginning," he added, "it did not seem so bad."

Dusque nodded in understanding. "And now?"

It was Tendau's turn to sigh. "And now, it is different."

"Why now?" Dusque asked, hoping that his answers would somehow guide her.

"I thought," he admitted, "that the Empire would leave us alone. And I believed that nature should be allowed to take its course. But after the Battle of

Yavin, we were no longer uninvolved. The Empire decided to leave a garrison stationed on Ithor. Like so many other worlds, the Empire had implanted themselves like a blight on us. It was then that my eyes were opened." He stopped and looked into the small fire and did not continue for several long moments.

"I believe in the Mother Jungle," he said eventually, "and disease is a part of her mystery. By design, it serves a purpose, as do famine and competition for territory. All of these things are unpleasant for some to observe, but a single part in a larger cycle. But when one starts to tamper with nature, the disease that should be checked runs rampant instead. I believe the Empire places the galaxy out of equilibrium. It is the duty of every individual to find and restore balance.

"So," he sighed, "to answer your question, I am a biologist who works for the Empire. I do not know for how much longer, though. Does that make sense?"

Dusque was silent for a while. She weighed his words against what she felt inside. Finally, she said, "And just what does one do to return the galaxy to equilibrium?"

The Ithorian smiled at her. "My child, I do not have one answer for you. I wish I did. But each of us must make a journey to a decision that is for us alone. While my destination might be the same as yours, our paths must inherently be different."

Dusque pulled her knees up against her chest and

wrapped her arms about them, although she felt no chill. "And how do we know what our path is?"

Tendau reached over with his long arm and brushed her hair lightly. Dusque momentarily had a flash of her father. That gesture had been the only physical affection he had ever demonstrated to the sole girl in his brood. She was struck momentarily by a touch of homesickness, which she immediately banished.

"It will become clear to you," he said gently, "in time."

Caught up in the moment, Dusque confessed, "I met someone last night." The Ithorian said nothing, only nodded to her to continue.

"He said he was with the Alliance," she said quietly, lowering her voice even though there was no one else as far as the eye could see. "And he said he needed my help." She looked at the Ithorian imploringly. "He . . . knew things about me."

Tendau nodded gravely. "Dusque, there are very few secrets in this galaxy. You should know that. After all," he added, "even our job is to unravel secrets at the most basic, genetic level. We are all watched as though under a microscope. We are all known to one degree or another."

She shifted uncomfortably. "I guess I thought I was under the radar, so to speak. I guess I thought no one really noticed me. I mean," she added, "I never get any recognition at the labs. I got used to thinking of myself as invisible. And," she finally admitted, "I think I liked being overlooked."

"It is a shadow of a life," the Ithorian said, "and one I have been guilty of, as well. I put my desires before the needs of others. But you have only been overlooked out of fear. Willel fears you because he knows that you will surpass him in ability soon enough."

"So what do I do?" she asked.

"You decide what you can live with and what you cannot bear to witness any longer," he stated flatly.

"Is that what you've decided to do?" she asked. "I thought I saw you talking to someone unusual last night," she offered, suddenly feeling guilty that she had spied on him.

The Ithorian, however, took no visible offense. "Child, we do what we have to and we choose what to live with. Nature must, however, be kept in balance. And those things that are unnatural should be removed—otherwise chaos ensues."

Dusque sensed he was finished for the moment and wouldn't tell her what to do. He had been clear enough that the choice belonged to the individual. As she started to toss dirt on the fire to smother the flames, she silently berated herself for how servile in her thinking she had become. Of course, she trusted Tendau, but did she really want him to tell her what to do? Or had she simply become so used to taking orders from her male colleagues that she was afraid to stand alone? She shook her head.

She started to put her backpack on, when she felt the Ithorian, unasked, help her with it. She smiled despite her mental debate. "Thank you," she told him and held his gaze for a long moment. "For everything."

"Child, when the time comes, you will see your path like a beacon before your eyes. Trust me," he finished.

"I do," she finally admitted.

"Now that that is settled, let's see about those bats," he said. And they headed farther into the trees.

Initially, finding paths through the trees had been simple. However, that did not last for very long. As they struggled with vines and branches, it became necessary to bushwhack their way through the increasingly dense jungle. The gray sky was blotted out by the thick canopy of trees, and Dusque felt claustrophobic. Almost no light was able to break through, and they had a hard time keeping each other in sight. By default, Dusque took the lead to clear a path for Tendau to follow. She could feel herself become winded, and the moisture-laden air was difficult to breathe. Each breath was an effort, and both were soon taxed. To make matters more challenging, their coordinates took them straight to a bog.

Seeing no way around it, they had no choice but to wade through it. Dusque went in first and held her arms above the waterline. Tendau followed, but seemed less uncomfortable than she.

"I hate getting wet," she mumbled.

The sun set, although it made little difference

where they were. Then Dusque noticed little points
of light that appeared to be dancing above the water, and she smiled despite her misery. The lights
turned out to be a kind of glow bug. There must
have been a hundred or so, and they bobbed and
fluttered just above the boggy water. She was so en-
tranced, she forgot where she was. When she realized Tendau hadn't commented on them, she turned
around to see why not. That was the moment she
realized he was nowhere to be seen.

"Tendau," she called again and turned sluggishly
around, tangled in the tall reeds. She drew her
Twi'lek dagger and slashed at the plants, her heart
pounding. She struggled forward, her splashing sending the glow bugs into a frenzy of buzzing. A cloud
of them dissipated in her wake.

"Tendau," she called again, fearing the worst.

"Here!" The faint reply seemed to come from
somewhere off to her left.

She slogged her way toward a clump of knotted
trees, grateful to find more solid purchase. As she
grabbed some of the heavy roots to hoist herself
out, a strong hand grabbed her wrist and yanked
her free of the murky water.

"I think I found their lair," he whispered. "At
least, it looks like what the Zabrak trainer mentioned last night." And he motioned for her to
follow.

Above the bank, nestled in a hillside, was what
appeared to be a cave. Dusque shook her head,

impressed that her colleague had spotted the lair with its natural camouflage and in the poor light.

"Good eyes," she told him. "I was so busy watching glow bugs, I didn't even notice I had lost track of you. Sorry," she apologized sheepishly.

"Don't worry," he replied. "I know if I had been in any real trouble, you would have found me."

Dusque pulled out a small halo lamp and switched it on. Its beam illuminated a small circle of dirt in front of her. She nodded to Tendau, and they approached the cave opening.

The entrance was large enough to house several packs of creatures. A quick perusal revealed nothing, although Dusque did stop to do a brief survey of the sopping grounds around the cave opening just in case. With a quick nod to Tendau, she entered the lair. He followed directly behind.

The first section of the den was cavernous, with a vaulted ceiling from which hung a few stalactites. Dusque crossed her arms reflexively as a cold breeze assaulted her. In the distance, she could hear the faint sound of water dripping intermittently. That and the few echoes of rockfalls were all she heard at first. There was no sign of anything living. Her faint light revealed several tunnels, each winding in a different direction. She turned her face from one side to the other until she could feel on her skin where the breeze was coming from. She motioned to Tendau with one of the hand signals they had developed since first working together, and they started their descent into the darkness.

Given the cave's acoustics, it was a challenge not to reveal their location to anything that might have been nesting in there. Fortunately Dusque's boots, made from the softest hides with soles sturdy enough for the most rugged terrain, were as quiet as though she were barefoot. And the Ithorian, although it was extremely challenging to match Dusque's abilities, was as silent as she. It was so dark within the cave that even with her light, Dusque was forced to run her hand against the side of the tunnel to keep from becoming disoriented. The rocks that formed the cave walls and ceiling were so unremarkable and so dark, it was difficult to visually tell which way was up at times. She found the effect almost nauseating.

As they descended, Dusque started to become discouraged. There was little sign of anything other than more rocks and tunnels. She was about to motion to Tendau that they should turn around when she heard an odd sound down farther to their left. She held up her hand and signaled to the Ithorian to hold up and listen. She saw him cock his head at an angle, and after a moment's deliberation, he nodded. He raised his hand and waved his fingers briefly: their sign for wings.

Dusque slid slowly around the corner, Tendau directly behind her. By her weak light, she saw a creature hovering over something about ten meters away. She couldn't make out much, but she was able to observe that whatever it was had a wingspan about as long as she was tall and what looked like a

wicked beak of sorts. It was hovering over a small
mound. Both she and Tendau held their ground and
watched as the creature dipped down over the
mound, settled on it for a moment, and then took to
the air again. The creature repeated the process a
few more times before flying deeper into the tunnels. Certain that it wasn't going to return in the near
future, Dusque and Tendau cautiously approached
the unattended mound.

Dusque dropped to her knees and saw that the
mound was the remains of a squall. Not indigenous
to Rori, it was a small, fur-covered mammal with
long ears and a distinctive, hopping gait. And the
one on the tunnel floor was a very dead specimen,
mostly likely the recent meal of a borgle bat. As
Dusque ran her hand over the corpse, she felt something wet and slick near the squall's throat. She
pulled her hand away and held it in the circle of
light from her halo lamp. Her hand gleamed back a
rich crimson in the dim light: blood. That was interesting: blood on the neck, but not much on the
ground around the corpse. That would suggest that
the borgle that had killed the squall was not just an
ordinary carnivore, but a bloodsucker. Dusque
flashed her stained hand in warning to the Ithorian.
She rose to her knees and moved down the tunnel.

Winding her way to the right, Dusque heard the
sounds of flapping grow. She reached a bend in the
tunnel and, using it for cover, carefully peered
around the corner. Several creatures were flapping
around in a cluster. None of them was as large as

the first one she had seen above, near the corpse of the squall. But she was able to get a better look at these specimens.

They were definitely bats, with leathery wings and fur-covered bodies. Their faces were elongated, and they had very pointed ears. From where she stood it was hard to tell if they had any type of claws on their feet, but Dusque assumed they probably did. The fact that they were blood drinkers was most likely the reason they were untamable. Any creatures this aggressive would have to be taken when they were extremely young, if one were to have any hope of training them to respond. One of the group suddenly emitted a high-pitched sound and flew off into the depths. The others followed, and Dusque seized the opportunity.

Shrugging off Tendau's warning grip, she slowly crawled over to where the young borgles had been fluttering. There she discovered the remains of what must have been a nest. She grew excited when she saw that while there were no juveniles present, there were tufts of downy fur caught in the nest itself. She deftly pulled out her sample containers and collected all the bits she could find. She gave Tendau the sign for success and was sliding back toward him when an odd reflection caught her attention.

There was something glinting in her light off in a far recess of the tunnel. As Dusque moved closer to it, she could see that yet another opening appeared to descend even farther down. What had caught

Dusque's attention was a bone, picked clean. And she saw that there were more reflections down the partially concealed tunnel. Since neither she nor Tendau had spotted any other living thing in the caverns besides the bats, including the smallest insect, Dusque's curiosity was piqued. Those bats' feeding habits were blood drinking. This was most likely the work of something else. She wondered what other creatures might be living in down among the bats. She couldn't resist a quick reconnaissance. Tendau shook his head, but Dusque held up one finger and disappeared into the gaping maw.

She felt more cold air brush against her skin and realized that this was the source of the chill that she had felt when they entered the cave system above. Her lamp revealed almost nothing. The darkness seemed to swallow it up and was absolute. Dusque felt a stab of dread, and the hairs on the back of her neck stood on end. She was starting to reconsider her plan when something bumped into her from behind.

Stifling a scream, she turned and realized the Ithorian had followed her. She smiled, although she knew he couldn't see it, and continued into the darkness. With him near her, Dusque was more sure of herself. However, as she came across more and more bones, each one a different size, her certainty began to falter. With no definite way to tell how big the cavern was, she was starting to understand that it was littered with bone cairns in every niche. She wished that she had thought to mask her and the

Ithorian's scents before they had begun their exploration. And then she heard a flapping in the dark. They both froze in their tracks.

Unlike the sound the other bats had made, this was slow and deliberate and powerful. Dusque knew it was near and was torn between her desire to see it and her growing fright. She shook her head and told herself that this was exactly the reason she had become a bioengineer: to discover new things and to understand them. She knew there was no turning back. So she steeled herself and continued deeper into the black cavern. Feeling her way against the wall, she knew Tendau was still behind her. And as she felt the wall curve, she came around to an eerie sight.

By her weak light, Dusque saw a mound of bones as tall as she was and nearly eight meters long. And atop that skeletal throne was a monstrous borgle. Heart pounding, mind racing, Dusque estimated the beast was at least five meters long. While it resembled the others in almost every other detail besides its size, there was one other striking feature: the bat had glowing, hateful, yellow eyes. In fact, they were almost hypnotic in their power. In the pit of her stomach, Dusque suddenly understood why the fingerless trainer had said they were evil incarnate. She reached back and squeezed the Ithorian's hand so hard that she nearly broke his fingers. She found herself frozen in her tracks and hazily wondered if it was the borgle's doing.

As Tendau started to tug her back, the mutant

bat let out a shrill screech, and from somewhere below, Dusque heard the fluttering of hundreds of
wings. The Ithorian pulled harder, and she suddenly
felt freed. The two turned and started to run at a
breakneck speed. Tendau's small pistol and her dagger would be of no use against the sheer number
of bats.

As they stumbled through the tunnels, it was
Dusque's turn to grab her friend and pull him
along. She could feel the breath burn in her lungs,
but her fright had galvanized her into action and
given her a burst of energy. Just as she thought she
felt claws grab at her hair, she saw the weak light of
day ahead. With the entrance to the cave in sight,
they both increased their speed and tumbled, rolling
out of the cave and partway down the slight hill.
They lay in a heap, gasping for air, weapons drawn
and at the ready. But nothing followed them out.

Dusque rolled onto her back and let a sigh of relief escape. After she had a moment to collect herself, she started to giggle. Her giggles grew into
full-fledged laughter and then Tendau joined in. They
laughed until they were breathless again, and then
Dusque pushed herself on one elbow to regard her
friend.

"Did you see the size of that thing?" she asked,
amazed.

"It would have been hard to miss it," Tendau
quipped, "seeing how it filled the whole vault."

Dusque smiled but found herself sobering up. No
longer giddy, she said seriously, "Aside from its ob-

vious size, that thing was wrong . . . somehow." She found she didn't have the words to describe how she felt about its overpowering malevolence.

"Yes," Tendau agreed. "There's no denying that that creature was a mutant—an abomination of evil. Sometimes it is easy to pick that out, isn't it?" He gave her a pointed stare.

"Yes," she agreed, his real meaning perfectly clear to her. "Sometimes it's easy to tell something is wrong. But sometimes it isn't," she argued.

With that, she knelt and rummaged through her pack, checking to make sure her samples had survived their hasty departure. The containers were unbroken, and she was glad the trip hadn't been wasted after all.

"If only we could've sampled that thing," she murmured.

"You amaze me, child," Tendau admitted. "You really do at times. We're lucky the thing didn't sample *us.*" He stood and straightened his tunic. "Now let's return before you get us into real trouble."

FIVE

As dawn broke with its thin, pink tendrils snaking across the sky, they made good time heading back to Narmle, even though they were exhausted from their flight from the cavern. Dusque, elated at their relative success, could not resist stopping to take a quick survey of some small warrens that she had noticed on their way out to the caves. While she was sampling, she thought she heard a low growl not too distant from where she and Tendau were working.

"Do you hear something?" she asked him quietly.

"No," he replied.

"I think something's been following us," she told him.

"Child, you are imagining it. I think we are both still somewhat on edge."

"Just the same, let's keep moving, okay?"

"Of course." And they packed up their equipment and continued on.

Suddenly, the low growls that Dusque was certain she had been hearing stopped entirely. Rather than relieve her, though, it made Dusque's hackles rise. Before she could even turn around to say another word to Tendau, the jungle exploded around them in a cacophony of snarls and screams. Dusque realized that one of the screams had come from her.

A huge tusk-cat came crashing out from the thick brush. Weighing easily four times as much as Dusque, it had two very prominent canines protruding from its jaw that lent its kind their name. The feline was sand colored with a very long tail and strong haunches, although its fur looked mangy and patchy. Dusque and the Ithorian tried to dart for cover. Dusque made it to some trees, but Tendau was not so fortunate.

The tusk-cat bounded after the Ithorian without hesitation. Dusque could see that he was fumbling for his blaster, his fright and his exhaustion making him clumsy. The tusk-cat was about to pounce on him, and Dusque knew he didn't stand a chance. Seeing him in mortal danger, she acted without thinking.

Unsheathing her dagger, she rushed at the charging tusk-cat. With a leap, she landed partially on its back. As soon as she made contact with the cat, she locked her arm around the creature. Surprise and momentum were on her side, and Dusque diverted the feline's attention away from Tendau and onto herself.

The large cat galloped around like an unbroken tauntaun, trying to buck the offending weight off it. Dusque, at the same time, tried to slash at the cat's throat, but it managed to snap its jaws dangerously close to her hand in retaliation. The sharp teeth caught her on the arm and Dusque screamed in pain. She managed not to drop her dagger, but she lost her grip on the cat. The tusk-cat bucked again and Dusque went flying across the small clearing, landing hard on her side. The enraged beast turned and charged. Dusque rolled off her side onto her back and raised her small dagger in the air just as the feline leapt.

Tendau, having freed his blaster, dropped to one knee. For a brief instant, Dusque could see him take aim. Then her vision was eclipsed by the sight of the tusk-cat, jaws spread wide, descending on her. She brandished her dagger forward and aimed right for the center of the cat's throat, knowing the gesture was fruitless but refusing to give up. As the feline landed, the air around them was filled with a blinding red haze. Dusque heard the tusk-cat howl and snarl in rage and pain just before collapsing on top of her. She wasn't even sure if her knife had struck its mark. The weight of the cat forced all the air out of her lungs. She dimly thought she heard the whine of another blaster shot slice through the air. Vaguely, she realized the cat was suffocating her. Dusque tried to push against the body, to no avail. She found it difficult to draw in a breath, and more colored lights danced and flashed behind her lids as she grew light-headed.

Slowly, Dusque felt the cat start to move.

"Dusque," she heard a muffled voice call.

She started to push the cat in the direction it was

already moving, and as part of the feline cleared her head, Dusque could see the Ithorian above her. He was straining against what Dusque now recognized was deadweight. The tusk-cat was finished. Although her hands were somewhat pinned, Dusque used her knees and legs to try to help Tendau move the carcass off her.

She gave a hard shove, grunting with the exertion. Between the two of them, they moved the cat far enough so that Dusque could pull herself out from under the dead animal.

"Are you all right?" Tendau asked with great concern. He knelt down next to her and ran his hands over her bleeding arm.

"I'll be fine, I think," she said and grinned ruefully. "Good shot."

"Sorry I wasn't faster. Let me retrieve your pack and tend to this," he added, indicating her arm.

Dusque pulled away at the torn fabric of her sleeve and examined the wound. It looked relatively superficial to her. "Leave it," she told the Ithorian. "We shouldn't stop for this. She probably wasn't alone."

The Ithorian returned to her side and started to rummage through her bag. "I haven't heard anything else. If she was with her pack, they would've descended by now." Looking at her bloodied clothing, he added, "That smell would've driven them into a frenzy."

"You're probably right," Dusque agreed after some thought. She watched as he laid out a ground cloth for a somewhat sterile field and pulled out bandages and a few stimpaks. She sat cross-legged and offered her injured arm out to Tendau. Carefully, he cleaned and dressed her wound.

They managed to return to Narmle and Moenia without any further incidents. Despite her wounds, Dusque enjoyed the quiet trek through the wilderness. But once they reentered the city, all the doubts she had tried to dismiss came rushing back like waves crashing on a shore. Once again she recognized how fortunate she was to have a friend and colleague like Tendau in her life. *He helps me and supports me and I'm lucky to know him. But what can I do for him? I take and take and stay safe. I work for the Empire, but I don't embrace their beliefs any more than I've embraced those of the Alliance.* And when she thought of the Rebels, her mind drifted back to the black-haired agent who had haunted her since they had first locked eyes.

Maybe, just maybe, like Finn said, by choosing not to take a chance, I've been choosing not to live. What does that make me in the end? she wondered.

The spaceport was crowded for the return flight to Naboo. As Dusque looked around, absently rubbing her wounded arm, she saw many folks who appeared tired and scared. She suspected they had come to Rori to answer some call to adventure and had been beaten back. Realizing their mistakes, they were fleeing back to those things that they knew. But, Dusque noted to herself, they had all taken a chance. At least they could comfort themselves with that knowledge during the long nights ahead of them.

The shuttle flight wasn't long, but Dusque was haunted the whole way. And while she had accused her mother of becoming a shadow back when she lived at home, Dusque suddenly feared the fact that maybe she had been the ghost in her family all along. Perhaps the time to choose had come. And yet she still felt torn.

"What should I do?" she asked the faint reflection that stared back at her from the shuttle window. But that specter had no answer for her. She sulked in silence.

When the shuttle touched down, there was a huge rush of people. Travelers spilling out of the shuttle were replaced by nearly as many eager to get on. Dusque was shoved and jostled and she remembered why she liked being in the field so much, even if it meant that she was being hunted by something decidedly bigger than she was. Folks of all classes with all manner of baggage were milling about in the open-air arena of the shuttleport. Some had released their pets, and an extremely large peko peko hovered obediently near its owner. The blue of its skin was dazzling in the morning sun. Dusque noted that the Naboo tended to revere them less as living things than as trophies. It was the Gungans who kept them as pets.

While Dusque was admiring the reptavian, she unknowingly lost track of Tendau. By the time she had retrieved her small pack, he was nowhere to be found. She turned and turned, pushing against the crowd of people, trying to locate him. She wasn't worried so much as curious where he had gotten off to again. While she was searching, she thought she caught sight of the black-haired Rebel, Finn. In spite of herself, Dusque felt her heart skip a beat. A Gungan trader walked past her, his falumpaset trailing behind him. The quadruped was nearly three times as big as Dusque, with packs and equipment strapped to its back. As it passed by her, it obscured her view. She ducked her head from one side to the other, trying to catch a glimpse around it, but by the time the gray-skinned creature had moved past, Finn was nowhere to be seen. Dusque scanned the crowd briefly and then dismissed him as a mirage, conjured by her imagination since he had been weighing so heavily on her mind. Then a ripple of activity went through the already bustling crowd.

Dusque was tossed around by the throng. As she pushed back to keep her balance, she started to become worried. Something was not right. A few of the travelers started to yell. Over the growing din, Dusque could hear the heavy tread of armored feet echo across the stone walkways, approaching rapidly. The shuttle departed so suddenly that its blast knocked a few of the disembarking passengers off their feet. Dusque found herself on her stomach, blinking dust from her eyes. She raked her hair from her face, and when her vision cleared, she could see Tendau about ten meters away. He was completely surrounded by white-armored stormtroopers. The sun, which had actually broken through the heavy cloud cover that always seemed to shroud Moenia, winked and glinted off their armor. Dusque squinted against the glare and saw that a dark-clad Imperial officer of the Security Bureau was reading to the Ithorian from a datapad he held in his hand. Although he was surrounded, Tendau was making no attempt to flee.

Dusque was not so reserved. She sprang to her feet and started to shove her way through to reach him. But those who had recovered their footing were backing away collectively from the tableau in front of them. Some tried to run for the exits, while others crouched and cowered fearfully. Dusque was in a state, her emotions making her rash. First she knocked down a small Bothan woman holding a basket of fruit, then she ran up against a newly formed wall of spectators. She grabbed a Rodian by the shoulders and tried to yank him aside. But the crowd had bunched up and there was nowhere for Dusque to move him. He turned angrily and looked at her coldly with his multifaceted eyes.

"Watch what yer doin', woman," he yelled at her.

"I've got to get to him!" she cried and strained to see past the gawkers who were now riveted by the scene.

"No, you don't," he warned her, "trust me on that. They've got a warrant for the Hammerhead's arrest and execution."

"What?" Dusque demanded. "What has he done? What's going on here?" All the while, she was trying to force her way closer, to no avail. Almost sensing the impending danger, the crowd was no longer trying to move away. Another line of stormtroopers moved into formation, creating a solid line in front of the spectators, this time to keep them back.

"I heard someone up front say he was a traitor," the Rodian replied distractedly. "Sold some information or bought some. Who knows?" He turned to get a better look.

Horror-stricken, Dusque saw that the Imperial officer was putting away his datapad, his pronouncement finished. He signaled to three of the troopers, and two of them seized the Ithorian by his long arms. He made no move to struggle as the two dragged him toward an open section of the spaceport, followed by the third, who was brandishing an E-11 blaster rifle.

"Nooo . . . ," she moaned quietly. She tore at the shirts and sleeves of those around her in an effort to burst free. But the more she pushed, the more she was shoved back. At one point, she was certain that Tendau saw her. He shook his domed head sadly and let it hang down. She cried out to him, freeing one hand between the troopers to wave imploringly. He raised and lowered his hand, signaling for her to stop: death ahead, it meant in their private language.

Her fear and rage made her reckless, blind to the imminent danger all around her. "You don't understand," she screamed at the officer. "You're making a terrible mistake!"

The officer glanced over in her direction. He cocked his head and tried to find out who exactly was screaming at him. His hand dropped to his sidearm, and Dusque was too frenzied to notice the implied threat in his actions. She was starting to scream again when a strong arm wrapped itself around her waist and yanked her backward, nearly off her feet. She twisted wildly against whoever was pulling her away from the front of the crowd, but she couldn't take her eyes off Tendau.

The two stormtroopers who had pulled him toward the far side of the shuttleport now stepped away from him, although they kept close enough in case he tried something. But the Ithorian simply raised his head to look at the sky. The third trooper faced him from three meters away and drew a sight on him with his blaster.

"Ready," the stormtrooper said, not really asking a question.

Dusque grew limp and found herself using the arm that still held her as support, instead of struggling against it. "No," she whispered, her eyes wide with disbelief.

"Now," the officer ordered. The crowd had grown deafeningly quiet.

The Ithorian dropped his gaze to look directly at the soldier, then spread his arms wide in an almost welcoming gesture. The stormtrooper fired his blaster rifle once, the red beam slicing through the morning air with a deadly whine. It struck Tendau directly in his chest. He convulsed inward and crumpled to the cold stone. He twitched once and then was still.

Dusque screamed out and bent forward, feeling as if the beam had struck her, as well. She lifted her head, and a snarl of defiance escaped her lips. She dragged a forearm across her moist eyes and tried to launch herself at the officer, but another arm encircled her and she felt herself wrenched farther away from her target. She fought against the grip and twisted around to come face-to-face with Finn. She was dumbfounded. The Rebel spy used the opportunity to drag her farther back into the crowd toward the main exit of the shuttleport.

"What?" she finally managed, more out of surprise than any conscious thought.

"We need to get out of here," he whispered urgently, still pulling her by the arm.

Dusque shook herself free of his grip and twisted back to the knot of onlookers, her face like that of an avenging spirit. Finn ran back and caught her up in his arms and forced her to turn away.

"If we don't get out of here now," he repeated, "we will both die and that will serve nothing. Don't make it a wasted death!"

Dusque felt as if she were moving through a dream. Tendau's death echoed in her head and her heart. She deflated and let him hustle them both out of the shuttleport, past those who craned their necks to get a better look at her dead friend and those who thanked their fortune to still be standing. Once out of the launch area, she vaguely noticed the ticket terminal and the small groups of people chatting and having a few drinks before their departure.

As she was rushed past them, she couldn't help but think how wrong it was that they didn't know Tendau was dead; that they didn't care that he was gone forever. She couldn't comprehend that he was gone. And she couldn't understand how Finn had come to be there to save her at just the right moment. She raised a hand to her head, suddenly hot and claustrophobic. Finn kept them moving.

Once outside, Dusque drew in a few deep drafts of air. Almost directly opposite them, past a crafting station, was a lively cantina. Finn started to take them in that direction, and Dusque hadn't regained her senses enough to question him. She found it easier to let him pull her around than to actually process what she had just seen. At the entrance to the cantina, however, she abruptly froze.

"Not in there," she whispered. She couldn't take the thought of being surrounded by noisy people, laughing and talking and carrying on.

"Right," Finn agreed. "Too many eyes. No way of knowing who might be in there." He pulled her past the cantina to the back of the building. It was on the periphery of the city proper; the only thing behind it was a bit of a brick road that faded into the swamps and marshes. The building wall curved, and soon enough they were both out of earshot of anyone. Dusque leaned her back against the cold stone wall and closed her eyes, oblivious to the two tracks of tears that trickled down her hot cheeks. She remained motionless for several long moments.

When she opened her eyes and faced the black-haired agent, there was a hard expression on her face. "Get out of my way," she said through tight lips, her emotions at war with themselves. She needed to let them vent, and Finn provided a convenient target.

Finn didn't release his grip on her arm, though he relaxed it a little. "And where do you think you're going? Are you seriously thinking of marching back over there? And doing what, exactly?"

"There has to be justice," she demanded. "There has to be. And I want answers."

"Listen to me closely," he said, moving so near to Dusque that she could almost count his individual eyelashes. "As far as they are concerned, justice has been meted out. Go back there, and they'll serve justice on you, as well."

"What are you talking about?" she cried, his words making no sense to her. "How could Tendau's death be justice?"

Finn looked around to see if anyone had heard her call out. Satisfied that they were still undiscovered, he continued, "Your colleague traded information with Bothan spies. He betrayed the Empire."

"What?" She shook her head. "He was a scientist. All he ever did was look for answers to nature's secrets. He didn't trade them." But she thought back to the other night in the casino and the Ithorian's conversation with the stranger—a conversation he had never explained. And now would never have the chance, either. Had something illicit transpired between them?

Finn appeared to be unconvinced. "Well, in the eyes of the Empire, he was a traitor. And even his position couldn't save him from a traitor's fate." He looked at her meaningfully and Dusque recalled their only other conversation, when he had warned her that her job was no guarantee of safety or anonymity. It certainly looked as if that had been true for Tendau. Could it be true for her, too?

"And if they haven't already," he continued, "they'll brand you a traitor right along with him."

"What?" she asked. She felt as though she couldn't stop asking the question, couldn't stop walking through a horrible dream.

He let go of her arm and continued more softly, "You worked with him almost exclusively, day and night, out in the field. You tell me how they could not suspect you. Is there someone else in your labs who would stand up for you, speak on your behalf and proclaim your innocence, your loyalty to the Emperor?"

Dusque stopped in her tracks. She knew that back in her sterile world, none of the others would say a word. And she had done nothing to set herself apart as a staunch supporter of anything. "No," she finally said. "No one would. In fact, some would be glad to see me go." She thought about what she sadly realized had been her last night with her only friend. She thought about how he said that nature must be put right, no matter the cost. And she thought about how she had done nothing like that. "And make no mistake," she warned him, "I'm not innocent."

Finn looked slightly surprised by her last admission. He stepped back imperceptibly and ran his hands through his unruly hair. "Then you're already a part of the Alliance?" he asked, confused.

"No," she answered, "but I'm guilty just the same."

"Doesn't matter now," he told her. "We need to get off this rock. If we don't, they'll capture you for sure. Trust me on that."

A frown crossed her features. She looked down at her torn and dirty shirt and trousers. She realized that she had only her small pack on her and nothing else. Her belongings as well as Tendau's were back at the Hotel Aerie, just outside the city. "What about my things?" she asked. She knew it was a foolish question, but focusing on the mundane was helping her cope. "Everything is back in our—my rooms," she corrected herself and felt a lump form in her throat, her voice suddenly husky with emotion.

"There's no time. You don't have a choice any longer. We've got to go," he said. "We'll keep outside the city limits and stay on the perimeter." He started to move, but Dusque held her ground.

"We don't have time for this," he said, walking back to her. "Do you not understand the gravity of the situation? It's not like you have a choice any longer." The exasperation was clear in his voice.

She regarded him steadily. "Oh, yes I do," she replied. "I do have a choice."

His black eyes grew stormy. "You're right, you do. You can stay here and die, or you can join the Rebellion."

"It's not that simple," she whispered, confused again.

"Nothing ever is," he said gently. "Then come with me for the Hammerhead's sake," he added, and Dusque momentarily bristled at his casual use of the slang for Ithorians. "If you don't believe in me and what we stand for, then come with me because of what they did to him. Come with me for revenge."

Dusque swallowed her fear. She felt churned up inside, unsure of her emotions. What he said made sense at a basic level. It was the least she could do for her fallen comrade. *Maybe,* she thought, *maybe I can't right nature for you, but I can avenge you. That I can do.*

"All right," she agreed. "Let's go." And she placed her fate in his strong hands. *For now,* she thought to herself. *I'll trust you for now.*

SIX

Finn led the way, keeping them close to the stone buildings on the edge of Moenia. From across the swamps, Dusque heard the cry of the peko peko. Subconsciously, she started to estimate how far away it was—probably twenty meters—as though she were actually going out to track the reptavian.

But those days were gone, she corrected herself.

The spaceport, it turned out, was even closer. Finn stopped and turned to Dusque.

"I can see the shuttle from here. We're going to have to run for it," he explained, and then a gentleness suddenly came over him. "Can you do it?"

Dusque was confused. His concern for her made her feel moved and angry at the same time.

"Yes," she said.

"Let's go," he said, and they burst out running across the brick courtyard. Up the steps and past the throng of travelers, they ran at full speed. No one paid them any mind, however, and only one passenger even glanced at them. Dusque realized, as they weaved their way through the lounge into the docking bay area, that Finn had timed it almost perfectly. They didn't stand out in their haste because the shuttle was nearly ready for departure. In fact, a Trandoshan doctor almost bowled them over in his hurry to board.

Finn slowed down enough to toss their travel tickets at the protocol droid that was busy trying to collect and organize vouchers.

They and the medic were the last to board the shuttle. As Dusque sank wearily into a seat and strapped herself in, she looked about the cabin. It was a ragtag and motley group that shared the transport with them. With the exception of the medic and themselves, she thought most of the others looked like questionable sorts. Some carried weapons whose capabilities she couldn't even begin to guess at, and others appeared to be hunters. It dawned on her that she had no idea where they were going—but if the passengers were any indication, it was not a nice place. She resolved to ask Finn about it as soon as they took off. She was just going to close her eyes for a moment first . . .

The next thing Dusque was aware of was someone insistently shaking her shoulder. She was so tired; she tried her best to ignore it. But the shaking only grew steadier the more she turned away from it.

"All right, Tendau," she murmured and weakly waved one hand, "I'll break down the camp. Just give me a bit longer."

"We're here," Finn whispered, capturing her fluttering fingers in his grip.

Dusque's eyes flew open at the unexpected touch and the sound of the strange but increasingly familiar voice. She blinked her eyes to clear them and gazed around the ship. She saw that most of the passengers had disembarked. She and Finn were some of the last to leave.

"That was fast," she said.

For the first time since they'd met, he flashed her a genuine smile. "How would you know? You slept the whole time." He rose to his feet and offered her a hand up. "I understand, though," he added when she looked down at her lap. "With everything that happened . . ."

Dusque ducked her head and refused to accept his hand. She felt suddenly guilty for having rested at all. She thought that she should have maintained some kind of vigil for her lost friend, but instead she had slept like a child the first moment she'd had a chance to. "I'm fine," she told him brusquely and moved past him.

"Stubborn," he muttered, following behind.

Dusque smelled the heat before she felt it. She climbed out of the ship and squinted against the sun. Without waiting for Finn, she moved away from the landing area and found herself a vantage point. From there, she shielded her eyes and quickly scanned the area. Dust filled her nose, and a warm breeze caressed her cheek.

The area where they had landed was mountainous, although she saw a valley to the south. The sun was just breaking above the range, and the sky was a yellow-pink. Directly in front of the shuttle was a bridge that led to a rather large outpost. The buildings, constructed mostly from sandstone and other local materials, almost faded into the harsh landscape. And there was no mistaking the smell of rotten eggs in the air. The bridge crossed a river not of water, Dusque surmised, but of sulfur. She put her hands on her hips and turned to Finn, who was watching her.

"Well?" she asked him.

He stepped over to her side. "Aren't you even curious where we are?"

"Lok," she replied. "Obviously."

"How did you know? As far as I was aware, you've never been here before."

"I'm a biologist, first and foremost. And I'm good at my job," she announced without a trace of vanity. "Just because I've never been here doesn't mean I don't know about the planet."

Finn raised his eyebrows. "I'm impressed."

"The sulfur rivers gave it away," she admitted, pointing to the canal ahead of them.

Finn smiled broadly and Dusque thought he was pleased. "They do reek a bit, don't they?"

Dusque nodded. "It's because of the sulfur that the kimogilla developed such a tough hide. I've only seen one sample of it. Amazing, adaptive feature on the beast."

"Not to mention they're one of the most venomous creatures in the galaxy and can swallow a Wookiee whole if the mood strikes them. If we're lucky," he added, "we won't see a single one of those monsters while we're here."

It was Dusque's turn to be surprised. "You know your creatures."

"I know Lok," he corrected her.

"And that's why we're here?"

Finn nodded. "I needed to get you off Naboo, and while this place isn't somewhere you'd describe as safe, it is safer than the Emperor's homeworld."

Some thirty meters away, Dusque saw a spined snake slither out of a rock cairn and strike at one of the flightless birds indigenous to Lok. The bird was dead before it hit the ground. While the snake dislocated its jaw to accommodate its meal, Dusque looked at Finn.

"No," she agreed, "I would definitely not think of this place as safe. Why here?"

"I've got some connections," Finn told her.

"There are members of the Alliance here?" she asked. She knew they had to hide themselves well from the ever-vigilant eyes of the Empire, but Lok was a hellhole. As she kicked at the skull of a small scavenger beneath her feet, she wondered how desperate they must be to hide among the snakes and the dead.

"No," Finn admitted slowly, "not the Rebels. The ties I have to my connection go back farther than that. I used to . . . do things for him."

"Who?" she asked.

After Finn checked to see they were alone, he said, "Nym. All of this here is his stronghold."

"I know that name," Dusque remarked thoughtfully. Realization spread across her face after a moment. "Isn't he the pirate who's been raiding supply transports along the Corellian Trade Spine?"

"How did you know that?" he asked, nonplussed.

"He intercepted several shipments designated for my group. When I tried to find out what had happened to the supplies, his name was bandied about. It delayed a project of mine for some time."

Dusque regarded Finn with a keener eye than she had before. She had actually heard quite a bit about Nym and what he was capable of—or, at least, accused of being capable of. The lanky man standing in front of her not only worked covertly for the Rebels but, by his own admission, had even older ties with one of the most fearsome pirates this side of the galaxy, renowned for looting the hyperlanes of the Core Worlds. She looked at him and wondered what he was capable of. And she wondered what she had been drawn into.

No, she corrected herself, *I didn't just fall into this.* He was, after all, right. There had been no security for Tendau and Dusque in their work. She had chosen to do this, and she'd chosen to trust the man in front of her. Now she was going to have to see where her choice took her.

"So you do know about him," Finn replied.

"Well, not only does he have an impressive ship of his own, but he has been amassing a small fleet here, as well. We should be able to get some covert transport."

"And just why would Nym help us, if he's not with the Alliance?"

"Let's just say that he owes me a favor and the time has come to cash it in," he replied grimly.

"Must have been a big favor," she mused.

"It was," he admitted, with a lopsided grin. "Remind me to tell you about it someday."

"I will." She smiled back. "So, assuming he'll help us, where do we go from here?"

"We go on to Corellia, but that's not our final destination," he said. "I don't know where we go after that."

"What?" she asked.

"It's a safety measure," he said slowly, and Dusque sensed that he was choosing his words very carefully.

"How does that keep us safe?" she demanded.

"It doesn't," he replied, shaking his head. "It keeps the Alliance safe. If we fail, no one else will suffer from our deaths."

"I don't understand," she continued. "Everyone who joins must know they're risking their lives and the lives of those around them."

"You're right," he agreed, "but you don't understand. You don't really know what the Empire is capable of."

"I have an idea," she replied. "And I'm still here with you, willing to take my chances."

Finn scrutinized her for several moments. A hot breeze carried across the small plateau they were standing on, and some of Dusque's hair blew across her face. Gently, Finn reached over and pushed the offending strands away from her gray eyes. The gesture was almost a caress, and Dusque felt unsettled. "Doesn't matter," he said. "Everyone betrays those they love to the Empire eventually; there's no choice." And he gave her a sad smile.

"There is a choice," she returned. "The problem is, sometimes we make the wrong one."

Finn seemed to contemplate her words, weighing them carefully. Dusque thought that it was as though he was wrestling with something.

He probably hadn't expected her to be serious, she thought. He was probably going to underestimate her just like everyone else did. Well, he was in for a surprise. If she could avenge Tendau, then any price was worth it.

The silence between them was growing uncomfortable. "So where do we find Nym?" she asked.

"Follow me," he told her, leading her away from the shuttleport. Dusque realized that there was little need to hide on this planet; for the moment, they enjoyed safety amid the anonymity of refugees and renegades. There was one thing that concerned her, though.

"What if there's a price on my head?" she asked as they moved across the bridge that led to the collection of sandstone edifices comprising Nym's stronghold.

"Shouldn't be a problem," he told her as he swatted a rather large fly away from his face.

Dusque pursed her lips. "That really must be a big favor that he owes you."

"Well—" He turned his head to look at her. "—the favor wasn't that big. I just don't think the price on your head will be all that high." He held a serious face for a moment longer and then smiled at her.

"Nice," she replied. "Bounty humor."

"Come on," he said with a slight chuckle.

As they moved around the stronghold, Dusque saw a group obviously preparing for a hunt. Most wore armor of varying degrees and quality. Several were checking the readiness of their weapons and supplies. A Mon Calamari was counting out his supply of lecepanine darts and testing the strength of his wire-mesh traps. And a few even had their own animals with them. A full-grown gurrcat paced next to his master, and a Bothan was feeding her young bantha some of her travel biscuits.

A well-armed human male walked over to them, and Dusque felt her pulse quicken. His chest shield winked in the sunlight. She noticed that Finn had edged his hand slightly toward his hip and realized that he must have a blaster secreted under his travel cloak. She breathed a little easier knowing he was armed.

The man stood in front of them and looked them

both over appraisingly. He nodded at Finn and let his gaze linger a little longer on Dusque. Normally, she would have been offended by his stare, but she bit back her indignation, understanding that drawing attention to themselves now was not in their best interest.

"We're looking for a few more to join us," he began in a gravelly voice. "Want to group up?"

Finn stood just forward of Dusque and said, "Not today, friend. We're busy."

The hunter leaned against his polearm and blocked their path. Slightly taller than Finn, he tried to emphasize his height by looking down at Finn in an exaggerated fashion, using his weapon for balance. "I wasn't referring to you. I meant the lady, and I am not your *friend*," he added with a touch of menace.

Dusque was slightly surprised when Finn didn't do anything. The hunter shifted his weight to lean closer to her. "Now," he repeated, "how about it?"

Before Dusque could do anything, Finn swept his leg in an arc and knocked the polearm out from under the hunter. Without the weapon for balance, the man toppled over onto his face. Finn was on him in a flash. He straddled the larger man's back and drew his concealed weapon. With a scout blaster aimed at the fallen man's head, Finn said through gritted teeth, "I said we were busy and that means the lady, too. Understood?"

Shown up in front of his snickering crew, the hunter nodded without saying a word.

"Good," Finn told him and then stood up, holstering his weapon with practiced ease. He nodded once to Dusque and then helped the shamefaced hunter to his feet. As they walked away, Finn tossed back a parting remark over his shoulder. "And you were mistaken. I *am* your friend. If I wasn't, you would be dead."

Maneuvering around the bustling streets, Finn seemed right at home to Dusque. She was certain he had been there before, and obviously for a fair stretch. He ducked and weaved through the alleys and byways until they were standing in front of a cantina.

"If he's in town," Finn explained to Dusque, "he'll be here." He pushed open the door for her, and they walked in.

After the bright sun, it took Dusque a few moments to adjust to the dim lighting of the bar. Off to one side, a lone Bith played a slitherhorn. There was a nalargon next to him, but it was not being played. Probably too early in the day, Dusque thought. Perhaps the rest of the Bith would perform later. Very rarely did the baggy-headed aliens travel alone through the galaxy; they tended to tour in groups. Because they saw sounds in much the same way others saw color, they made excellent, if expensive, musicians. Nym, she reasoned, must be very wealthy.

Several Zabrak milled about the bar and were busy discussing animals. Dusque caught bits and pieces of their conversation. They, like the group outside, were planning a hunt. But they were hoping to capture several species for training, not trophies. She almost wished she could go with them. Lok boasted some of the harshest geography and climate in the galaxy, and Dusque marveled at the way nature had allowed its creatures to survive and adapt.

Finn walked around the bar toward a seating area in the back. It was deserted, and Dusque suspected they were out of luck. But then she saw Finn approach a partially hidden door and continue farther into the recesses of the cantina. She hurried to follow him, enjoying the cooler temperature of the darkness.

Rounding a corner, they entered another room. It was hazy and filled with smoke. A few human men sat at a small table in the corner, lost in their conversation. A Twi'lek female wearing a few strategically placed pieces of cloth undulated seductively in another corner of the room, dancing to music no one but she appeared to hear. Toward the back, reclining on a couch carved out of the sandstone, was the person they were looking for. Finn walked over, and Dusque followed close behind.

It was impossible for Dusque to tell the age of the pirate sitting on the couch. He could have been forty or four hundred. Although he was sitting, she estimated he was at least two meters tall. What she could see of his green, hairless body was heavily rippled with muscle. He had pronounced brow ridges that cast strange shadows over his red eyes, and while he didn't have a nose like humans did, he did have the suggestion of nostrils that ended in two tendrils hanging to his chest. Several thicker tendrils sprouted from his scalp and hung about his shoulders like hair. He wore bits and pieces of armor carefully placed, and carried two blasters at his hips and at least one armband of additional ammunition. He sat effortlessly enough, drinking what looked like Vasarian brandy from a large mug and nodding in time to the Twi'lek dancer's movements. She noticed he had placed himself at the back of the cantina, with a good view of the room and near another half-concealed door. A kusak lay curled at his feet. The partially armored canine was a fearsome species that, if tamed, was loyal to the death. She saw he was stroking the animal absently with his free hand. While he might have appeared unaware to the casual observer, Dusque realized he was extremely tactical in his positioning. He was no one to be taken lightly.

When he saw Finn, a slow smile of recognition crossed his face. Dusque noticed that it did not reach his eyes, however. They glowed a deadly crimson.

"Finn," he said easily, "what brings you back to my doorstep?" He cast an appraising eye over Dusque, but in a discreet way, far from the obvious ogling of the hunter from outside. "And in better company than the last time I saw you." He motioned for them to sit and join him at his small table.

Finn pulled up a chair, flipped it around, and straddled it with his arms across its back. Dusque got herself a chair and waited for Finn to start talking. She found, however, that she had a hard time diverting her gaze from Nym. He was an impressive specimen, and she racked her brain trying to decipher what species he was.

"Hungry? You look like you could eat me alive," he told her, and Dusque shook her head. It dawned on her that she had been far less subtle in her observations of him than the reverse.

Finn started to speak, but Dusque interrupted him. "I'm sorry for staring," she apologized sincerely. "It's just that I never thought I would ever be fortunate enough to see a Feeorin in my lifetime."

Nym regarded her shrewdly for a long moment. She could see Finn shift uncomfortably on his chair, and she wondered if she had somehow offended their prospective savior by her statement. But Nym broke the tension by dropping his head back and laughing with a deep, throaty bellow. When he straightened his head, he nodded in acknowledgment to Dusque.

"Nobody has ever said they were lucky to meet me." And then he turned to Finn and said, "*Much* better company than last time. Now that you've brightened up an otherwise boring morning, what do you want?" There was no kindness in the question.

"I need a favor," Finn told him straight out. "I need a ship."

Nym leaned back and stroked his chin for a moment. "That's a big favor. And what do you need a ship for?"

"I need a ship that'll get us as far as the Core Worlds," Finn explained. "That's all you really need to know."

Nym cast a sidelong glance at Dusque and replied, "I doubt that's all I need to know. There's a good story here." Changing his tack, Nym asked Dusque, "But how the ▓▓ did you get mixed up with this gravel maggot?"

Dusque didn't wait for Finn to say anything. "I was in the wrong place at the right time." And she smirked at Nym, sensing that she shouldn't give him any ground.

Nym grinned back and nodded his head. Facing Finn, he asked, "What do you want with a ship, anyway? It's not like you could pilot the thing."

"What?" Finn sputtered, and by the look on Nym's face, Dusque understood that for this round, Nym had won. He had flustered Finn first. "I'm a ▓▓▓▓ good pilot."

"Maybe a good *copilot*, but you're no good on your own. It takes a special breed to fly solo," Nym pronounced.

Finn's jaw had a rigid cast to it. Dusque, wondering what he was biting back on, was impressed that he wasn't getting too wrapped up in the dance of male dominance. "Regardless of what you think, a two-person ship is what I need. And you owe me," he added, not above using a deadly tone, too.

"Don't have one," Nym grunted. He gulped down his brandy.

"What do you mean you don't have one? Lok is littered with wrecks. Surely you've got a few that are in commission?" Finn demanded with some exasperation.

"No," the pirate replied calmly. "None are up and running. There were some complications on our last run on the Corellian Spine. But don't get yourself worked up."

"Why not?" Finn asked.

"Just because I don't have any ships operational doesn't mean I can't get you a ride. I can arrange transport for you and your lovely cargo." He looked at Dusque. "Or you could stay here with me for a while. I could tell you a lot about my species."

"It's a very tempting offer," she said, playing along. She reached over and casually dropped her hand by the kusak, letting it sniff her. When she was sure it was comfortable, she rubbed it along its haunches. Nym and Finn were clearly amazed that the beast tolerated her touch.

"Maybe some other time," she offered, sounding regretful. "Right now, I have some business to finish. And I need him to do it."

"Another time then," Nym agreed and winked at her. He returned his attention to Finn. "I can get you the ride, but it'll cost you."

"I don't believe you. After what happened on

Dathomir, you would deny me this? And what about that little misunderstanding between you and the Gray Talon? Have you forgotten all of that?"

Dusque caught her breath at the last one and felt her eyebrows trying to climb into her scalp with surprise.

"What was between us then doesn't equal what you're asking for now. Even you should realize that," Nym reasoned.

"That's it, then. Come on, Dusque. We'll find someone else to deal with." Finn rose to his feet and offered his hand to Dusque. She looked at Nym. The pirate had a smug expression on his large face. Dusque suspected he was the only game in town, and what was more, both he and Finn knew it.

But those like Nym always wanted something, she thought. That was part of what drove them on. For them *having* was not nearly as sweet as *wanting*. She and Finn just needed to find out what Nym wanted.

"It seems a shame we couldn't do business together," she announced.

"Business is a different matter. I can always do business," Nym said.

Finn slowly returned to his chair, but not in the slumped-over posture he had adopted when they had first sat down with the pirate. Reading his body language, Dusque knew he was tense and she guessed that the meeting had taken a turn he hadn't anticipated.

"What do you want?" Finn asked Nym finally.

The pirate stretched back against the naturally carved sandstone and idly scratched at his kusak's ear. "There is something you could do . . ."

"What?" Finn asked again, his irritation barely masked.

"North of here is a small box canyon. There's a group of corsairs camping there, and they have something that belongs to me," he explained. "I want it."

"What is it?" Dusque asked.

"A portion of a hyperspace map. I want it for my 'collection,' " Nym told them. "Get it for me and I'll see that you get to where you're going, no questions asked."

"How big a camp?" Finn asked.

Nym made a dismissive gesture with his mouth. "Three or four at the most. Easy for you."

Dusque knew what the next logical question should have been, but figured Finn was too smart to ask Nym why he didn't bother to retrieve it himself. The answer was plain: the task was extremely dangerous.

Finn shook his head slightly. "Fine, we'll do this for you. But this is the last time, Nym," he added in a deadly tone.

The pirate smiled lightly, leaned his head back against the rough, unfinished wall, and closed his eyes. "Not the first time I've heard that. And I'm sure it won't be the last, either.

"Head north, over the plateau and then down

into the canyon. You can't miss their camp," he said. "Get my map."

Finn nodded curtly and stood. Sensing that Nym was finished with them, Dusque rose to her feet, as well. As they started to walk toward the entrance, Nym called out to them once more.

"Take the back door," he told them, hooking a thumb in the direction of the passageway Dusque had noticed when they first sat down. "And feel free to help yourself to whatever supplies I've got laying around back there. You might need 'em." With that, he resumed watching the dancer, who hadn't paused through their entire conversation. They were dismissed.

Dusque, closer to the door, opened it, but noticed that Finn moved up to stand slightly in front of her. Certain that the pirate couldn't hear them, she whispered, "I must be important, the way you always shift yourself to cover me."

Finn looked at her with some surprise. "Of course you're important." But Dusque could almost bet that he hadn't been aware he was doing it. She wasn't sure what to make of him—or what she was starting to feel when she was next to him, either.

They walked through a narrow, dimly lit passageway that emptied into what appeared to be a storeroom worthy of a small army. Along one wall was a massive collection of rifles, pistols, and bandoliers of ammunition. Another wall was covered in swords and knives, and yet another boasted an impressive collection of traps and snares. The last wall had a modest collection of clothing and armor. Dusque immediately moved there.

She thumbed through the various pieces of armor and camouflage. She rejected a chest plate that looked too heavy: in the heat of this volcanic world, she wanted something that wouldn't weigh her down. She found a jumpsuit of a light weave and pale color. She had just started to take her torn tunic and pants off when she sensed that she was being watched. She glanced over her shoulder and saw that Finn was over by the blasters. But he wasn't reviewing the inventory. Instead, his black eyes were riveted on her. She returned his gaze and then turned away, flustered.

He's done it to me again, she thought.

She dressed rapidly, exchanging everything she originally had except her hide boots. Then she selected a pair of thin leather gloves to protect her hands and a pair of goggles brown-tinted to save her eyes from the intense glare of the sun. At the wall with the knives, she chose a light, single-arm sword. She lunged forward a few times with it, testing its weight and feel. The craftsmanship was superb, and she absently wondered where Nym had pilfered the weapon from. Finally she added a small knife to her boot and, feeling suitably outfitted, turned around to check on Finn.

Obviously at some point he had stopped watching her and gone on to select a carbine rifle to add to his personal arsenal. He had also exchanged his dark cloak for a lightweight tunic and matching trousers. Twin bandoliers of ammo crisscrossed his chest, and she saw that he had chosen a pair of hide gloves, too.

"Good idea in case there are more spined snakes, or worse," Dusque told him. She rummaged through the clothes until she found a visor. She pitched it to him.

Finn caught it easily enough in his hands.

"It'll save your eyes," she explained, "and make some of the local wildlife easier to spot right before they strike you dead."

Finn tossed the visor in his hand once and looked at Dusque. "Nice," he said, mocking her earlier words. "Biologist humor." But he slid the visor on.

"Let's go," he told her, and they stepped out into the burning heat that was midday on Lok.

SEVEN

"How are you doing?" Finn called back to Dusque.

They had been running for some time now. The sun was beyond its apex, on the decline, but it was almost impossible to feel a difference in the temperature yet. The ground felt hot and dry under Dusque's booted feet, and she was beginning to feel a burning in her muscles. But rather than succumb, she was starting to revel in the fact that her body was being tested by the bleak and foreboding landscape and she was meeting it head-on.

For the most part, they both kept silent, for fear of alerting anything to their presence. Dusque spotted some incredible specimens of snakes and birds, not to mention some desert plants that she had never seen before. She wished there had been someone to witness it with her—someone who would have found beauty in every bit of scrub and parched plant.

Tendau would have been amazed, she thought. When her mind drifted to the fate of the gentle

Ithorian, she felt a lump form in her throat and had to blink back tears. No matter what he had done, he hadn't deserved to die like a cur, shot dead in the streets. Even in its style of execution, the Empire had tried to strip him of his dignity. But Dusque had watched how he faced his death with courage and honor.

I'll make them pay for that, she vowed.

They were heading into a canyon, Dusque realized, noticing the way the rock walls seemed to be closing in on them in from both directions. The sky was stained a rosy pink and Lok's sun was like a flaming, molten ball just above the horizon, sinking fast. Finally, there was a subtle cooling to the burning air. In short order, she knew it would be freezing on the volcanic planet's dark side. With the change in temperature, the daytime animals would be looking for their burrows and the night hunters gradually waking up.

Catching sight of a rock cairn off to one side, Dusque lit upon an idea. She dropped farther behind Finn and veered over to the cairn, slowing her pace. A few meters from it, she stopped completely and pulled a wire-mesh trap from her sack. Holding it in her left hand, she slid bit by bit on the ground until she was right up against the cairn. Carefully, as though she were handling an active thermal detonator, she began to shift some of the smaller rocks until she found what she was looking for.

Nestled in a ball against the remaining rocks for warmth was a spined viper. The cooler night air had already slowed the animal's metabolism enough that its senses were somewhat deadened. It didn't even notice that Dusque had removed some of its protective shelter. As she was about to reach in, she heard Finn come up behind her. Without looking away from the viper, she held up her free hand in warning to him. He stopped in his tracks, and she could see from the corner of her eye that his hand had dropped to his blaster.

Dusque picked up a small pebble and tossed it into the lair, just in front and to the side of the viper's head. Dulled by the lack of warmth, it struck out at the pebble much slower than it would have earlier in the day. She knew she had one shot. As it lunged forward, she thrust her leather-clad hand into the cairn and grabbed the creature by the back of the neck, careful to avoid the venomous spines along the dorsal part of its body. She yanked the reptile out quickly and stuffed it into her mesh trap without a moment to spare, not even giving Finn time to react. Certain the snake was secured, she placed the trap into her travel sack. Then she sat down and realized she was sweating slightly in the cool breeze.

Finn dropped down near her, although she noticed he kept a slight distance and one eye on the slowly undulating pack. "Why'd you do that?" he asked. "We're not collecting, we're retrieving for Nym."

Dusque, confident that the viper was trapped and her bag was sound, slung the pack onto her back.

She stood up and set off in their original direction. Over her shoulder, she tossed back, "You never know when one of these might come in handy." He nodded, but she could see that he wasn't entirely convinced. Still, he did seem to accept her word, and she was pleased that he trusted her judgment despite the fact that he didn't really understand her actions.

By the time they reached the canyon, night shrouded the land. Off in the distance, a large moon could be seen peeking over the rim of the eastern canyon wall. Silhouetted against its white glow were two objects. One was very obviously a large tent, with distinctive rooftop points stabbing into the sky. The other might have been a structure, as well, but it was somewhat smaller than the tent. The pair were close to each other, situated on the top of a plateau. It was a perfect vantage point. The occupants had a clear view in all directions, which made a covert approach almost impossible.

Both Finn and Dusque crouched low, leaning against the canyon wall. Finn whispered into her ear, "Corsairs."

Dusque nodded, and now that Finn had broken the silence, she said, "Which way do you want us to go?" As soon as she said it, she realized that she already trusted his abilities enough to let him make the call.

Finn rummaged through his smaller pack, pulled out a pair of electrobinoculars, and adjusted the range. Cupping his hands over them, he turned toward the encampment and for several moments took readings and made observations. Finally, he slid closer to Dusque and handed the binoculars to her.

"See there?" he asked her, and guided her hands toward the direction he had been viewing. "As best as I can tell, it looks like there are two of them, and they're drinking."

Through the electrobinoculars, Dusque could see two figures huddled around an outdoor fire. One was squatting near it, presumably tending the flames, and the other leaned casually against a tent pole, taking a long swig from a bottle. The only one Dusque could see clearly was the one standing up. He was one of the Nikto species. She estimated that he was almost as tall as Finn. His yellow skin and almost complete lack of brow ridges or horns told her that he was one of the M'shento'su'Nikto race that had evolved in the southern region of Kintan. Instead of fins, they had long, prominent breathing tubes along the backs of their heads. Because the species had very little musculature in their faces, they often had blank, unintelligent expressions and were sometimes mistaken for idiots or dullards. But that was far from the truth. The Nikto could be deadly in their single-mindedness.

"I thought Nym said there were three or four," she replied as she handed him his electrobinoculars.

"He did," he replied as he stuffed them back in his travel pouch. "But I was watching for some time and I didn't see any others. You?"

"No," Dusque answered. "We'll need to be extra cautious, regardless. Those Southern Nikto are able to use their breathing pipes to detect vibrations. They could hear us long before they see us."

"Hmm, that's the trick then," Finn said. "Let's see if there's anything that can help us there." He pulled out the electrobinoculars and scanned the canyon. Not twenty meters from the north side of the plateau base was a small herd of very large snorbals. Dusque followed his gaze and nodded when she saw the herd of large herbivores, scavenging for food with their split trunks.

"That might do it," she agreed, "provided we can get them to go in the right direction."

"One thing before we go in there," Finn told her.

"What?" Dusque asked.

"There is no reasoning with these pirates, you understand? We have to go in and take them out. Hesitation means death," he explained.

"I understand," she told him, though she wasn't sure she did. "But how can you be sure they're the right ones?"

"While Nym and I . . . disagree on some things, I do know he wouldn't have sent us on a wild Bantha hunt. He sent us directly to this camp, so these are the ones. No mistakes there."

"I suppose . . ." she said nervously. "Well, I'll follow your lead."

"I can't see any other way," he added. Dusque wondered if he had said that for the benefit of her conscience or his own.

Finn scurried along, low to the ground, and Dusque flanked him. When they were about ten meters from the grazing herd, they split up and started to circle the animals from opposite directions. One of the snorbals picked up its head, and Dusque knew they had no time left. She waved to Finn and started to move closer to the animals without shielding too much of her approach. She saw Finn doing the same thing from the other side. One after another of the herd pricked its ears, and as a group they started to move loudly up the incline of the plateau.

Dusque and Finn continued to steer them slowly up the plateau, toward the corsair camp. The two humans trailed behind them, using their heavy footfalls as cover. When they were fifteen meters below the camp, Finn signaled to Dusque. Together, they moved so suddenly that the animals startled and burst into a run. Dusque and Finn took advantage of the pounding stampede to sneak up to the perimeter of the camp.

Sliding along on their bellies, they could see that the animals had had their desired effect on the renegade pirates. Both Nikto were on their feet and watching the animals cut across the plateau. As the creatures began their descent of the other side of the incline, the Nikto who had been tending the fire drew his blaster. Dusque could feel her heart pounding and her mouth going dry. She tensed, preparing to feel his laserfire. But the pirate drew a bead on the departing animals and opened fire on them instead.

He struck one, and the two corsairs chuckled between themselves. He took aim again, squinting along the sight, and continued to fire. That prompted his companion to draw his weapon, as well, and try to best him. Dusque figured she and Finn had only a few moments. She motioned to Finn and the pirates. He looked surprised until she reached for her backpack. He grinned crookedly and gave her one sharp nod. He took aim and waited for Dusque. She shook her sack twice and flung the enraged contents as the two corsairs continued firing.

The spined snake shot out of the opened trap and sunk his fangs into the Nikto closer to the tent. The pirate screamed in rage as the venomous reptile attached itself to his cheek. The Nikto tried vainly to pull the creature free of his face, but the viper coiled its body around his waist and resisted all attempts to dislodge it. The corsair's screams of rage attracted the attention of his companion, who had been too busy picking off snorbals to notice the other's predicament. The unbitten pirate lowered his blaster as he started to turn around, a vaguely perplexed look on his smooth face. Finn seized the opportunity and started blasting.

The unbitten Nikto tried to bring up his weapon and return the unexpected fire, but Finn's aim was dead straight. The shot caught the pirate across the chest and the force of the blow spun him around. He was dead before he hit the ground. Finn moved forward to finish the second, but stopped when he saw that the pirate was mortally wounded. The stricken Nikto fell to his knees and then landed face-first on the parched ground. His death was fast but not easy as the viper's venom paralyzed all of his autonomic functions. Dusque moved up and watched the life begin to drain from his face. The viper slithered off and disappeared into the cold darkness, once more in search of a warm den.

While Dusque knelt down near the Corsair she had effectively killed, Finn trotted over to the small structure near the tent. By the firelight, he recognized it as a locked container.

"They must have been guarding the cargo, waiting for someone to pick it up. The map's got to be in here," he told her. "It won't take me long to slice the lock." Dusque nodded in agreement.

While Finn set to work on the electronic code, Dusque watched the bitten pirate slowly expire as his breathing and his heart stopped. She had mixed feelings about her part in all of it. She knew that, given the chance, they would have killed her, but the reason she was out here was her own doing. She tried to balance her need for revenge with taking the life of someone who wasn't really part of the Empire *or* the Rebellion. But before she could debate the morality of her actions any further, she was grabbed forcibly from behind and thrown to the hard ground, stunned.

Something pressed hard into the small of her back—she guessed it was her attacker's knee. He was mumbling drunkenly as he stripped her of her weapons. Then the weight lifted, and when she turned her head, she could see him stumbling away, shaking his head as if he were trying to clear his thoughts. Finn obviously hadn't heard the third corsair's arrival. He must have cracked the code, because the large container was now wide open. Only his lower legs and his boots were visible as he rummaged through the illicit goods. Dusque didn't have enough air in her lungs to call out a warning to him.

The quickly sobering Nikto staggered over, yanked Finn by the ankles, and dragged him free of the container. Startled, Finn didn't have time to reach his blaster before the Corsair pinned his arms under his heavy legs so he could keep his own arms free. As he straddled Finn, the pirate began to punch him repeatedly in the head. Dusque, all but forgotten by the enraged Nikto, pushed herself to her feet. She stumbled over to where the pirate sat, locked in a struggle with Finn.

She may have been unarmed, but Dusque was not without her resources. Hardly thinking, she threw herself at the pirate's back and fastened onto him tightly. The Nikto barely slowed his assault on Finn, even though he now had two to contend with. But he didn't realize what Dusque knew.

As a bioengineer, she was aware of his biology and his one weakness. Enduring a stabbing blow to her ribs from the corsair's elbow, Dusque managed to clamp her hands on his two breathing tubes and refused to let go. It took a moment for the enraged Nikto to realize what she was doing to him, and by the time he did, the lack of air was already taking its toll. He slowed his assault on Finn and turned his waning attention onto Dusque.

Rising to his feet, he stepped over the inert Finn and swung his own body into the metal container. Dusque winced in pain as her back smashed into the cold steel, but she didn't loosen her grip. The pirate whirled about and reached back, clawing his hands across Dusque's face and arms. With one last burst of strength, the air-deprived Nikto got hold of her forearms and managed to pry them free of his breathing tubes. Keeping his grip on her arms, he swung her over his head and slammed her to the ground in front of him. Blinking hard, Dusque looked up and saw him raise his arms over his head, locking his hands together into one fist. But before he could deliver what would surely have been a deathblow, his head suddenly turned to an awkward angle with a strange *pop*. His arms fell limply to their sides, and he toppled over to her right to lie in an unmoving heap. Dazed from his attack, Dusque couldn't quite process what was happening.

Suddenly a bruised Finn filled her vision. She watched as he moved the pirate completely off her and knelt next to her. He put his hands under her arms and raised her to a half-sitting position. While Dusque shook her head, she could feel Finn's hands run up and down the length of her. She winced when he touched her back, and the bright stab of pain sharpened her focus.

"Hurts?" he asked her.

"A little bit. Not so bad, though," she replied, and tried to flex her shoulders and stretch her spine somewhat. She looked at him through the tangled mass of her hair and saw the beginnings of a bruise flowering across his left eye, but otherwise he appeared no worse for the wear.

He looked at her with some concern. "Really?" he asked again.

She shakily rose to her feet unaided. "I'll be fine. What about you?" Tentatively she touched his swollen cheekbone. He flinched, jerked his head back, and caught her fingers lightly with one hand.

"I've been better," he admitted and then flashed her a roguish grin. "But I've been a whole lot worse, too." He looked at her through his own tousled hair, and somewhere Dusque managed to find a smile.

"Did you get the map?" she asked, feeling uncomfortable again and wanting to say something to break the strange mood between them.

"I was about to," he told her. He hooked a thumb at the dead Nikto. "Until Handsome interrupted me." He led Dusque around the slain pirate and added, "That was very quick thinking on your part, especially considering how much bigger he was than you."

He turned his attention back to the container and didn't see the rosy flush stain her cheeks. His words carried a great deal of weight with Dusque. It was the first time a man other than Tendau had ever given her any praise for her abilities in the field. She became even more flustered and busied herself by craning over Finn's shoulder to see what was in the storage unit.

Bits of metal and gemstone winked out at her in the moonlight. She could see blasters and other, more exotic weapons, as well as a cache of documents and credits. Finn tossed out a few datapads and other bits and pieces, mostly weapon powerups and the like.

"I found some datachips," he called out to her. "Need to check 'em with my datapad." After a few moments, he said, "Got it. It's the only one of the bunch that's a map. It better be the right one," he continued.

He emerged with a datachip clenched tightly in his hand. Dusque returned his smile and was momentarily surprised when he handed it to her to carry. "I can't wait to see the look on Nym's face when you give it to him," he explained. She accepted the treasure and placed it in her small sack. She also recovered her sword and her mesh trap. She hated to waste anything or leave anything behind. The last thing she did was toss handfuls of dirt onto the dead pirates' fire. She kicked at the embers and ground them under her boot soles. When she was done, she turned and saw that Finn was watching her.

"We have Nym's prize, so let's go collect our reward," he told her.

They walked down the plateau, and Dusque sensed that Finn was keeping a slow pace in deference to her injuries. While she was hurt, she noticed that the more she moved, the more she limbered up. She appreciated his concern and was also glad that when she appeared to be able to handle more, he increased their rate accordingly.

Except for the cries of a few perleks out scavenging, they saw nothing else on their return trip. The sky was clear and another moon rose in the distance. *Or is it a planet?* Dusque wondered. Tendau had always been better at celestial geography than she was.

Nym's stronghold loomed up in the distance like a grave marker. Dusque wondered how many the Feeorin had buried in his career. She nearly jumped out of her skin as a gurk came screaming toward her, howling and arms raised. She drew her sword, but lowered it when she realized the hairy humanoid was only a whelp, the most threatening thing about him his screams. Finn had already turned to see what was wrong, his hand reaching for his blaster, so Dusque signaled that everything was fine as she trotted past the youngster. She didn't sheathe her weapon, however, until she was well inside the stone wall surrounding the stronghold.

Even though it was the dead of night, they encountered a lot of traffic. If anything, Dusque thought, there were even more hunting parties arriving and leaving than they had seen earlier. Groups of well-armed and eager killers continued to gear up and head out, even though others were returning blood-ied and wounded and unsuccessful. She remembered how she had felt during her own trials, and how ex-hilarating it was to challenge her mind and body's endurance. *Perhaps,* she mused, *it's that challenge that drives them to test themselves.* She noticed the remains of the group that had accosted her and Finn on their arrival on Lok. The leader who had made advances to her was very obviously missing. Dusque shuddered and jogged to catch up with Finn.

The cantina was a hive of activity. The rest of the Bith band had arrived, and the place was alive with chatter and music. An incredible variety of species was packed into the large room, and Dusque and Finn had a little difficulty threading their way through the jocular crowd. Dusque noticed, though, that there was an almost frantic air to the festivities, as though the revelers knew that this might be their last celebration before whatever fate had in store for them in the harsh and unforgiving terrain of the volcanic world.

They managed to squeeze their way past a pair of rambunctious Wookiees and wind their way back to the concealed room where they had found Nym before. As he had been in the morning, the pirate was seated on the naturally hewn-out seat, his kusak curled up by his feet. This time, though, he was not alone. Seated next to him was a human male, and opposite them both was a very tall Wookiee.

The human and Nym were obviously in the throes of a heated discussion—a very private one. They stopped arguing when Dusque and Finn entered the room, and Dusque sensed that some agreement had been reached between them. The human stood up and glanced at Dusque with a cursory, appraising eye, then turned back to Nym.

He looked tall, but Dusque had a hard time judging his height accurately because the leanly muscular man stood somewhat slouched, a posture that gave him a lackadaisical air. She suspected he did that to lull others into a false sense of security. With brown hair and eyes to match, he was handsome by human standards, if a bit scruffy around the edges, maybe thirty standard years old. He was dressed in casual pilot's garb, but Dusque's eyes grew wide when she saw he had the Corellian Bloodstripe running down the length of his black pants. That was an honor few earned.

"Finn," Nym began, breaking off his discussion with the other man, "You've got the map?" His red eyes flicked over to Dusque. Without any preamble, Dusque brushed past the human and laid the map down on the table. Nym cocked his head in acknowledgment of their accomplishments and tucked the map, unopened, into his tunic. Dusque wasn't sure if he did that to show his trust in their honesty or if he simply did not want the strange human and the Wookiee to view its contents.

"Good. Now, about my end of the deal," the pirate lord continued. "There's a small transport waiting for you in my starport. You'll be flyin' with a Mon Cal, but Han and Chewie here are gonna escort you all the way to Corellia. Seems you run in the same circles," he added slyly.

Han nodded in salute to Finn, while winking at Dusque. The Wookiee howled a salutation to them, as well, before rising to his full, towering height. Han turned his attention back to Nym and his demeanor grew serious.

"Listen, Nym," he began, speaking freely now, "there's still a lot of credits to be made working for the Alliance. We could use your help, and I can arrange for high-risk, high-paying jobs."

The pirate shook his head. "We've gone over this, Solo, and you know where I stand."

It was Han's turn to shake his head in disappointment. "I know what you're thinking," he told Nym. "I was there once and you're wrong. You think that no one's gonna bother you, locked up here in your personal fort. Well, sooner or later the Empire will find you, and they will shut you down." Dusque heard the genuine passion in his words, his casual demeanor forgotten for the moment.

Han looked at the pirate one more time before heading for the door. "Get your stuff. We're leaving," he tossed over his shoulder, businesslike, to

Dusque and Finn, and left with the Wookiee trailing behind.

Dusque thought about his words and how closely the conversation mirrored the one she and Finn had shared. All around her, she was finding accomplished people who firmly believed in the Rebel Alliance. She was starting to wonder how she had avoided the whole conflict for so long, buried away in her lab as Nym was in his fortress. She was starting to see that both were just elaborate prisons of a sort.

"Finn," Nym said, "you an' me, we're free of each other. Understand? Take the transport, but this is the last favor I do for you. Or the Alliance."

Finn saluted him in return. "We are quit of our debts." He turned and started out of the room.

"And good-bye to you," Nym said, addressing Dusque with mock gallantry. "I hope our paths cross again."

Dusque surprised both of them by winking at the pirate lord. "You never know. The galaxy is full of surprises. Oh—" she tapped her sword, "—I'm going to hang on to this. Something to remember you by."

Dusque could still hear the Feeorin's hearty laughter as she and Finn made their way toward the small starport. She didn't know much about ships, but the small one in front of them seemed adequate enough. A Mon Calamari was standing near the landing gear.

"I hope he flies better than he looks," Dusque

whispered to Finn, eyeing the pilot's mangy clothes and tarnished weapons with concern.

"Me, too," Finn grinned. "But if Nym recommended him, he'll be one of the best."

When the Mon Calamari pilot saw them, he waved them aboard. "She's no cruise liner, but she does what she has to. And with the *Falcon* flying escort, this trip should be a breeze," he told them. Inside, Dusque and Finn found seats crammed among all sorts of cargo and junk. As they strapped in, Dusque could hear the Mon Calamari signal to Han.

"Peralli to *Falcon*. All cargo is secured. Ready for departure."

"Copy that," came the static-laced reply. Dusque wondered when the communications equipment on this ship had last seen maintenance. "*Falcon* out."

"Hang on," the Mon Calamari shouted back to them. "This is going to be a little rough."

Dusque gripped the arms of her seat when the transport shuddered to life. As they left Lok for Corellia, Dusque looked at Finn and wondered what lay ahead.

EIGHT

"Now that we've jumped into hyperspace," Peralli said, "you've got some time. Nym sent me a message. He said that you"—he pointed to Dusque—"can help yourself to that small crate over there. He wanted you to have something a little more practical than that skinny gurnaset sticker to remember him by, whatever that means." The Mon Calamari shrugged his shoulders and ambled back to the cockpit.

"Wonder what Nym's got in mind for you," Finn said. He unbuckled himself and maneuvered over to the small crate. Dusque did the same.

"Let's open it up and find out," she replied.

Finn grabbed a metal bar and pried the top loose. Inside the small crate was an impressive selection of blasters, all new and shiny. Dusque briefly recalled Tendau's weapon and how there seemed to be something vaguely sinister about it, like unspoken betrayals.

"Not bad," Finn murmured as he rummaged through the contents of the container. He pulled out various styles of blasters and checked their power supplies. Dusque was impressed with how comfortable he was with each type, easily disassembling them and reassembling them again after verifying their condition.

"What'll it be?" he asked her when he was finished.

"Doesn't really matter," she confessed, "because I don't know the differences between any of them."

"You've never used one of these?" he asked her.

"Not in my line of work. Survival knives, some fencing, and hand-to-hand techniques are all I've ever practiced or used." She lowered her head, afraid that she had disappointed him and that he must now have found her wanting.

He surprised her again. "Then we better rectify that while there's time," he said easily, without a hint of derision in his voice. "C'mere."

Dusque moved closer to the crate. Finn pulled out four different models of blasters and handed two to her, while he hung on to the other two himself. He nudged a few scraps of metal and other crates aside with his foot and cleared a path to a small workbench. He laid his blasters down and then had Dusque add hers to the lineup. He arranged them, then picked up the first one on the left, a long, slim one, and held it up, barrel pointed away, for Dusque's inspection.

"This is a sporting blaster," he explained. "It has a manual sight here just in front of the cooling coils on the barrel. It's light and easily concealed. Go on," he urged her. "Take it."

Dusque accepted the weapon from him and felt the heft of it in her hand. It was very light, weighing not much more than a decent survival knife. While she balanced the item in her hand and tried to become more familiar with the feel of it, Finn moved up beside her.

"The downside to this weapon is that it doesn't have a very powerful charge and it burns up power packs pretty quickly. Also, it uses a manual sight, so there's more room for error. Actually," he continued, "it's more the weapon of the nobility than anything else."

"Then it's no good?" she asked.

"Don't discount this little one so fast," Finn told her. "You can swap out power packs pretty quickly and, if you need to sneak a weapon in someplace . . ." He paused. Moving to stand behind her, he pointed out a small recessed button on the blaster above the trigger.

"See there?" he asked her. She nodded and found herself standing taller as he stood closer.

"Press this and she pops into three pieces: the grip with the power pack, the main body with the blaster components, and the barrel. Give it a try."

Dusque found that the gun came apart readily. Without waiting for his instruction, she snapped its parts back into a functioning weapon. "That could be handy," she agreed coolly, trying not to show how pleased she was by the obvious approval on his face.

He took away the sporting blaster and handed her the next one.

"This is a DH-seventeen blaster," he explained. When she took it from his hands, he moved even closer to her.

"Heavier than the other one," Dusque remarked.

"Yep," he agreed. "Longer range than the sporting model and longer-lasting firepower." He wrapped his hand over hers. It was warm and dry and strong.

"The safety release," he told her, "is above the trigger. See?"

"Mm-hmm," she agreed, studying the pistol. "Is that the power pack?" she asked, pointing to a unit above the trigger, near the barrel.

"That's right," Finn replied, sounding delighted that she noticed. He released her hand and stepped back. "On the other model it was in the grip itself. These are a little trickier to take out, but can still be removed quickly when you get the hang of it."

"Pros and cons?" she asked.

"It can blast through stormtrooper armor, but not a ship's hull, so this is a good choice for close fighting on a ship. And on the low-power stun, it can knock someone out cold. It's normally semiautomatic, but this one's been juiced to fully automatic. See?" he asked as he pointed out the modification.

"The downside with that is you burn up packs very quickly and can even overheat the outer components if you're not careful. And it's illegal for any nonmilitary personnel to possess."

"Oh," Dusque said, and held the weapon out as though she were targeting something. Finn moved behind her and placed his hand over hers again as she sighted down the weapon. He guided her head with his other hand.

"It's got a scope," he explained quietly, "not a manual sight. Notice the difference?"

Dusque faltered for a moment when she felt his body touch her back lightly. As much as she wanted to deny it, there was a current that ran between them. It excited and frightened her at the same time.

"I do," she finally said. Finn was quiet for a minute, and when he stepped over to their arsenal, Dusque was certain he let his fingers trail over hers longer than he needed to. He busied himself with his next selection, and Dusque wondered if he needed to collect himself. When he did choose another, she realized she had seen one like it before.

"The other pilot, Han Solo, carries one like that," she said.

Finn gave her a grin. "Very good," he complimented her. "You obviously studied him pretty closely," he added after a moment's thought, and Dusque could've sworn there was just the touch of jealousy in his voice. Even while she felt exasperated, she knew she was also pleased.

"Well, I did have a hard time taking my eyes off him," she told Finn innocently and watched his jaw clench. She bit back a laugh. When he didn't respond, she began to wonder if her teasing had gone too far. She was about to say something to make up for it, but then the storm cloud lifted from his face and he smiled back at her, although it was not the easy smile of a moment ago.

"Anyway," he began, ignoring their last exchange, "the DL-forty-four is what's known as a heavy blaster." He tossed the weapon at her, and Dusque needed both hands to catch it. She wondered if he was mad at her.

"You're right," she said, "but I can still carry it one-handed."

Finn nodded. "And you can fire it that way, too. But this weapon is really designed for close-quarters combat, and it uses up power packs even faster than the DH-seventeen.

"The nice thing, though," he continued and leaned in, "is this right here." He pointed to a small unit in the grip. "That device vibrates the grip when you're low on power, so you know to switch out packs. Downside with this weapon is you have to be a good shot. You can't just blast away and hope for the best, or you'll burn out the pack. And the button above the grip but below the sight is a quick release for the power pack."

He took that one away and handed her the last weapon on the table. It was longer than the others.

"This is the E-eleven blaster rifle," he told her. "Go on, take it."

Dusque was a trifle hesitant because he still seemed angry with her. Finn appeared to sense her discomfort and eased off a bit. "You can do it," he told her. She accepted the rifle and realized she needed both hands to hold it comfortably.

"It has a range almost three times that of a blaster."

"It's heavier," Dusque admitted. "I don't think I could hold this with one hand."

"Most can't. If you see under the barrel, there's an extendable stock that'll help your aim."

Dusque fumbled with the mechanism and Finn assumed his earlier pose, standing behind her and cradling both her and the weapon in the circle of his arms. He snapped the stock partially open, forming a triangle under the gun.

"Now hold this up and look through the scope," he instructed her.

Dusque saw that the view with this one was different. "It's not like the others," she told him. When he responded, he spoke into her right ear and his breath sent shivers through her once more.

"It's computerized so that you can aim in the worst conditions. Doesn't matter," he continued, "low light, haze, or smoke won't affect your shots. For more stability—" He paused and pulled the stock toward Dusque, opening it fully. He placed it against her shoulder. "—open this up."

He stretched his arm against the length of her left one and there wasn't a part of their bodies that wasn't touching. Dusque wasn't sure which of them was trembling.

"The switch over here," he continued softly, "is

so you can vary the power setting from stun to something . . . more . . . powerful." He hesitated.

Dusque was no longer listening to the words he was saying. She leaned her body against his and found his solidity comforting. She didn't know which one of them lowered the weapon, but it slid to the floor with a dull thud. His hands trailed up her arms and he gripped her shoulders firmly. His breathing came out in short puffs that tickled her neck, and chills ran up and down her spine.

"Dusque," he whispered.

"Yes," she replied in kind.

"I-I . . ." He faltered.

"Yes?" she asked gently, overcome with an emotion she feared to name.

"I-I can't," he finished and pushed her away from him.

Dusque reeled slightly as she regained her balance, and she was surprised at herself for having relied so much on his strength to support her. She leaned forward to grip the workbench and take a deep breath.

When she had composed herself, she saw that Finn had a torn expression on his face. She wondered if he was frustrated by pushing her away, or upset that he had allowed her to get too close to begin with. And then his words about the Empire came back to her, how he believed that everyone betrayed those they loved to it eventually.

As Finn started to speak, Dusque held up a hand

and placed it against his lips. "It's all right," she said. "I understand. It's the Empire, isn't it?"

Finn did not speak for some time, but stared at her with his black eyes. Dusque thought she might drown in those inky depths. When he finally did answer, his voice was hard and almost cold. "Yes," he agreed, "it is because of the Empire."

Dusque wondered what atrocity they had committed against him or, most likely, someone he had loved to leave him so cold and hateful now. The realization came to Dusque that while he knew so much about her, his past was shrouded in mystery. She had learned a little on Lok, but there was so much left unsaid between them.

"What happened—" she started to ask him, when the Mon Calamari returned.

"Strap yourselves back in," he ordered, totally unaware of what he had interrupted. "We're about to drop out of hyperspace."

"You heard the man," Finn told her, and she wondered if he was glad he didn't have to answer her question.

She turned away from him and picked up the DH-17. "I think I'll take this one," she said, changing the subject herself. She didn't want to force him to talk if he was unwilling to open up. She grabbed a holster from the crate and an armband with power packs. When she had added the weapon to her gear, she sat down and strapped herself in.

From the only viewport in the cargo area, Dusque could see the slashing rays of hyperspace travel streak by, and then the stars stopped their mad dash. She breathed a sigh of relief, glad that they were almost there. But her relief was short lived. Suddenly the shuttle rocked hard to the left and then the right. Had she not been buckled up, Dusque knew she would have been slammed against the wall with the rest of the cargo. As the ship bucked, she could see laserfire from the starboard portal. They were under attack.

"What is it?" Finn shouted, struggling with his restraints.

"Imps," the Mon Calamari yelled. The tension and fear in his voice were unmistakable.

"Blast it," Finn hissed. "They're never in this sector." He freed himself just as the ship took another hit; he was thrown hard to the floor.

"Watch out!" Dusque called as a crate broke free of its moorings and slid dangerously close to him. He sidestepped the deadly object and it smashed into the far wall, goods spilling out everywhere.

She saw that he managed to struggle into the cockpit, and then she lost sight of him. She debated joining them forward, but realized she had absolutely nothing to offer them other than a distraction. She knew less about the workings of ships than she did about guns. She held on to her restraints as the ship was tossed about like a piece of driftwood at sea and hoped that Finn was as good a copilot as he had proclaimed on Lok. Between the blasts, she strained to hear what they were saying up front.

"Solo, do you copy?" the Mon Calamari shouted. "We're under attack."

"I've kind of got my hands full here at the moment," came the *Falcon* pilot's clipped response.

The ship took another hit, and Dusque was nearly torn from her seat by the force of it. They were in serious trouble, she realized, and she wondered if she was going to perish out in the void of space with her friend's death unavenged and her life unremarkable.

I've done nothing with my life, she mused, and the waste of it tormented her more than its imminent loss.

"Give me that comm," she heard Finn's rough voice demand.

"What?" Peralli cried out.

Dusque heard what she thought might be a struggle of sorts before the ship took another dangerous hit. No longer bucking, the transport started a dangerously steep descent. While Dusque held on to the arms of the seat out of useless fear, she heard a whine and an explosion. Oddly, it sounded like it had come from within the cockpit.

"Finn!" she screamed. She clawed at her straps, suddenly more afraid that he had perished than that her own death was close at hand. As she fumbled to find the buckles, she was momentarily relieved to hear his voice. It sounded as though he was talking to Han, saying something about their position. As she released the last strap, she realized that the ship

was plunging ominously downward at an increasing rate. The attack, however, had ceased.

She held on to the support structures and crossbeams to keep from crashing forward as she made her way toward Finn. Smoke obscured most of her view; she could see that the tiny cockpit was filled with the acrid stuff, and part of the control panel was sputtering. As she clung to the doorway, she could also see Peralli slumped forward in his pilot's seat, his communications gear askew on his large, fishlike head, his eyes rolled back. He was dead. Finn was straining his muscles as he fought with the controls.

"What—" was all Dusque managed to stutter.

Without looking up, Finn said through gritted teeth, "Too late to save the ship. Too late."

"What about the *Falcon*?" she asked.

"Han managed to clear the fighters," he replied.

There were no longer any in sight, she noted, and she wondered why the fighters hadn't stayed to finish them off. Filling the clear canopy of the cockpit was the planet Corellia. It looked so peaceful, Dusque thought, blue-green and white against a velvet background. But as it grew larger and larger, she realized that they were accelerating.

"Get yourself strapped back in," he shouted to her, "and brace yourself for planetfall."

Dusque swung around. She climbed over boxes and loose gear, fighting to regain her seat. There was too much in the way—too many items that had not been properly strapped down—and the ship rocked and swayed as gravity pulled it through the atmosphere. She slipped and fell back. On her hands and knees, vaguely aware that she was crawling *up,* she reached out for the seat. Her fingertips touched it, then the ship shuddered, and she stumbled. With a great push, she lurched to her feet, intending to launch herself at her seat. And then she heard Finn scream out, *"This is it!"*

The ship slammed to a shattering halt and Dusque felt herself falling, suddenly airborne. She hit something hard and then she felt nothing more.

Somewhere in the blackness, Dusque could feel herself floating. She was warm and comfortable and felt quite free. There was, however, a persistent tugging and a voice somewhere deep in the void. She tried to ignore it, preferring the cool darkness to the sounds and sensations calling to her. She moved away from it and when she did, she felt a sharp, stabbing pain. Suddenly colors blinked and swirled around her, shattering the peaceful darkness. And from somewhere, she heard a moan. Then she realized the sound was coming from her. She blinked hard several times and slowly opened her eyes completely. It took some time before she was able to focus, and when she did, she was amazed.

She was lying in a heap in what remained of the cockpit, her limbs askew, covered by bits of crates and other debris. She could feel wetness behind her and tasted blood. She tried to move and winced again. She realized it was the sharp stab in her side that had roused her to consciousness—that and the voice that still called out to her frantically.

"Dusque!"

"Here," she answered weakly and then tried again. "Here!"

Debris started to fly off her, and Dusque realized that she was less injured than she had originally thought. She was mostly pinned. As a large piece of equipment was lifted from her chest and shoulders, she could see Finn standing above her. Worry and concern were etched on his face. Blood seeped down his forehead; he was frightening to behold. But Dusque was grateful to see him alive.

Without saying a word, he reached down and removed the last bit of wreckage off her legs. He leaned down and scooped her up into his arms. She stifled a cry of pain and, as he carried her up toward the main cabin, she realized why he had moved her without checking for other injuries first. Over his shoulder, she could see that the cockpit was slowly flooding with water. The body of the pilot lay there, partially submerged.

"Peralli," she said weakly.

"He's dead," Finn stated flatly, a grim expression fixed on his stony visage. He maneuvered them over to the workbench, which was only slightly tilted. He laid her down with surprising tenderness and ran his hands over her legs and arms, checking for injuries. When he moved up to her waist and left side, she winced in pain.

"Feels broken," he told her, referring to at least one of her ribs.

"No argument there," she agreed.

"I'm not sure what else might be injured," he told her, worry softening his voice.

Dusque propped herself up on one elbow and moved to sit up. Finn tried to restrain her initially, but she shook her head and waved his hands away.

"No time for that," she replied and clenched her jaw. "What about you?"

"Nothing, just a few scratches," he said, dismissing her concern. He left her side and started to search the piles of gear that had been thrown about the cabin.

"What are you doing?" she asked him, keeping one eye on the water that had now filled the cockpit. At least, she thought, the Mon Calamari had been returned to the water in the end.

"Looking for a medkit to fix you up," he explained angrily. "We are going to have to get out of here soon."

"Forget about it." She winced. "Grab the straps from that chair. They'll do."

Finn managed to find one of the flight chairs and cut the straps free with a knife he had tucked up his sleeve. When he had freed two of them, he stumbled back over to Dusque. She sat upright and raised her arms out to her side. The pain in that simple movement was excruciating, and she realized that she looked like Tendau had in his final moments, arms spread.

"Do it," she told him.

He nodded to her once and placed the first restraint around her chest. As soon as he had the free end threaded through the buckle, he began to tighten it. Dusque groaned with the discomfort.

"More," was all she managed to say.

He exhaled heavily and cinched the strap tighter. Dusque bit back on a moan and then breathed a little easier.

"Do the other one," she told him.

As he applied the second makeshift brace, she leaned against him with her outstretched hand. "How did the pilot die?" she asked, to take her mind off the pain.

Finn was silent as he tightened the second brace. "We took a hit in the cockpit," he finally said. "He didn't make it."

Dusque hazily thought that he seemed to be hiding something. She wondered if he had somehow made a mistake and that had been the reason for the pilot's death. And if his abilities with a ship were not what he had said they were, what else, she wondered briefly, might he have lied to her about? She dismissed the thoughts as soon as he looked up at her through his tousled hair. She realized that she didn't care about herself or anything else at that moment; she was just glad he was alive.

"I thought I'd lost you," he said shakily. He touched her face. "I thought . . ."

"I did, too," she answered him and managed a smile through her discomfort. She placed her hand across the straps and breathed in experimentally. "It'll do," she pronounced.

Finn helped her up. "Grab what you can," he told her. The water had reached the main cabin. "We've got to move."

She eased herself off the table and found that the straps were holding: there was much less discomfort the more she moved around. She found her small pack and strapped it to her back. She wasn't able to find her sword, but the blaster was poking out from under some circuitry. She wound the holster around her hips and even found an armband of ammo floating past her feet. She noticed, as she ducked below hanging wires and jagged metal, that there was little else that was salvageable.

Finn was near the back hatch. He was squatting in the water, and Dusque realized that he was placing charges around the door. The door lock must have been jammed, she deduced. She slogged through the nearly waist-deep water to stand beside him.

"Now what?" she asked.

He placed the last charge and turned to look at her. He had a worried expression on his face.

"I'll manage," she replied to his unasked question.

"I'm going to have to blow the door. I've got charges placed in the cockpit, as well. I'm going to blow that first," he explained, "and then the door. As soon as I do, the seawater is going to rush in behind us first, and as the air escapes, hopefully it will push us out the hatch."

Dusque nodded. "As soon as we get out," she

told him, "and you can open your eyes, let out a little air. Your bubbles are going to head to the surface, so follow them."

He nodded in return. "Grab on to something, okay?"

She wrapped her arm around a metal beam. "Okay," she told him, and started to take several quick breaths to blow all the carbon dioxide out of her lungs. Then in one big breath she filled her wounded chest with as much air as she could possibly hold. She saw Finn do the same. He locked eyes with her and held out a detonating switch. He pressed down on one switch and then the other. Twin explosions rocked the doomed vessel, and Dusque found herself thrust out into the depths of the Corellian ocean. Once again, she was lost in the darkness.

NINE

Dusque was being buffeted around. She shut her eyes tightly, but could do nothing about the cold water that immediately filled her nostrils. One thing she had neglected to tell Finn was that she was absolutely terrified of deep water. And she was in the grip of that fear now. It took all that she had not to scream, though she knew it would do no good. When she finally built up enough courage, she opened her eyes.

She was swirling and tumbling about, unable to tell what was what. The water around her was frothy from the plane wreckage, and Dusque felt panic start to build within her. She momentarily forgot her advice to Finn, finding it impossible to tell where any of the bubbles were heading. Through blind luck, she managed to see the remains of the shuttle. She fixed her frightened gaze on it and realized that it was getting smaller the longer she looked at it. Her scientific mind kicked in and overrode the fear.

Of course, she scolded herself, *gravity has taken*

hold of it and it's sinking. If it's going that way, then
I'm headed the other.

Without another thought, she kicked up as hard
as she could. Though she feared the ocean, she was
able to swim. Drowning was a great motivator and
teacher.

Remembering what she had told Finn, she let a
little of her precious air escape from her mouth and
saw the tiny stream of bubbles move past her eyes.
That told her that she was headed in the right direction. She swung her arms down in great passes and
kicked as hard as she could. But the burning in her
chest let her know that she didn't have much time.

The combination of her injuries and her fear
caught up with her. She let out a bellow, and giant
bubbles exploded from her mouth in an underwater
scream. She saw strong foam no more than a few
meters directly above her. With a final thrust of her
arms, and spots winking in and out of her vision,
Dusque broke the surface.

Her ragged gasp for air sucked in some salt water,
and she started to hack and wheeze. She retained
enough presence of mind to tread water, and now
that she was breathing in air, her fear started to re-
cede. It was still there, but it was no longer overwhelming. When she finally cleared her sore chest,
she started to swim in ever-widening circles, calling
for Finn.

"Over here," she heard, and she turned about
wildly, searching for the source of the voice, pray-
ing it was Finn.

Eventually, she spotted his head bobbing in the surf some ten meters away. Beyond him, she could see something almost equally gratifying: a shore. She started her clumsy strokes over to where Finn was, pausing frequently to get her bearings and catch her breath. Her fear may have receded, but it wasn't that far in the distance. Between her sore ribs and clumsy strokes, she was a pathetic sight.

"Thank the Force," Finn said and Dusque thought it almost sounded like a benediction from his lips. "I thought I'd lost you again."

"N-no," Dusque sputtered. She found it difficult to swim and talk too much.

"Are you all right?" he asked.

Kicking furiously to stay afloat, Dusque answered, "I will be once we're on shore."

Finn scrutinized her and she could see he realized that she was close to panicking. "We're close now," he told her encouragingly. "Follow me."

Dusque struggled along behind Finn, and she was certain he had slowed his pace considerably to accommodate her poor form. He asked only once if she needed help, and when she refused, he didn't ask again. But she saw him turn his head back frequently to make sure she was following. Even though the shore wasn't far off, he veered toward a clump of large rocks, and she knew he was doing that for her sake so she wouldn't have to ask for help. She felt the now familiar mix of exasperation and pleasure over his actions.

He was slightly ahead of her and called back,

"Let's climb out on those rocks and catch our breath, okay?"

"Mm-hmm," Dusque agreed, holding her mouth shut against the water. As they neared the outcropping, the water broke against the coral flats and grew choppy because of it. She could see that even Finn was being buffeted around by the force of it. But he still worried about her, not himself.

"There are some reeds or something here that you can grab hold of," he called to her, and started to swim in the direction of the vegetation he had seen. Even though she was nearly exhausted, something in what Finn said didn't make sense. There shouldn't have been any reeds or the like growing in the surf. It took her muddled mind a moment to realize what it was he had seen.

Finn was about to reach for one of the two stalky reeds when Dusque screamed out. He turned back toward her and didn't see those two stalks raise themselves out of the water and hold themselves above his head menacingly.

Realizing that swimming to him was out of the question, Dusque reached for the blaster she hoped was still in its holster. It was. She pulled the blaster free and flipped the safety like Finn had shown her on the shuttle. "Down!" she screamed at him.

She released a volley of blasts in the general direction of the arachnid creature. More by luck than skill, a few of those blasts caught the monster dead-on, and it crumpled back into the water. She didn't know who was more surprised by her shooting: her or Finn. She held the blaster tightly in her fist, afraid to try to holster it while the waves knocked her around. She swam awkwardly over to Finn, growing more tired by the second.

When she reached his side, she gasped, "Maybe we can stop here for just a moment or two?"

Finn smiled broadly. "For you, we can even stop for three. Is it safe, though?"

Dusque wasn't too tired to realize that he was asking her for her evaluation of the situation, even though she was floundering and sputtering like a child.

"L-looks clear," she gasped, and watched as Finn pulled himself up onto the rocks, carefully avoiding the dead spider creature. He braced himself and pulled Dusque from the water. She gasped at the pain in her side, but she didn't care. She was overwhelmed with relief to be out of the water. For a few seconds, they both sat there, gasping and shivering. Just as Finn was about to say something, the creature sprang to life and shot toward them.

Before Dusque could let loose with another round of laserfire, Finn unsheathed his knife and drove it into the creature's back. It fell flat in a chattering heap, all of its many limbs splayed out. And from where Finn had stabbed the thing, black ooze started to pool. He reached for his knife, but Dusque caught his forearm.

"Watch out," she warned him. "That black ink is venomous."

Finn carefully extricated his weapon and cleaned

it off with a piece of his torn tunic. He inserted the sharp blade back under his sleeve and Dusque figured out that he must have some kind of mechanism under there to release the blade when triggered.

"It was probably dead when it skittered over here," she told him after she had caught her breath. "Just a reflex action."

Finn regarded the meter-long arachnid with some disgust. "Just what was that thing?" he asked her.

"A dalyrake," Dusque explained. "They're more common on Talus than Corellia, but, as you can see, they can be found here, as well."

"And that black stuff is toxic?" he asked. Dusque would've laughed if her side didn't ache so. When he asked the question, he looked for the entire world like a little boy both disgusted and fascinated by a creepy-crawly.

"Yes," she answered with a smile. "They can live on land or in the water indefinitely. What they do quite often is find a solid perch near water and dangle in their front two arms as lures. They wait for some unsuspecting fish to swim by and spear it with their venomous talons." She smiled more broadly, wondering if he grasped the implication of the explanation.

"So what you're telling me is that I was nearly killed by something that hunts fish . . ." He trailed away.

The corner of her lip twitched in amusement. "That's right, Finn," she said, emphasizing his name.

He looked at her and said, "Isn't that ironic?"

The next thing she knew was they were both lying on their backs, laughing at the absurdity that a man named after a part of a fish had almost been killed by something that frequently preyed on them.

"O-ow," she said, gripping her side and sitting back up, composing herself after the much-needed release of tension.

"Let's get to shore and get you some medical attention," he told her. "It's not too far now."

The idea of reentering the water sobered Dusque up. She scanned the shore and tried to estimate how much farther it was until she would be on dry land. *Only about fifteen meters or so,* she thought. *I can do it.*

"Yes, you can," Finn told her as if he had read her thoughts.

"You're right," she said in return. "I can."

Finn slid into the water and Dusque followed him in more slowly, favoring her injured side. The water felt colder after their time on the rocks, but Dusque steeled herself, knowing they would soon be back on land. Glancing ahead to the beach, she thought she saw something glint bronze in the setting sun. She saw that Finn noticed it, too; he seemed wary as he swam ahead of her. As soon as he was able to, he stood up and waded partially to shore. Then he stopped and waved, and Dusque realized that the bronze glint she had seen was a metallic figure, who responded to Finn's wave with a salute.

As Finn turned and waded back in to help her out, Dusque asked, "Someone you know?"

"Droid that works closely with someone I work for," was all he said as he helped her from the water.

Seeing that the droid was a protocol unit, she sighed inwardly.

"Hello, there," he introduced himself. "I am See-Threepio, human–cyborg relations specialist." And he even managed a half bow.

"How did you find us?" Finn asked as he guided Dusque up the shore.

"We tracked your descent," the droid explained, "and I was sent out here just in case."

"In case one or both of us survived?" Finn said wryly. He cocked his head toward Dusque. "We need to get her to a medcenter."

"I'll be fine," she told him, eager to get away from the water.

"There are several competent Too-Onebees where we are going," C-3PO assured them, "if you can wait. It would be better that way, if possible, but it is a long walk from here and some parts are quite steep."

"I'll manage," she assured Finn, almost ignoring the droid completely.

"All right, but we'll take it slow," he finally agreed. He put his arm lightly around her waist, and Dusque didn't mind the support.

As she and Finn walked up the beach together, C-3PO led the way.

"Oh, dear, I hate sand. It always lodges in my

gears." He turned and looked at Finn. "Did I ever tell you about the time on Tatooine when I . . ."

He droned on and on but Finn and Dusque hardly noticed a word he said.

The walk to their final destination was long and difficult. Several times, Dusque had to readjust the tension on the makeshift bandages around her rib cage. But she didn't slow down, and they made fairly good time.

It was not the first time that she had been on Corellia, but Dusque had never been to the area they were hiking through. As best as she could estimate, they had crashed fairly close to Tyrena. C-3PO seemed to be leading them northwest, up into the hills and mountains, but when she asked Finn just how far they had to go, he surprised her with his answer.

"I have no idea," he told her.

"Haven't you been to this camp before?"

"I haven't been to that many, and this one is a closely guarded secret because of who's there right now," he explained.

"Doesn't it get frustrating?" Dusque asked. "All the secrecy . . . How is it different from the tactics the Empire uses?"

Finn studied her closely for a moment, and Dusque wondered if she had offended him. However, she was too sore and too tired to try to defend herself, so she just breathed in the soothing forest air and waited for him to reply.

"You're right," Finn said after a long pause. "Many of the tactics are the same. That's the danger in all of this," he continued more softly. "You have to keep your motives true, or you could find yourself on the other side with no idea how it happened."

Dusque wasn't sure what to say to that. She and Finn continued on without speaking. C-3PO was a different matter: Oblivious to whether anyone was listening to him, he rambled on and on about the difficulties he faced in his day-to-day operations. The only time he was silent was when Dusque spotted a pack of canids between a few of the tall trees and hissed at him to be quiet.

"Unless you want to be trampled by those rooting pigs, shut up," she whispered urgently.

Finn flashed her a winning smile and they passed the animals in the brush without incident. For the remainder of the hike, C-3PO stewed in what seemed to be offended silence. Dusque was not put out by it in the least.

As they trotted down the incline of yet another hill, Dusque saw a small collection of stone structures, all very flat and probably no more than one level above ground. From the look of the place and Finn's earlier comments, she got the impression that the camp was temporary, which made sense, since the Rebels never knew when they'd have to flee suddenly. Still, there were several fortifications, and she could see sentries patrolling about.

They were greeted by a soldier who recognized

C-3PO and waved them in. He looked very young to Dusque, but what surprised her more than his age was the fact that he seemed genuinely glad to see that they had arrived safely, strangers he had never met before but who shared his dreams. Dusque nodded to him, and he gave her a smile and a quick salute before sobering and resuming his duties of scanning their surroundings, his weapon at the ready.

They headed down a stone walkway and entered one of the largest edifices in the compound. The place was teeming with Rebel soldiers, but few spared the newcomers more than a cursory glance. Dusque assumed that this was because they had obviously been cleared by security. She watched as C-3PO walked over to a compact command center, where he was accosted by a small R2 unit. The little white-and-blue domed droid beeped and chirped excitedly at C-3PO.

C-3PO grew more animated. "Yes," he told the little droid excitedly, "it was extremely dangerous, but I managed to maneuver them through it and arrive here safely."

Dusque, smirking at C-3PO's version of the tale, chuckled when the R2 unit emitted an off-pitch squawk and the protocol droid stiffened into an offended stance. Her laughter caused her to wince again.

"Threepio," Finn called out, "where's your medcenter?"

The bronze droid broke away from what looked like the beginning of an argument with the R2 unit and pointed out where Finn should take Dusque. He then returned to his squabbling with the little droid. Dusque suspected they were great companions and probably carried on like that for hours at a time. The fact that many of the Rebel soldiers moved past them without interest seemed proof enough to her that her reasoning was sound.

Finn escorted Dusque around the complex. She was amazed at how much activity was going on, among not only human soldiers, but other species and droids, too. She couldn't remember her lab ever being this active over anything. Compared to the Rebel base, her lab was passionless—that was the only word she could think of to describe it. The thought depressed her. As they passed by what seemed to be someone's office, Finn paused and stuck his head in the door. The office occupant, a young man with hair as black as Finn's and dressed in a pilot's suit, waved to them.

"Wedge," Finn greeted him, smiling hugely.

"Finn!" The man called Wedge started to rise.

"Hold on, buddy," Finn said, raising one hand, palm out. "Let me get her to the medics and I'll be back. We need to talk."

Wedge nodded and sat back down behind his desk, as serious as he had been when they had first passed by. Dusque wondered how the Rebels managed to remain so focused and so dedicated. And then she wondered if most of them had someone like Tendau in their past, driving them on. More than likely, they all did, she mused.

"Here you go," Finn said, ushering her into a tiny but well-stocked med room. A 2-1B droid stopped adjusting some equipment and glided over to them.

"How can I assist you?" it asked.

"I think I've got some cracked ribs," Dusque told it. "Would you take a look?"

"Of course," it replied. "Please sit down." And it indicated a nearby bed.

"You'll be okay?" Finn asked.

"Go ahead and catch up with your comrade," she told him easily. "Everything's fine now." And with those words, she leaned back on the bed. The relief to be here, where she could be treated at last, was too much for her: her control started to splinter, and all the agony she was in was written on her face. Seeing that, Finn hesitated.

"I'll only be a few minutes," he assured her.

With closed eyes, Dusque waved him away. "I'll be fine." And he left.

While the droid passed a scanner over her ribs and back, Dusque studied the bustling base from her cot. Through the open doorway, she could see various personnel moving about, as well as C-3POs, binary loadlifters, and other draft droids. In the center of the hub stood a tiny woman. Dusque estimated that the petite, brown-haired whirlwind was a good head or so shorter than she was, but what the woman lacked in stature, she clearly made up for with drive.

As the 2-1B started to treat her broken ribs, Dusque could see that the woman appeared not only to be helping by carrying supplies, but also to be giving orders. It slowly became clear to Dusque that it was the woman who was in command at this base. She marveled at how that could be. Having spent her entire life in service to the Empire, she had never come across a woman who held any sort of rank even close to what she suspected this woman did. And she looked no older than Dusque.

Dusque felt something emotional inside herself shift. Surrounded by these Rebels, from the young sentry at the gate willing to die not out of fear of retribution from his superiors but for a dream, to the petite woman in white who commanded the respect of those around her, Dusque realized that theirs was a dream worth dying for. The words that Tendau had spoken to her in what seemed to be a lifetime ago on Rori crystallized for her.

When the time comes, you will see your path like a beacon before your eyes, he had told her, and she realized he was right. She had found her way.

"Your ribs are bruised, but not broken," the 2-1B announced, interrupting her reverie. "I'm applying bactabandages to help speed the healing."

Dusque breathed in a shallow sigh of relief and was surprised to find that it didn't hurt. Whatever the 2-1B was doing to her ribs, it was certainly getting rid of the pain. As soon as the droid was finished with her treatment, she got up and moved about experimentally.

Finn returned looking grim, but his expression

lightened when he saw that she was up and maneuvering around without pain. "How do you feel?"
he asked her.

"Good as new," she informed him. "Actually,
better than new."

He looked at her quizzically. Dusque decided she
would share her epiphany with him, so he would
truly know she had embraced his cause.

But he cut her off before she could start. "Good
to hear. We need to go now and receive the rest of
our orders," he explained, his grim expression
back. "We're almost out of time."

Realizing how serious he was, Dusque sobered
up, as well. "Lead on," she told him. She turned
and thanked the med droid, then followed after Finn.

Together they wound their way around the
labyrinth that was the base and made their way to
the second floor. There, near what Dusque thought
might be a large-style holoprojector, was the woman
in white. There were a few others in the room, but
most were busy, taking readings or communicating
with other troops stationed elsewhere. The only
other person in the room was a young man who
looked only slightly older than the eager sentry by
the gates.

With blond hair streaked by the sun, he was obviously someone who had spent his few years outdoors. He was dressed simply enough in a shirt and
trousers, but a strange, cylindrical device swung
from the belt at his hip. She didn't recognize the
technology, and that puzzled her, because she

prided herself in knowing all the latest equipment. When she looked up, she realized that his sky-blue eyes were staring intensely at her. There was something ancient about those eyes, and she shivered, although she wasn't cold. She broke away from his gaze when she heard the woman address Finn.

"I'm so glad you're both here and safe," the small woman said sincerely. Dusque thought her eyes looked warm and comforting. "When Han reported that you had been shot down, we feared the worst."

"How is he?" Finn asked, and Dusque heard a hard tone in his question. The woman did, as well.

"Don't worry, Finn," she said, laying a comforting hand on his forearm. "Han's fine. It was a near thing, but he and Chewie escaped the Imperial fighters. I don't know how he does it," she added with a chuckle, "but that bucket of bolts he calls a ship got him away again." She was silent for a moment and Dusque thought she sensed more than just comradelike concern for the dashing pilot.

"I cannot say how glad I am that you are all right," the woman continued, addressing Dusque.

"Thank you," she replied and, after a brief hesitation, asked, "Who are you?"

The petite woman and Finn exchanged a short glance between them. "You didn't tell her?" she asked Finn.

"No point in it until we got here," he answered, "if we got here at all."

"Finn and I have known each other for more

years than I care to name. I am Leia Organa," she introduced herself. "I'm sorry, I wish we had more time, but we don't."

"I understand," Dusque replied. She thought that she knew the name from somewhere, but she wasn't sure. "Can you still use me?" she asked. "Since the Empire executed my friend, I might no longer be in good standing with them. And all this will have been for nothing."

Leia nodded. "We heard about what happened to Tendau. I'm sorry," she added, and Dusque was touched by her sympathy. Leia was a military leader, but she clearly had not lost sight of her compassion, or the awareness that it was real people who perished, not numbers on a datapad.

"We weren't able to discover why a warrant was issued for him but, fortunately, none has been issued for you," Leia went on.

"So her cover is still valid?" Finn asked.

"Yes," Leia replied. She faced Dusque. "Because of your background in xenobiology and your title as an Imperial bioengineer, no one will question why you would explore such a relatively unpopulated planet. You can move about without arousing too much suspicion. That's why we needed someone in your position, with your impressive abilities. No one less would do. And because of your personal history," she continued, "I hoped that you would be willing to help us."

Dusque was suddenly overwhelmed by the reality of the situation. Finn had said much the same thing to her when they had first met, but she had not understood; she had been unable to see past her own insecurities. Now, seeing the large number of people Leia commanded, she understood. If all the Princess had needed was a body or someone of moderate ability, she had ample supply right here in the hidden base. But Leia had asked for *her*. She was momentarily speechless.

"Judging by what it took for you to get here, I don't think I'm wrong in my presumption," Leia added.

The choice was truly before Dusque, and she knew her answer would change everything. It was a chance to make a real difference. And there would be no going back. For the first time in her life, Dusque felt no fear.

"I want to help," she answered.

Leia studied her appraisingly, then nodded curtly. "Good," she said without fanfare. "Your superiors don't know where you are, do they?"

Dusque shook her head. "I didn't report in because I didn't want to give them any idea where I was, especially if there was a chance I might be wanted."

"Safe thinking," Leia said approvingly.

"And don't worry," Dusque added, flushed with pleasure at the compliment, "I haven't been off their radar long enough for them to be concerned yet."

Leia nodded. "That's good. Now," she said, all

business again. "The list we need to recover is on Dantooine."

Dusque heard Finn let out a deep breath and she wondered why he had been holding it the whole time. *Probably afraid I was going to back out,* she thought.

"We had a base there for some time," Leia explained, "until someone betrayed us. Fortunately, we were able to evacuate the entire complex in under a day. In that haste, however, we were forced to abandon and destroy some supplies and information. This list of contacts and sympathizers was encoded into a holocron by several different agents, some of whom are no longer alive. No one person has ever known all the names in order to protect the contacts—this holocron is the only place all these names appear together. Several Rebels were able to hide the holocron within the ruins of an ancient Jedi temple for safekeeping just days before Alderaan was destroyed." She paused, and a shadow crossed her face. "These are dark times for us."

Dusque suddenly remembered where she had heard of Leia before. She was a former Senator— and Princess, if memory served—from Alderaan. Dusque looked at her thoughtfully. Here was a woman who had lost everything, faced overwhelming tragedy, and found the strength to continue and to persevere.

"We need to retrieve that list before the Empire does," Leia continued after a moment's silence.

"We know now that the Empire is aware of the list and has sent agents after it. Time is of the essence.

"I want you two to find the holocron and bring it back to me here. If you aren't able to return with it safely, then destroy it. Don't even risk transmitting the information back to us. Better those named remain anonymous and alive than fall into the hands of the Empire."

Dusque looked at Finn and then back at Leia. "We can do it," she promised the petite powerhouse. "We won't fail you."

"There's an exploration shuttle waiting for you at the other end of the base. There's no more time," Leia finished. "You need to leave now."

As Dusque and Finn left the chamber, Leia quietly breathed, "May the Force be with you."

When the two had left, Leia sighed deeply. She hoped that they would be successful. The holocron was a vital piece in the effort to overthrow the Emperor and restore freedom to the galaxy. If nothing else, the people represented on that list deserved their safety and their lives. But she also realized that she might have just sent another two people to their doom.

She turned and saw Luke. "Why were you so quiet?" she asked. He appeared deep in thought, and she moved closer to him and lay a delicate hand over his. "What is it? Do you sense something?" She found herself trembling slightly with concern.

His burgeoning powers both frightened and in-trigued her.

Luke had a faraway look in his eyes. When he fi-nally spoke, it was as if from a great distance. "I don't know exactly," he said, "but I have a bad feel-ing about this." And then he grew silent.

Leia wondered just what her newest recruit and one of her oldest allies were flying into.

TEN

The shuttle was waiting for them at the far end of the base. Finn had been strangely quiet on the way there, and Dusque wondered what he was so worried about.

"What is it?" she asked as they boarded the tiny ship.

Finn scrutinized her silently. The quiet was maddening. Dusque couldn't understand his behavior.

"Please," she entreated him, "tell me what you're thinking."

Whether it was the tone of her voice or the look in her eyes, it had the desired effect on Finn. He relented a little.

"I was just thinking about what you said back there, to Princess Leia . . . You meant it, didn't you? About the Alliance, that is. This isn't just for the Hammerhead anymore. You believe in this cause?"

While she winced inwardly again at his casual reference to Tendau, she excused his choice of words, realizing that with all the death he must see, he would have to desensitize himself to a certain extent to

187

deal with it all. She decided he needed to hear her words again, as reassurance that she was with him all the way.

"When you first brought me into this, I wanted only revenge for Tendau," she said. "You're right. But after what I've seen and done, I realize that the Alliance is the right path. And I believe it here," she finished, placing a hand over her heart. "Please trust me."

Finn seemed to be struggling with something internally.

"Don't you believe me?" she asked.

He swallowed hard. "I do now. I thought you just wanted to see blood spilled for your colleague, and I'll admit I was willing to leverage your anger to get your help. But I did doubt that you believed in any of this, and I figured our mission was a one-time deal for you. Now, though . . ." He trailed away.

Without saying another word, he turned and busied himself with checking their supplies. Dusque smiled to herself, sure she understood his turmoil. Now she was the one who knew what to do and had a purpose equal to his. She guessed he was frightened by the implications. So she went to inventory some of the other equipment on board, and left him in peace.

The Rebel forces had supplied the small vessel well. There were fresh clothes, perfect for explorers and surveyors. Along with datapads, rudimentary camp supplies, and electrobinoculars, there was also a well-stocked medkit, along with portable

stimpaks and plenty of small containers for samples. There was almost everything that Dusque
would have asked for herself if she were on an ac-
tual mission to sample genetic material.

Finn had moved away from a workbench area
and squatted on the floor, feeling the grooves of the
floor panels. When his fingers caught on a release,
he opened up the cover to reveal a cache of a different kind. He motioned for Dusque to come over.
When she did, she whistled appreciatively.

There was a deadly array of blasters and short-
range rifles, along with survival knives and a few
other weapons. There was also an electronic lock
breaker, comlinks, sensor tags, and even several
thermal detonators. She looked at Finn and felt the
gravity of what they were walking into.

"If something happens," he said, answering her
unasked question, "we blow the list and everything
else. Nothing left."

Dusque found she didn't have the words to answer him, so she nodded silently.

There was a whistle from the comm unit, and
they turned in unison. Finn slid into the pilot's seat
and grabbed the headset. Dusque finished up the inventory and prepared herself for the flight.

"Go ahead," she heard Finn say, but because he
was using the headset, she couldn't hear who was
on the other end.

"Yes," he answered, "we're set to go now. There'll
be no further communications until we return with

the item. Finn out." And he pulled the headset off roughly.

He was tense, she thought, as she was. But she also wondered if he was a little unsure. Since the crash on the Mon Calamari's vessel, Dusque had had a nagging doubt about his piloting skills. Maybe, she thought, he was having them now, too. She wondered how she could help.

She stuck her head in the cockpit. "You know, you don't have to hide what's being said anymore. I understand the risks, so don't feel like you need to shield me."

"We're in the business of secrets," he answered, "and so are you, now. 'Fraid you're going to have to accept that. It's almost time, so you'd better strap in." With that, he turned his attention to the myriad switches and flashing lights that made up the control system. Dusque ducked back out and went to get settled in her seat.

"All set?" he called out after a minute.

"Just strapping in now," she replied. She pulled the sturdy restraints over her shoulders and across her torso, locking them in tight.

"As soon as we're out of the gravity well, feel free to come up," he told her.

The shuttle shuddered a little as it rocketed through the atmosphere, and Dusque thought briefly that she was coming to hate space travel almost as much as C-3PO seemed to, judging from one of his many tales of anguish she hadn't managed to tune out completely.

Not what she had hoped to hear, but she understood his concerns. "All right," she replied.

For nearly an hour, he gave her the basic rundown on how the ship operated, from using the deflector shields to jettisoning cargo if needed. Dusque tried to take in as much as possible, but was daunted by the enormity of the job. Finally, perhaps sensing her growing frustration, Finn stood up.

"I'm going to go back and change, get geared up, so I'll leave you to it for a while," he told her. "We've made the jump to hyperspace, but go ahead and go over the controls for yourself. Holler if you have any questions." And he moved toward the rear of the shuttle.

Dusque sighed and went over the mental checklist he had given her. She had newfound respect for pilots, because even with all the technology at their disposal, doing the job well was extremely difficult. She thought that if she had to, she could probably get the thing up in the air, but wasn't sure she'd be able to fly it beyond that, and she didn't even want to think about landing. She studied the controls, but the more she looked at them, the more they all started to look alike. She was rubbing her eyes in frustration when a signal blared, startling her. She glanced at the board and was pleased to realize that she remembered what the signal meant: it was time to drop out of hyperspace.

Finn came hurrying up front, wearing a standard-issue, all-weather environmental suit.

"We'll be in orbit shortly," he told her, sitting

down. "Why don't you go and get changed? You have a few moments before we have to strap in for landing."

As Dusque hurried back, she felt her mouth dry out. She was approaching the moment of truth, and the thought of the task that lay in front of them made her heart pound. Her fingers trembled slightly when she snapped the closures on her environmental suit and strapped on the sport blaster that was permissible for nonmilitary personnel. Telling herself to relax, she stuck several power packs into her sack and strapped on a survival knife. Then she decided to conceal a heavy blaster inside her tunic. Her outer cloak was fabricated from tough fiberplast, so she took the calculated risk that the weapon would be hidden well enough.

Then a flash on the auxiliary control board caught her eye, and she turned to look. Had that been a blip on the radar monitor? Wanting to be sure, she stared at the monitor and waited. After a short time, it happened again. It was as though something was following them, trying to stay just out of range.

She ran forward to the cockpit. "Someone is following us!" she told Finn.

"What are you talking about?" he asked, sounding incredulous.

"Look at the radar!" she exclaimed, waving her hand at the monitor as she slid into the copilot's seat.

For several long moments, both of them watched the monitor.

Finally Finn sighed and shook his head. "There's nothing there," he informed her.

"But there was," she insisted.

"Look," he told her, reaching out to lay a hand on her shoulder, "we're both tense. You probably saw a meteor or an asteroid shoot by. It's a very common mistake new pilots make."

Dusque sat there, frustrated, with her arms crossed. She was sure she had seen something on the screen. Rather than argue with Finn over it, since without proof it looked like a losing battle anyway, she took up a silent vigil over the monitor, determined to catch it out. However, the screen remained accusingly blank, and Dusque started to think it had been a natural celestial occurrence after all.

"We're coming up on the Imperial outpost," Finn announced at last. "Get ready for landing. And no sign of anything following us," he added without mockery.

"I guess I imagined it," she admitted, feeling foolish. She wanted him to think she was competent—and then was annoyed with herself for caring so much what he thought of her.

As soon as they landed, they were contacted by the outpost command center.

"Prepare to be inspected," a voice announced over the comm unit. Dusque and Finn exchanged a tense glance before Finn responded.

"Hatchway open, we're ready for boarding," he said into the comm.

The heavy tread of armor reminded Dusque of the spaceport on Moenia, when the stormtroopers had come for Tendau. Her blood pounding in her ears, she struggled to maintain an outward look of calm. Finn appeared stoic, but then he winked at her just as a stormtrooper entered the cockpit. That one gesture relieved her of an immense amount of tension. She inhaled deeply and stood to address the trooper.

"Everything in order?" she asked, seizing control of the moment.

"We're still checking your cargo," the armored stormtrooper replied through his transmitter.

Once again, Dusque was struck by how impersonal, how inhuman, every aspect of the Empire was. Even a voice lost all warmth when heard through their armor.

"Your clearance codes, please," the stormtrooper added.

Dusque handed him her credentials, along with Finn's falsified ones. The stormtrooper was momentarily put off when he saw that Dusque was the senior member of the group. Judging by his reaction, Dusque guessed he had never come across a woman in charge before. He continued to scrutinize them, and Dusque wondered just how good a job the Rebels had done with Finn's forgeries.

"Everything appears to be—" the stormtrooper began, before he was interrupted.

"Come back here and take a look at these," another officer said.

Dusque's heart skipped a beat. She looked once at Finn and her mind raced. She was afraid that she had somehow not secured the panel correctly over their cache of weapons. Nausea swept through her when the first stormtrooper called her name.

"Come back here." It was clearly not a request but an order. Finn moved to join her, but Dusque, her arm by her side, discreetly waved her hand to stop him.

"If need be," she whispered, "I can make a run for it and you can blast out of here."

She hoped he understood what she meant. If they were found out, he might be able to pilot the ship away while she distracted the stormtroopers by bolting out of the hatch and running. That way, at least one of them would survive. For a moment she was taken aback by this new Dusque: never before had she been so willing to put herself directly in the path of death. And certainly not for anything so nebulous as a *cause*.

"Yes?" she asked, and was proud of the fearlessness in her voice.

She stepped back into the main cabin and saw that several stormtroopers were gathered in a knot. She could not see what they were looking at.

"Explain this," he ordered, and Dusque feared the worst. She chewed her lip slightly and looked at the open hatchway, estimating how long it would take her to reach the outside before she was either apprehended or shot. Before she could decide, however, the stormtrooper turned and faced her, holding something out to her.

Dusque let out her breath very slowly. Instead of some illegal weapon, the soldier had one of her collection tools in his gauntleted hand.

"It does look rather evil," she replied easily, "with the trigger and the pointed dispenser unit, doesn't it? It's a liquid suspension device."

The stormtrooper cocked his head and studied the unit again. "What?" he asked.

"Here," she said, and plucked the device from his fingers. "Sorry, but I don't want you to get the stuff on yourself. It's highly viscous."

"What do you use it for?" he questioned.

"It's just one of the tools I use to preserve specimens and as a component in medical stimpaks. Don't see much of this stuff out here, do you?" she commented, assuming an air of authority.

"No," he replied, "I don't see much of anything out here."

She nodded in commiseration. "This isn't the most glamorous assignment for me, either. Probably because I'm a woman," she groused.

The stormtrooper nodded and ordered the rest of the troopers off the ship.

"Looks like everything is in order here," he told her. "Don't want to make this more difficult for you than it already is," he added quietly.

"Thank you very much," she responded and flashed him a grateful smile.

The stormtrooper left with the others and Dusque

went back to the cockpit. Finn stood up with a pleased expression on his face.

"Nice," he told her. "Very nice."

"Nothing to it," she sighed and then chuckled. "Let's move it."

"After you—" He bowed at the waist. "—fearless leader."

Dusque grabbed her pack and slung it onto her back. She made one last check of her gear, while Finn did the same. Certain they had everything they could think of, they stepped out into the base and sealed up the ship.

Dusque was struck once more by the sterility of the Imperial base. As she stepped out into the square, small clouds of dust puffed up from the red dirt. There were several flat buildings set up, but the place seemed like a ghost town compared to the Rebel base. There were almost no people around. At first glance, all Dusque saw were a few troopers and a lone Bothan who appeared to be surveying, filling a container with some type of amorphous gemstones. The outpost seemed to be the loneliest spot in the galaxy.

As they moved past the military lookout, a uniformed soldier came running after them. Dusque felt her heart rise up in her throat and she saw that Finn had slipped his hand inside his travel cloak. She did the same, her blaster easily within reach.

"Wait," the officer called. "We're not finished with you both just yet."

Dusque turned around, Finn less than a meter behind her. "I don't understand," she said gruffly, forcing a bravado she did not feel. "What is the matter now? You've held us up long enough."

The officer regarded her with openmouthed surprise.

"I am an Imperial bioengineer. The Emperor will hear of this treatment when I am finished with this mission. If you think this post is as remote as it can get, you are sorely mistaken," she finished with a touch of disdain.

"You haven't logged in for our records," the officer replied shamefacedly. "We don't get many visitors, and the stormtrooper who passed you through forgot. It's required."

"Oh," Dusque said and proceeded to act as though she was somewhat mollified by the officer's obsequiousness. "I suppose that won't take very long."

The officer pulled out a datapad and stylus. He noted her credentials and then Finn's.

"That should do it, then," he said. Then he looked at his information and frowned. "Ah," he cleared his throat.

Dusque turned back around with an angry look on her face. "What?" she asked, sounding extremely put out.

"I need to fill out a reason. Why . . . um . . . are you here? We heard no word of it."

"I am part of an advance group, scanning this world and other unpopulated ones in the Outer Rim," Dusque said.

"For what purpose?" the officer asked and Dusque thought he seemed genuinely curious.

"For future colonization," she said.

"Oh . . . ," he replied.

"Play your sabacc cards right, officer, and you might be the lead garrison for the next major Imperial base," she finished with a flourish.

As she suspected, the officer perked up when he heard that he might actually be in command of something other than a forgotten post on an empty world. He didn't even look down at his datapad after that. He straightened up and gave Dusque a genuine salute.

"We're in order here. Good luck and let me know if we can be of any further assistance to one of the Emperor's bioengineers." Then he added, "We have heard of some smuggling activities going on north of here. Perhaps I should send a small detachment with you?"

"I appreciate the offer," she told him. "Officer . . . ?"

"Fuce," he replied, "Commander Fuce."

"I appreciate it, but I suspect your men don't have the training and skills needed to take samples and conduct surveys. Without that, they would only slow us down. But I appreciate the offer and the warning. And I'll make sure my superiors know how well informed and helpful you've been. Thank you," she told him.

He saluted again, then turned on his heels and marched back to his station.

Dusque and Finn navigated through the small outpost without any other incidents. Dusque was vaguely aware that except for a few disreputable types hanging about the tiny, nearly deserted cantina, there was no one else around. The place had been forgotten by enemies and friends alike.

When they finally cleared the compound walls, whatever pretense of civilization had existed within those boundaries disappeared. The view opened up to rolling hills and savannas. The lavender grass that grew rampant on the planet turned the entire countryside a soft purple as far as the eye could see. As Dusque was scanning the horizon, the dark clouds finally released their moisture. Big, heavy drops started to fall. She held out her hand and smiled at their luck.

"Perfect," she said to Finn. "This will help mask our scent from several species of the local wildlife."

"It is perfect," he agreed with a strange look in his eye. "You handled yourself very well back there. I was impressed."

Dusque found herself blushing at his praise and she lowered her head. "I was scared," she admitted. "Really scared for the first time in my life. And I wasn't scared for me—I was frightened for all the people on the list, all the people back at that base, all the nameless souls in the galaxy. But most of all, I was afraid for you."

She felt his hand under her chin, warm and dry, as he tipped her head up.

"I can't believe I've met someone like you in my

life now, here at this moment and we should be involved in this . . ." He shook his head sadly.

"I know," she told him. "There's no time. But if we're successful . . ." She trailed off, unwilling to presume anything.

He pulled her into his arms and kissed her passionately. For a moment, under the boughs of the twisted biba tree, there was no Galactic Civil War, just two people.

"We have here," he said when the kiss ended, "and we have now. There's no point in dwelling on a tomorrow that may never come."

It was Dusque's turn to stare at him. "But we *have* to believe in a tomorrow," she insisted. "Otherwise there is no purpose in today."

Finn pulled himself away from her and composed himself. "You're right," he agreed eventually. "Sorry, I was caught up in the moment."

"There's no need for apology," she told him.

"No, there is." But he didn't explain. Instead he turned away from her and pulled out his scanner, took a brief reading, and then pointed to their left. "North by northeast," he announced. "We haven't got much time."

Troubled, Dusque let him take the lead, and they entered into the uncharted wilderness of Dantooine.

ELEVEN

With the Imperial base far behind them, Dusque and Finn moved quickly but cautiously. The purple fields were littered with all kinds of flowers, and at unguarded moments Dusque found herself thinking that Dantooine was one of the most beautiful planets she had ever seen. It looked like some wild, unkempt garden that had gone to seed. Beyond the lavender hills, olive-colored steppes framed the sky. Even the rain, which continued to fall, and the ominous roll of thunder in the distance couldn't dampen how she felt.

As they jogged along a small gully, Dusque wondered what was going through Finn's mind. She knew he cared about her, and she was past the point of denying to herself that she felt something for the lanky, black-haired Rebel. If it hadn't been for him, she thought, she probably would have been killed with Tendau. His fortuitous arrival had saved her from that certain fate, and he had given her a goal into which to channel her rage and frustration. He had been the one who had started her down the path. If for no other reason, he would be special to her. But nothing was ever that simple.

Before she could think on it further, she heard a thumping in the distance. She slowed her pace, and Finn did, too. They slowly climbed up a steep hill and dropped down to their bellies at the apex. Off to their right was a herd of very large creatures. Dusque berated herself for being careless enough to nearly blunder into them.

She suddenly realized that this was exactly why Finn was being so strange and removed. He knew better than to let anything else cloud his judgment on something so crucial as their mission. She told herself she should do like him and remain focused.

The creatures stood three times as tall as a human, but most of that height came from the neck and head. They had thick, squat bodies with four short legs. Their hide was light on their bellies and darkened along their backs. Wide stripes added to their camouflage, so that when they tired of grazing and lay down, they became difficult to pick out on the steppes. And their elongated heads were covered with horns.

"Piket longhorn," Dusque whispered to Finn.

The ground rumbled under them when one of the animals decided to lie down for a nap. It ungracefully tumbled onto its side, as though dead.

"They're not going anywhere now," Dusque commented.

"Are they aggressive?" Finn asked.

"Not normally. Occasionally there is the rogue

one to worry about, but mostly they're peaceful grazers."

"Big grazers," Finn corrected, and she saw he had regained his dry humor.

"Very big," she agreed. "But if they're staying, we are going to need to move around them. And we need to watch for other, deadlier creatures. Believe it or not, these guys are the prey, not the predators."

"Great," Finn replied, raising and lowering his eyebrows. "I'd hate to see whatever it is that eats them."

As they moved quietly back down the hill, the thunder grew much closer. The sounds helped mask any noise they might have made. As they ran back up the opposite side of the gully, Dusque and Finn saw another herd of piket ahead of them. Off to their left was a long, narrow lake that went on for a fair distance, and they both realized they had no choice. They secured their gear and dived in.

Once a little way out from the piket, Finn pulled on Dusque's arm to get her attention. She turned around fearfully, treading water, and they looked at each other.

"Let's cross over to the other side," he said, pointing away from the piket.

Sputtering water, Dusque said, "But if we go on like this, hugging the shore, we can get past them and not lose too much ground."

"I know," Finn replied, "but getting out sooner makes more sense."

"Don't do it just for me," she argued, paddling about awkwardly.

"We won't lose that much time," he assured her. Without waiting for an answer, he started to swim to the other side.

Dusque shook her head angrily and followed him, frustrated with herself for letting him take over, and with him, for taking over.

"Sorry," she mumbled after he gave her a hand out of the water.

"You save us from stumbling into a pack of very large animals and you apologize?" He grinned. "So we take the scenic route, so what?"

They started up again, although they had to veer to the west because of the lake. The rain started to slow, but the sky was still an ominous gray, blending into the lavender hills. For a brief time, Dusque and Finn did not come across any other living thing, and the only sound that disturbed the silence was the soggy squish their boots made in the soft ground. Soon enough, though, several forms started to separate themselves from the misty hillside.

Dusque recognized the grazers immediately. Thune, they were called. There were five of them. Each was the size of a small shuttle, with a massive head and legs and gray hide that appeared wrinkled and hard. One lifted its head and looked directly at the two humans, and Dusque could hear Finn's sharp intake of breath. From the center of the thune's face swung a huge, noselike appendage; thin, full ears circled its head like a halo or a collar.

Dusque touched Finn's arm. "It should be okay to move through them, provided we don't make any quick movements," she whispered.

Finn eyed the beasts warily, especially noting their very large feet. "You sure?"

"Yes," she replied. "We'll be fine so long as they don't stampede."

"Terrific," he muttered under his breath.

With caution, they started to walk slowly through the group of five individuals. Dusque couldn't keep from smiling. She had never had the opportunity to observe these magnificent creatures up close. The temptation to touch one of them was overwhelming. She reached out a hand and lightly trailed her fingers against the thune's tough hide. The creature didn't even seem to know that something had touched it.

Suddenly, one of the other thune began flapping the collar of its ears rapidly back and forth.

Finn moved up beside Dusque and gripped her arm. She could tell he was tensing to bolt.

"It's okay," she told him. "That's not a threatening gesture. She's just trying to cool herself down."

"She's fanning herself?" he asked in disbelief.

"Sort of," Dusque replied. "Her ears are filled with thousands of blood vessels, and as you can see, the skin is fairly thin there. By flapping her ears, she cools the blood in that area and then that blood courses through the rest of her body, lowering her overall temperature."

"Oh." Finn sounded only marginally convinced.

Dusque laughed gently. "Come on, it's safe. See?"

She pointed to the largest thune. "The matriarch is moving them away from us."

Together they walked through the herd's territory and kept going, trying to regain the ground they had lost. Suddenly, Finn grabbed Dusque's arm.

"Down!" he whispered urgently, and yanked her into some bushes.

She looked at him in surprise, and he raised his finger to his lip, signaling for quiet. She watched as he drew his blaster and started to crawl along, low to the ground. When he waved at her to follow, she pulled out the heavy blaster she had brought with her and crept after him. She was rewarded by a look of surprise.

"Where'd that come from?" he asked. "What happened to the small one?"

Dusque shook her head. "A woman's got to have some secrets."

Finn's mouth turned up in a smirk, despite the situation. But his good humor faded as soon as he turned his attention to what was just below the hill. He motioned for Dusque to take a look. Down in the small valley below, there were humanoids moving about.

There were about seven that she could see, and all but one were male. Larger and more brutish looking than the average humanoid, they were covered in thick, dark hair and wore simple animal hides and furs. They carried about only the most rudimentary tools—clubs and stone-head axes—and they were hunting.

"It might get a little rough here," Finn warned.

"Why?" she asked.

"We've lost some time because of our detour; we can't afford to lose any more, with what's in the balance." He started to take aim.

Dusque pushed his barrel aside. "We can't. Those are Dantari. From the few accounts that exist, they are peaceful, simple people."

Finn regarded her for a moment. "Are those few worth all the many lives that are at stake?" he asked with deadly seriousness.

After brief deliberation, she said carefully, "I think that if we were to hurt these people, we would be no better than those who serve the Empire. The people on that list want to help the Rebel Alliance, and that means that they are willing to risk their lives for complete strangers, no matter what the species. These are exactly the lives that they are willing to sacrifice themselves for."

Finn slowly lowered his gun. "I guess you're right." He sounded sheepish. "I just want to get that device and blast out of here."

"I know," she answered. "So do I. But I don't want it this badly."

Finn nodded, but he looked frustrated. Turning away from her, he began crawling back the way they had come, and Dusque followed in silence. Neither spoke until both were certain they were downwind of the Dantari.

"We're going to have to go farther north than we

planned and then cut eastward," Finn whispered at last.

"We'll need to keep our eyes out for any more of those people. Normally, they just range along the ocean," Dusque told him, trying to recall what she had learned of the Dantari in her studies. "If they've come this far in to hunt, they may be part of a larger group."

He nodded but did not reply. Dusque wondered if he was angry with her for telling him what to do, or angry at himself for not thinking things through more on his own. He remained silent as they rushed to detour around the Dantari and start regaining the ground they had lost. The rain tapered off, but the skies stayed overcast. Dusque, uncertain how to mend what felt like a breach between them, left him to his silence. But when she saw something decidedly unnatural in the distance, she spoke without thinking.

"What's that?" It looked like a flat object on a hill. As they crept closer they saw, rising out of the mist like some mythical creature rising from its own ashes, a modular structure.

"Well, I'll be . . ." Finn exhaled.

"What is it?" Dusque asked again, more nervous now that she could see several other, similar structures beyond the first one.

"It's the old Rebel base," he told her. When he saw her unease, he added, "It's been abandoned for almost two years. Come on."

"I thought we needed to make up for lost time," she reminded him.

"I just want to make a quick check that nothing was left behind," he explained, starting to run up the hill toward the base.

"But Leia said that the Imperials were already here. Don't you think they would've found anything if it had been left behind?" Dusque asked, jogging along beside him.

"They don't always know where to look," he told her.

"What happened here?" she asked as they arrived at the outer walls of what she was beginning to realize was quite a substantial base.

"I only heard the story secondhand, but I'll tell you what I know." He seemed about to go on when he stopped and turned to the right. Dusque looked past him to see a long canine-type creature pacing back and forth. Either it hadn't smelled them yet, or it didn't care.

"What is it?" Finn asked.

Dusque squinted to try to make out the creature. "I think it's a huurton. Probably a huntress, if she's on her own. Umm, maybe we should put a little distance between us," she suggested. "She could be very deadly."

"Right," he replied, and he led the way to an opening in the wall.

Once inside the old base, Dusque saw that it was a huge facility. In the structures closest to them, some of the windows were smashed and doors were ajar. Plants had started to grow over the buildings, and the whole area was desolate and somber. She wondered what it must have been like when it was alive with people.

"What happened?" she asked Finn again.

"As I understand it, this base was quite successful for many years," he began as they walked slowly through the facility, "most likely because of its remote location. I don't know how it happened or even how the Rebel soldier found it, but about a year and a half ago, someone slipped an Imperial tracking device into a cargo shipment.

"By some good fortune, it was discovered and the word went out to evacuate. These structures—" He stopped to tap on the wall of the one that they were passing on their left. "—are put together out of temporary, self-constructing modules. They were crafted to be movable at a moment's notice."

"Then if they left them behind, the Rebels must have had to flee really quickly," Dusque mused.

"As I understand it," Finn replied, "they all got out within a day."

Dusque inhaled deeply, trying to picture the hundreds, if not thousands, of troops who must have streamed out of the buildings. "I guess they made it just in time," she said.

"Supposedly, the Imperials didn't find them until Leia told them about the base," he added.

Dusque stared at him in shock. "*What?* Leia would never betray anyone!" She told herself she couldn't be that certain about someone she barely knew, but somehow she had absolutely no doubts about Princess Leia's personal strength and commitment to the cause.

"She was a prisoner on the Emperor's Death Star," he told her gravely. "From what she told me, they tortured her and used mind probes, but she didn't give them the location of the Rebel base. Then they tried a different ploy: they threatened to destroy her home planet. So she gave up the location here"—he waved an arm to indicate the ruined base around them—"on Dantooine."

"I guess I can understand . . . ," Dusque said. "But the fact that she betrayed the others still seems . . . inhuman."

"No, no, you've got it wrong! She already knew that the base had been evacuated. It was only a matter of time before the Imperials would have raided it."

Now the story was beginning to make some sense. "She thought it would buy her more time."

"Yes, but they destroyed Alderaan anyway."

Dusque nodded in understanding. When she thought back on it, she remembered hearing that scientists from a different department had been working on a project of some magnitude a year or so before the destruction of Alderaan. Some of those same scientists had disappeared from their regular labs, and rumor had said that they'd been sequestered for some special project. She wondered . . .

"Would it have been so bad," Finn asked her quietly, interrupting her musings, "if she had betrayed the Alliance for those she loved?"

"I don't know," Dusque answered honestly. "I can't say with any certainty what I would do, in a similar situation. But I think we follow this cause because it's the right thing to do. And I think that has to come before any of our personal loves. While dreamers may die, the dream lives on."

Finn fell silent. She wondered if he had been asking more about her than about Leia's choices. Perhaps, she thought, he wondered if she would betray the Rebel Alliance for him. Once more, she felt as if she were being tested, and was afraid she had failed.

"Let's take a quick pass through the command center," Finn suggested, "and then keep going."

"All right," Dusque agreed, "but we should be really careful. If there was one huurton here, there are probably others."

"Right," he agreed. Then he looked at her. "I see that you were an even better choice to work with than I originally thought," he said. "It never even occurred to me to consider your expertise with animals."

"That's why they call me a bioengineer," she said lightly, trying not to smile too widely at his compliment. But she had a feeling he could tell she was pleased, because he flashed her a grin before turning to move on.

They passed a series of smaller structures all in a row before climbing a set of stairs that led them to the command center. A glance inside each open door showed that the smaller buildings were barracks—and that they had been pretty well ransacked by the Imperial soldiers who had searched the place. The state of the barracks did not bode well for what they might find in the command center, but it was still worth a look, Finn explained.

At the next level, they encountered a huurton mother and her pups. Seeing her, Finn paused and looked at Dusque.

"As long as we steer clear of her," she assured him, "we should be fine. She'll probably herd her brood away from us."

"Got it," Finn acknowledged.

Carefully sketching a large circle around the huurtons, they entered what had been the heart of the former base. Dusque was overwhelmed by the damage that had been done to it. Curious, she approached a series of control panels that seemed to have been looted, but not destroyed.

"Finn," she called, "take a look at this."

He trotted over to her and studied what was left of the equipment.

"Would the Imperials have done this?" she asked.

"No," Finn answered slowly. "They wouldn't have had any interest in looting. Not to this degree, at any rate."

"Then who?"

Finn thought for a moment and then said, "Remember, that officer said they had been having problems with smugglers."

"You're right," she said then. "I think he called them the Gray Talon. You think it was them?"

"Either them or someone else in the same profession. I saw more evidence of that over here." He indicated a smaller chamber. Dusque poked her head in and saw that it was a room that had probably been occupied by a higher-ranking officer. There was a long table that had been knocked over and shattered, the pieces scattered across the remains of a woven floor covering. The walls were bare, with the exception of one picture that was hanging askew. Dusque shivered, although the air in the base was not cold.

"What's the matter?" Finn asked as he stood next to her. "Cold?"

"No, I just want to get out of here," she told him. She felt as though a grave site had been desecrated, although as far as she knew, no one had died.

Finn nodded in silent understanding. "Just let me make one quick pass and then we'll leave, okay?"

"All right," she agreed, "but I'm going to wait outside. Call me on the comlink if you need me." As she left, she made sure to turn on the small, handheld communication device attached to her belt.

Outside, she made her way onto the observation platform. From there, she could see that several groups of huurtons had made their homes in and around the abandoned base. In a way, she found the sight oddly comforting. It was almost as though the fearsome predators were guarding the remains of the place so that no one else would defile it.

The rain had stopped completely, but darkness was growing as night approached. She worried that Finn had been right, that taking the longer route had been a mistake. Now they would reach the Jedi ruins in the dead of night, at the earliest. Not only would that make their search that much more challenging, but it would mean the night predators would be awake and on the prowl.

Finn came out of the command center and walked over to her. "Nothing," he said, in response to her quizzical look. "We might as well keep moving."

"Mm-hmm," she agreed. "But take a look: there's a good view from up here." She pointed to the lower levels. "See? There are huurtons over in the eastern and northern quadrants of the base. We'll need to avoid those areas when we leave. It's getting dark, too," she added, voicing the obvious.

"Yes, it is." He glanced up. "At least the rain's stopped."

She smiled. "What I meant was, I'm sorry my delay cost us the daylight hours."

Finn was silent for a moment. "Don't be," he finally told her. "Besides, it was my choice to take the time to explore this base," he added. "So we share the responsibility for the delay, and cancel each other out, right?" His grin made her feel a lot better.

Feeling lighter, she followed Finn through the deserted complex to another gap in the surrounding wall. As they trotted down the hillside, avoiding the various pockets of huurtons, Dusque paused to take a last look at the Rebel base. Shrouded in the mists, it seemed like a lonely guard, waiting for a time when such places would no longer be needed.

They headed off in an easterly direction, following the coordinates that Leia had given them before they had departed Corellia. The terrain became more hilly, bordering on mountainous, and the number of biba trees started to diminish, replaced by more conifers and evergreens. Small ferns dotted the hillsides, and the lavender grass started to thin out.

They stopped only once, to drink from a small stream that they passed. While they rested, Dusque foraged around a bit, using her halo lamp. She found some berries and even a melon. She shared them with Finn and ate quietly, wondering what would happen when they reached their destination. She was still musing while they got ready to move on, so she wasn't prepared when a large voritor lizard broke through from the underbrush and charged her.

Before she had a chance to draw her weapon, Finn's blaster shots lit the area like lightning. The lizard growled in anger but was delayed only long enough for Dusque to draw her own blaster and start firing. Even though it was attacked on two fronts, the two-meter-long lizard was not deterred. It used its clawed feet to dig into the soil and pull itself inexorably toward Dusque. She dropped to one knee to get a better angle. With its two prominent dorsal fins, she found it difficult to get a good aim on a vulnerable region.

Dusque felt her hand tremble, and for a moment she thought that she was holding on to the grip so tightly that her hand was cramping. But then she realized that what she was feeling was the vibration of the weapon, alerting her to the fact that its power supply was nearly depleted. Grateful for Finn's lessons, she gave the creature one last blast and followed that by tumbling to her right. Swiftly, she popped out the used pack and replaced it with a new one.

The creature spun around, trying to keep Dusque in sight. Lashing out with its impressive tail, it caught Finn unaware, knocking his feet out from under him. He fell backward. The lizard started to turn on him, and Dusque realized that their blasters alone weren't going to stop it. While firing with one hand, she fished around in her pack with the other. When her hand closed around the object she was searching for, she shouted to Finn.

"Move!"

Without any hesitation, he scrambled to his feet and started to run. As she had expected, bolting immediately made him the primary prey in the eyes of the lizard. Dusque used that opportunity to activate the device in her hand and run after them both.

"Keep running," she yelled. "Don't stop for anything."

She took careful aim and fired at the voritor. Angry, it swung its head toward her threateningly, snapping its vicious jaws. Dusque knew she had one shot. When the lizard lunged at her, she threw the thermal detonator into its mouth and dived away from the creature, covering her head with her arm. If she had missed, she knew the next thing she would feel would be the reptile's teeth tearing into her. What she felt instead was the sudden heat from the explosion of the tiny bomb.

She felt bits of the voritor's body rain down on her. And behind the incessant ringing in her ears, she could hear Finn calling her name. As she rolled around and brushed bits of the very deceased reptile off, she saw Finn limping toward her. She rose to her feet and shook her head, trying to clear the ringing from her ears. Finn appeared eager to aid her, because he grabbed her by the shoulders and started shaking her, too.

"You idiot," she barely heard him say. "You could have gotten us killed."

"What?" she asked. "I thought the lizard was about to do that for sure."

"That was a class-A thermal detonator. They're supposed to have a blast radius of twenty meters. The baradium core must have been compromised somehow."

"What?" she asked again, partially because she could still only hear about half of what he was saying, and partially because she couldn't believe he was angry that they were alive.

Finn relented a bit as he calmed down. "That was quite a chance you took," he said more loudly.

"Only option I saw left. Our blasters just weren't bringing the voritor down. They're notorious for incredibly tough hides. In fact, no one is even sure how long these creatures live. It could be hundreds, maybe even thousands of years," she explained.

Finn's stern face lost some of its resolve. He gradually smiled at Dusque, whose ears were no longer ringing as badly as they had been. Shaking his head, he said, "Leave it to you to give me a dissertation on the life span of a killer lizard right after you nearly blew us to bits along with it." And then he laughed.

"Well," she replied somewhat sheepishly, "I couldn't think of any other way to stop it."

He limped closer to her and gave her a brief hug. "Hey, we're alive, so who am I to complain?"

"You're hurt," she commented.

"Not bad . . . probably just a bruise from that thing's tail. I'll be fine."

She was unconvinced. "I've got a small medkit with me."

"Don't worry. I just need to keep moving, so it doesn't stiffen up," he told her. "I'll be fine."

"All right," she replied. "Are we close?"

"Just over the next ridge, if these coordinates are accurate."

Even as they started to climb the hill, Dusque saw smaller scavengers move in to finish up what remained of the dead lizard. Nothing went to waste on the harsh world; something was always waiting in the shadows to take advantage of the situation. That was life everywhere, she reflected. She was saddened by the thought that civilized beings seemed bound by the same laws of nature—Empire and Rebels alike, in a way. Except she was more convinced than ever that if hope lay anywhere, it lay with the Rebels.

There was a roaring in her ears. She shook her head slightly. She thought her hearing had cleared, but the roaring seemed to be growing in intensity rather than diminishing. When she reached the top of the hill, just behind Finn, she realized that the roaring had been not residual damage to her ears, but a massive waterfall some sixty meters away. It spilled out from a steep, treeless ridge. Still, it was what was in front of the waterfall that caused Dusque to catch her breath. As a moon struggled to peek out from behind some clouds, she could see from that weak light that there was a huge arch not too far away, as well as other crumbled relics of structures: the Jedi ruins.

TWELVE

"We're here," Finn whispered.

Dusque followed as he walked carefully down from their vantage point into the ruins themselves. She felt awed, though she wasn't sure why. Not much remained—just a huge foundation of what must have been a large building back in some distant time.

"What used to be here?" she asked Finn.

"I don't know. Supposedly a Jedi Master established a training center here some four millennia ago, but I think these were ruins even then," he told her uncertainly.

Dusque found herself drawn to a grand staircase that led up to the remains of a tower. She marched upward and almost didn't see that there was a break in the stone stairs. She caught herself at the last moment, arms pinwheeling madly as she regained her balance. She stood looking at the gap in the staircase and contemplated trying to make the jump, curiously attracted to the yawning darkness above. All that remained of the tower seemed to be its foundation, but she wanted to see it.

"Dusque," she heard Finn call.

She debated for a moment, but then turned and cautiously descended the ancient stone steps. Below, she saw Finn standing closer to another foundation, this one perhaps a quarter of the size of the one Dusque had been investigating. He had pulled out his portable scanner and was turning slowly in a circle.

"What are you doing?" she asked curiously.

"The holocron would have been tagged; I'm hoping to pick up a signal from the sensor," he told her. He continued to turn, and then stopped. "I think I've found it," he whispered. She could sense the suppressed excitement in his tone and stance.

"Where?"

He put down the instrument and faced the powerful waterfall. Dusque knew what he was going to say before he opened his mouth.

"Behind that waterfall," he told her.

"More water," she said.

"The last time," he promised her.

As they marched across the ruined courtyard in front of the tower, Dusque glanced at the large archway forty meters or so away. She thought she saw a strange, greenish blue flicker in the night.

"Did you see that?" she asked Finn, pointing. "It almost looked like a fire. But a strange one."

He looked over, then shrugged. "I don't see it,"

he said, and she was reminded of his similar comments on the shuttle.

As though reading her mind again, Finn added, "That doesn't mean there's nothing there. We'll look into it after we retrieve our prize, okay?"

"All right," she agreed, somewhat mollified that he was at least considering it.

Their footsteps echoed strangely on the deserted courtyard, and Dusque wondered how many feet had tread on the same stones over the generations. She found herself looking over her shoulder more than once. The place, though obviously deserted, seemed to possess some kind of spirit.

As they moved onto the ground behind the large foundation, Finn turned and looked at her. "Do you feel something?" he asked.

She nodded. "Since we entered those ruins. It was like someone was watching us. And something else . . . like something I felt once in a dream." She felt chills race up and down her spine.

"I just felt uneasy," Finn said. He didn't add anything more, but looked at her strangely. Then he turned without another word and waded into the water. Dusque steeled herself and followed after him.

The icy cold of the water had a sobering effect on Dusque. She no longer felt as though eyes were on her, and she was grateful that she could focus on the task at hand. Swimming close behind Finn, she swallowed hard when she saw that she was going to have to go right through the pounding water. She started to call out to him to wait, but his dark form disappeared under the rush of the waterfall. She realized she was going to have to force herself through.

She squeezed her eyes shut, took a deep breath, and plunged in. The sound was deafening, and she felt herself batted down by the sheer force. She pushed herself up and opened her eyes when she felt her head was out of the water. Then she saw that they had reached a ledge—part of an intricate cave system. Finn was standing only a few meters away, watching her. Uncertain whether to be proud that he wasn't helping her, or annoyed, she slung her leg onto the ledge and pulled herself up. She checked to make sure her pack was intact and then wrung out her wet hair. Flinging the tangled mane behind her, she caught up to Finn.

"How far down is it?" she asked.

"I'm not sure," he admitted. "The portable scanner seems to have shorted out."

Dusque saw that the small device did seem to have stopped functioning. She thought that the water might have caused it, although this type of scanner was designed to last a long time and withstand extremely harsh environments.

"May I take a look?" she asked, having used similar devices over the years.

Finn handed it over easily. Dusque popped open the back panel and studied the circuitry by the light of her halo lamp. It appeared as though a connection had come loose. She attempted to reconnect it, then flipped the device around and tried to recheck the coordinates. But the device only sputtered and flashed.

"You're right," she told Finn. "Looks like the connectors are fried." She laid the device down on the ground. "No use carrying the excess baggage."

"Because of the short, I'm not sure when I was able to last take a reliable reading, but it seemed that the holocron was probably no more than a couple of hundred meters down," he told her.

Dusque walked past him to look at the tunnels that lay before them. "Doesn't look like they descend very steeply, does it? What may only be a short distance down may take a little while longer to get to, if the slope stays gentle."

"We'd better get started," he told her.

"Hold on," she said. "Let me check one thing."

Finn waited patiently while Dusque rummaged through her pack. Buried under power packs and stimpaks, there was something she hoped she had brought. She smiled triumphantly when her fingers brushed against two small aerosol canisters. She pulled them out and handed one to Finn.

"What is this?" he asked, examining the container.

"I noticed there were a few on the shuttle. I just couldn't remember if I had taken them or not. I got a little turned around after the stormtroopers boarded the ship," she said. "Spray the entire contents all over yourself. It'll help mask your scent."

She started spraying herself, and after watching her dubiously for a moment, Finn did likewise. When he was through, he raised his arm up close to his nose and sniffed at himself. "I don't smell any-thing," he said, baffled.

"That's the idea. Hopefully, nothing else will either."

Dusque dropped her travel cloak in a heap by the malfunctioning scanner, afraid that its flowing material might catch on the rough tunnel walls. She turned to Finn and signaled that she was ready. Following her example, he had shed his outer garments and readjusted his weapons so that they were all accessible. He motioned for her to go, and she started down the tunnel, surprised that he had her take the lead.

As they suspected, the path descended very gradually. They both scanned the walls and recesses of the tunnel, not certain where the holocron might have been secreted or even how it might have been hidden. They walked slowly, trying to minimize the echoes of their footfalls. As the roar of the waterfall grew more distant, Dusque realized that there was moisture farther down as she heard the telltale patter of drips hitting the rock floor.

Of course there would be water, she told herself. How else could the tunnels have been formed? But the rock looked rough, as though it had been hewn by something, not smooth, as it would have been if water had worn it away.

She had just adjusted her halo lamp to give her as wide a view as possible when she heard the drips come from a surprising location. She and Finn were on a narrow bridge of sorts, something having eroded sections of the cave away. The view from either edge was dizzying, and she felt a moment of vertigo. Since the rock walls all looked identical, she momentarily couldn't tell which way was up or down, and she lost her center of balance.

Closing her eyes, she took several, long deep breaths and wrapped her arms tightly about herself. That helped ground her so that when she reopened her eyes, she no longer felt disoriented.

"Dizzying, isn't it?" Finn whispered.

"Yes," Dusque admitted, glad she wasn't the only one who had felt it. She moved to the edge of the natural bridge and peered over the side. The cave was honeycombed with tunnels, and she thought she caught sight of something skittering off deeper down. They continued on until the tunnel split into two divergent paths.

"What do you think?" Finn asked her quietly.

Dusque chewed her lip thoughtfully and glanced in both directions. "I think we should split up," she finally announced.

"*What?*" He sounded shocked.

"You were right earlier about time running out. We need to make up for lost time now," she declared. "This is our last chance to do that."

"Are you sure?" He certainly didn't sound convinced.

"Yes, I am. We've got the comlinks if we get into trouble, or if we find the holocron."

"Let's check and make sure the comlinks still

work," Finn suggested. "After all, if the scanner could short out . . ."

"Good idea," Dusque agreed and they checked their communicators. Both were still in working order.

"I'll go left," she told him. "And be careful, I think there's something down here."

"You be careful, too. Don't take any unnecessary chances," he warned. "I mean it."

"You should have told me that back on Corellia," she retorted, then winked at him. He flashed her a smile in return, and Dusque was startled by how his teeth gleamed back at her in the gloom, like those of some predator.

She moved slowly down the dark tunnel and felt a shiver. It had been easy enough while Finn stood next to her to tell him that they needed to split up, but now that she was engulfed in the darkness of the cave, she felt very alone and vulnerable. She had a moment of regret at her decision but still knew in her heart it had been the right one to make. And then she realized something: Finn had let her make the call. In fact, pretty much since they had left the abandoned Rebel base, he'd turned over the leadership reins to her. She didn't know what surprised her more: that he had done it, or that she had accepted it so naturally.

So much had changed, she mused. And although it felt like a lifetime, it had really only been a few days.

She shook her head in wonder and then froze as she heard something. At first, she tried to tell herself that it was just the water, but the sound was not rhythmic or predictable like the drips that echoed softly through the tunnel system. Swallowing hard, she slipped her hand down to draw her blaster. She felt only marginally better with the cold metal in her hand. But she still saw nothing.

As she walked deeper into the tunnels, she thought the path she had chosen was splitting again, but it turned out that it had simply widened, forming a natural pocket in the tunnel. When she directed her light into it, something glinted back at her. She felt a rush of excitement, thinking that she had discovered the holocron. It was a perfect place to hide it, she thought, off the main track as it was. She moved closer to investigate.

Her elation changed to disappointment and concern when the shining object turned out to be a humanoid skull. As she scanned the area, she saw a mostly intact skeleton stretched out and picked clean. Although not what she had hoped to find, it did confirm that there might be something else in the caves with them. She grabbed her comlink and signaled Finn.

"Did you find it?" Coming from the small speaker, his voice sounded tinny.

"No," she replied, "but I did find some humanoid remains. Keep your guard up."

"Copy that," he replied.

Dusque replaced her comlink on her belt and continued down the tunnel. She found that since she had verified the presence of predators, she was straining to hear every last sound. Without warning, she heard the scurrying again, and this time it was on top of her. From around a bend she hadn't detected, a large rodent came hopping straight toward her. She didn't even have time to draw her weapon before the monstrosity was less than a meter away. She held her breath and froze to the spot.

Larger than most canids, the creature appeared to be covered in armored plates. It had an elongated nose, which suggested that it relied predominately on its sense of smell. As it hopped on its larger rear legs, it paused almost on top of Dusque's boots. It stood on its back legs and sniffed the air curiously. Dusque didn't move a muscle and prayed the comlink wouldn't suddenly go off.

While the creature stood on her, Dusque saw something start to ooze from its clicking jaws. As the liquid hit the tunnel floor with a spatter, there was a slight sizzle. She realized that it was bile, a powerful alkaloid that helped the creature break down and absorb fats. Now she knew why the skeletal remains were so smooth. The corpse had been simply digested away. She realized that it was a bile-drenched quenker that stood on her feet, something not many saw and lived to tell about. While she sincerely wished that she would not be its next victim, the scientist in her hoped that she might be able to salvage a sample of the animal's genetic material off her boot when she got out of there.

After what seemed like an eternity, the quenker

lowered itself and hopped up the tunnel. Dusque let out a shaky breath, but her elation was short lived. She realized that she would probably have to pass it at least one more time before she got out of the cave. She wasn't sure how long the masking aerosol would last, and she was torn. She wanted to warn Finn, but she feared that if he had found himself in a similar situation, the sound of the comlink would undoubtedly startle the creature and alert it to his presence. She accepted that fact that he was on his own, and that it had been her decision, her choice to live with. She began to grasp the enormity of what Princess Leia must live with every day, and she wondered again how the woman found the strength to do it.

Taking a deep breath, she continued down the tunnel. She had to admit, it was an ideal spot to hide something precious. She couldn't think of a reason anyone would come down here, and the quenkers—she was certain there were more than just the one—would make excellent natural guards. She wondered if any Rebels had died secreting the holocron. And she wondered if she and Finn would share their fate.

If I die here, at least I will have done something with my life, she thought. *I'll be remembered, even if it's only for a short time.* The thought warmed her and gave her the courage to go on.

The tunnel wound sharply to the left and then opened into a large chamber. Once again, there were two paths to choose from and a healthy sprinkling of humanoid remains in both directions. Not too far ahead, Dusque heard more skittering and another, unidentifiable sound. She decided she didn't need to see what had made that particular noise, so she chose the tunnel that veered away from it.

As she moved to the right, she realized that she was no longer hearing water echoing in the distance. She suspected that the tunnel she had picked was going to come to an end soon, simply another offshoot that led to nowhere. Shortly she discovered that she was both right and wrong: The tunnel did end in another cul-de-sac, but it was not empty.

She was startled to see an arch made from three slabs of stone freestanding in the center of the recess, only slightly taller than an average human. There was no chance that it was a natural occurrence— the stones didn't look as if they'd been cut from any of the nearby rock walls. She was sure they had been very deliberately placed. After checking around and behind the arch, she holstered her gun and walked through.

On the other side of the arch was a circle of smaller stones, each one small enough that even Dusque could have placed them there herself. In the center was a small fire pit, and above it was a rudimentary spit. As Dusque examined it, she wondered briefly if one of the Dantari had somehow set up a small encampment there, but she dismissed the idea as illogical. While the Dantari were simple people, they were practical. Quenkers would not be worth hunting: the risk–reward factor was disproportionate. Someone else had been here, but because the pit was cold—which she verified by holding her hand over the ashes in the center—there was no way of knowing if whoever it was might still be in the area.

As she crouched near the fire pit, she had an odd thought. She thrust both of her hands into the ashes and started to root around. Stirring up a small cloud of ash, she tried not to cough aloud. She was about to give up, feeling foolish, when she felt something unusual in the ashes. She got her hand around it and pulled it from the fire pit.

Dusque stretched out her palm flat and held the soot-encrusted object at eye level. She gently blew the ashes from it and then caught her breath in amazement. A perfect cube, no bigger than her hand, twinkled in the glow of her halo lamp. Her mouth opened in awe as she turned the object first to the left and then to the right, studying it.

The outer edges of the object were etched metal, while a crystal matrix gleamed and pulsed in the center. She fell back on her rump, as though someone had punched her in the stomach. She knew how important the device was, but she hadn't expected it to be so beautiful. For several long moments, Dusque forgot everything else around her and stared at the delicate-looking construct. She had no idea how long she stared at it or how long she might have been mesmerized by it if her comlink hadn't suddenly chirped at her. Shocked back into reality, she scrambled to grab the communicator.

Before Finn was able to transmit anything, she whispered, "I've got it."

"What?" Finn asked.

"I found it," she repeated, still staring at the holocron.

"You are amazing," he replied, clearly elated. "Let's start back up. I was just checking in with you because I haven't seen anything down here."

Dusque was about to end the communication when she remembered the rats. "Finn," she added, serious once more, "be careful. The tunnels are full of quenkers."

"I don't like the sound of that," he replied.

"The aerosol seems to work, but I don't know for how long."

"Okay," he answered. "Meet you back up at the divide. You watch yourself," he added.

"Copy that. Dusque out."

She marveled at the holocron once more before tearing her eyes from it and placing it carefully in her sack. She took once last look around at the stone campsite and wondered who might have used it and what they might have known about the holocron. She couldn't believe that it had come to rest in the center of the pit accidentally. She was momentarily frustrated that she had a puzzle before her that she might never know the answer to. With a sigh, she resolved to let it go. She quietly left the strange chamber.

As she started up the tunnel, Dusque kept a watch for quenkers, but she didn't see any. Rather than be pleased, she found their absence disturbing. If they weren't near her, they were probably hunting something. She hoped it was the creature that had made the strange sound deeper in the cave. Then she heard several short bursts of blasterfire.

"Finn," she whispered passionately, and started to run.

As she rounded a bend in the tunnel, the sound of blasterfire was almost deafening. The echoes from the blasts sounded on and on. About twenty meters ahead of her, she saw Finn, blasters drawn. He was surrounded by three quenkers, each one dripping acidic bile. Although he was holding them back, she could see that they were starting to close in on him. She dropped down on one knee and, taking careful aim, started to blast away at the quenker closest to her.

"Dusque!" he yelled.

She continued to fire away at the creature, and a part of her rational mind was amazed at their resilience and wondered what in the chemical makeup of their bony hides made them so impervious to blasterfire. The rest of her wanted nothing more than to blast the creature into oblivion.

She could see that she had caught the attention of not only the quenker she was attacking, but also the one that was closest to Finn. Her distraction bought him a little breathing room, and he was able to reload his nearly empty blaster.

After what seemed an eternity, the first quenker showed signs of faltering. Unsteady on its back legs, it began to tremble. Redoubling her fire on it, Dusque edged closer, trying to stay in the optimal range for her weapon. She kept her arms outstretched, firing until her blaster was mostly drained. Fortunately, the quenker expired before her power pack did. The rodent tumbled to its side in a great heap and twitched once before lying still.

Dusque refreshed her blaster and started firing on the one Finn wasn't attacking. It had already suffered severe damage from both their weapons, and at her renewed fire it broke off its attack and hopped weakly down the tunnel. From the corner of her eye, Dusque saw that the quenker didn't get very far before expiring like its littermate. There was only the one left. But Dusque found she didn't need to assist much; Finn had basically already killed it. The animal was just too stubborn to know it was dead already.

"C'mon and die," she heard Finn say through gritted teeth. As though the quenker heard him, it promptly fell over, finally aware that it had, indeed, died.

Both Finn and Dusque were breathing hard. Dusque found that she was trembling from the exertion, but was elated with their temporary success. She smiled at Finn and leaned against the tunnel wall to catch her breath. She saw that Finn's chest was heaving, as well. Ignoring his exhaustion, he crouched down to poke at the dead rodent.

"Careful," Dusque warned. "The saliva coming out of its mouth has acid in it." But unable to resist, she knelt down and collected a sample of the bile in a specially sealed container.

"Is there anything on this planet that's not out to kill us?" he quipped when she was done.

Dusque, however, answered him seriously. "Well, there is the little fabool. It's a creature that just sort of bobs around like a balloon. It's pretty harmless."

Finn laughed. "I was joking!"

"Oh," Dusque replied. "I guess I can't stop being a scientist. We are what we are."

Finn grew silent and lost his smile. "You're probably right," he replied.

"We should get out of here before the smell of blood draws out more of these things," she told him.

"Before we go," Finn asked quietly, "can I see it?"

"Of course." Dusque realized that she wanted to see the holocron again, as well, part of her still not believing that she had found it.

She pulled it out of her pack and held it out on her flat palm. It twinkled in the low light of their halo lamps, and Dusque saw that Finn was as mesmerized as she was.

"Where was it?" he asked.

"There was an offshoot of the tunnel and what looked like a primitive campsite," she explained. "I found it there, but I have no idea whose site it was."

"And it was just lying there?" he asked.

"No, it was in the fire pit under some ashes," she answered slowly, thinking how foolish it sounded in retrospect.

Finn looked up with some amazement. "What made you look in there?"

"I don't know," she replied, shrugging her shoulders in bewilderment. "It wasn't logical, but I don't think logic has anything to do with this."

"No, I think you're right," he agreed. "And I think we should start to make tracks out of here."

Dusque started to hand it to Finn, but he refused. "You hang on to it."

She put it away, and together they started the long climb out of the cave. Somehow, perhaps because they were flush with success, climbing out didn't seem to take as long to Dusque as descending had. *Or it's because I'm not alone,* she thought, looking at Finn. He, however, was grim faced once more. Dusque knew that he must have been thinking that they weren't in the clear yet. She admitted to herself that she had forgotten that simply because she and Finn had the device didn't mean the Rebel Alliance did. There was still a long way to go.

Eventually, the roar of the waterfall grew louder and Dusque knew they were nearly there. She breathed a sigh of relief that they had managed to avoid any more quenkers. She honestly didn't know how much more their weapons could have handled.

Soon enough, the back side of the waterfall was visible to Dusque. She moved to stand near the water's edge, feeling the mist on her cheeks. Whether it was because they had been successful or just because she was alive, she reveled in the feel of the cool water on her skin. They had succeeded and they had done it together. With a gentle smile, she turned around to share the thought with Finn.

He was standing a few meters behind her, an unreadable expression on his face.

Concerned, she took a step toward him. "What's wrong?" she asked, puzzled.

"I'm sorry," he told her eventually, fidgeting with his hands. "I'm so sorry."

Something in his tone scared her. What could he possibly be sorry about? The only thing she could think of was the nearby water, but he hadn't seemed so anxious previously. And then she heard the sound of a power pack slamming into place.

"If you don't hand over that pack, you're going to be a whole lot sorrier," a voice from behind Dusque called out. She and Finn whirled around to see several humanoids step through the waterfall. Every one of them was armed, and every one of the weapons was pointed right at them.

THIRTEEN

The man who had threatened them stood in front of three others. He was as tall as she was, dressed in a mangy vest and pants. He wore two low-slung holsters, one on each hip. A few tufts of wispy blond hair poked through the torn hat on his head. His shirt was partially open, revealing a silver chain from which hung a pendant with a sigil that looked like a bird's foot. He had both his blasters leveled at Dusque.

"Are ya deaf?" he demanded. "Whatever you two got while you were in there is the property of the Gray Talon. Now hand it over."

One of the others moved up to cover Finn, who gave Dusque a helpless look.

"You heard him," the one beside Finn shouted. "This is our planet and what's here is ours."

"I'll one ask you one more time," the leader said, "before I go ahead and take what I want. Hand over your treasure. I don't take kindly to the idea that someone would want to rob me."

"Okay," Dusque replied, not trying to hide the

quiver in her voice. "Just don't shoot." She proceeded to root around in her bag.

"Hurry," the leader ordered her. He seemed to be enjoying her fright. "If you do, I promise I'll kill you quickly. If not, I can make you suffer for days. I'd like that," he said softly, "but you wouldn't. Pretty thing like you shouldn't have to suffer."

Dusque poked around frantically in her pack and then her fingers closed around what she had been searching for. When she stopped moving, the Gray Talon member with the two blasters flicked one of his weapons in Finn's direction.

"If you don't give it to me, I'll have my partner kill him right in front of your lovely eyes."

As she pulled the container out of her bag, she popped the cap with her thumb.

"Here it is," she shouted, and tossed the vial of quenker bile directly into the pirate's face.

Screaming in rage and pain, he dropped his blasters and clawed at his eyes. Dusque, seeing him double over in agony, grabbed him by his vest and pulled him close. She reached down with one hand and pulled her sporting blaster free. Using the leader's body as a shield, she started shooting at the two men who were still closest to the waterfall. She managed to kill one of the two pirates with her first shot. She missed the second, and he charged at her, knocking her under the water.

Finn used Dusque's distraction to the fullest. Swinging his right arm up, he triggered the mechanism in his sleeve that released a deadly knife into his hand. In one motion, he brought that hand straight up and under the pirate's rib cage. The Gray Talon member was dead before Finn had resheathed the bloody weapon. Then he turned and saw that the last pirate was straddling Dusque's motionless form, and that her head was completely submerged in the cascade from the waterfall.

"Get away from her," he screamed, launching himself onto the pirate's back.

Locking an arm around the pirate's neck, he wrenched him off Dusque. They both tumbled into the water, and a weapon fired once before everything became silent.

Dusque realized vaguely that she could stand up. Somewhere in the distance, she heard the whine of a blaster, but it was hard to make out over the pounding in her own ears. She staggered to her feet, drenched and sputtering. Disoriented, she couldn't tell what was going on. As she slowly regained her senses, she saw that the cave entrance was littered with bodies. She seemed to be the only one left standing. But where was Finn?

Turning, she saw him lying partially in the water, facedown, along with one of the Gray Talon members. That sight snapped Dusque out of her stupor and galvanized her into action. She ran to Finn on wobbly legs and pulled him from the water. She could see that he had a severe burn on his left leg, but otherwise he appeared uninjured. Struggling with his inert weight, she dragged him up onto the rocky ledge of the cave entrance and dug the medkit out of her sack.

She examined his burned leg and was relieved to see that it didn't look that bad. She used a bulb of antiseptic wash to irrigate the wound, then applied a small bacta patch on the most severe section of injured tissue. She was almost done when he began to rouse.

"Wh-what?" he asked, sounding confused. When he struggled to rise, Dusque held him down.

"Hold still for a few more moments," she told him gently.

He winced as she pressed the bandage to his wound. "Have you still got the holocron?"

Dusque realized she hadn't even thought to check for the device. She placed her hand in her pack and felt its now familiar sharp edges. "Yes, it's fine," she soothed.

"Get out of here," he ordered her, pain evident in his voice.

"No." She grabbed a stimpak. "This will help you get moving in a minute or so," she explained, as she injected him in his upper arm with a stim-shot.

"We don't know how many more of these guys might be lurking around." His voice sounded stronger, the stimulant already starting to take effect. "You need to get out of here now. Take the holocron and get out."

"Not a chance," she said again. "Don't go and

turn into a martyr on me now," she joked, hoping to distract him from his pain.

He stared at her with clouded eyes. "No chance of that ever happening."

Dusque chuckled, but he remained silent.

"Better give me another shot," he finally told her, "if you're going to waste your time waiting for me."

She adjusted the stimpak and treated him again. "I don't want to give you too much more," she told him. "The more I give you now, the harder you're going to crash later."

"If you don't treat me now and get moving, we won't have to worry about later," he told her, struggling to his feet.

Dusque could tell by the set of his jaw it was useless to argue. She put her right arm around his waist to steady him. She knew he was still in pain when he didn't protest her assistance.

"Okay," she told him, "one step at a time."

They hobbled over to the water and waded in together, like two creatures clumsily joined at the waist. Finn hissed as the cold water made contact with his leg.

"Should we stop?" Dusque asked him.

"No," he said firmly. "Actually feels kind of good against the burn."

She thought he was probably lying to humor her. The least she could do, she thought, was not slow them down further by trying to stop him every few meters. She guided him through the water as carefully as she could, desperately afraid that she might slip and lose her footing.

"Don't forget your weapon," Finn reminded her before they ducked under the waterfall.

"Right," she said, mentally berating herself for focusing so hard on Finn that she had already forgotten about potential danger. She pulled out her heavy blaster with her left hand, and Finn did the same with his right. With every step, he grew stronger—thanks to the effects of the stimpak—so that when they came through the falls, he was able to hobble about unaided. Keeping their backs to each other, they turned about and scanned the area.

"Looks clear," Dusque said guardedly.

"For now," Finn agreed. They walked slowly across the ancient courtyard, their steps the only sound in the night. The clouds had completely cleared, and Dusque could see a moon over the horizon. She tried to remember how many moons Dantooine had, but couldn't. The stars were brilliant, as they always were without the lights of civilization to compete with. She allowed herself to look up for a moment and take it all in.

When she lowered her head, she saw that Finn was also regarding the stars, but his expression was intensely serious. He seemed to be concentrating hard. Finally he turned to her and said, "This way," cocking his head toward the left.

Dusque was a little embarrassed that she'd been wasting time stargazing while he, the wounded one, was working on figuring out their position. She wondered if she could ever hope to live up to Finn's—and Leia's—confidence in her.

They walked slowly at first, to accommodate Finn's injury. The longer they continued, however, the better he was able to pick up the pace and walk more sure-footedly. Dusque listened carefully for sounds of animals or other people. Hearing none, she took the chance of initiating a conversation.

"I'm sorry," she said.

"Sorry about what?" he asked, obviously surprised.

"For what happened before," she told him, not wanting to elaborate any more than necessary.

"I don't get it," he said. "Why would you be sorry?"

She sighed. "For what happened back at the waterfall. You tried to give me a signal and I missed it."

He continued to look at her blankly.

"When you said that you were sorry," she explained. "You know, when you tried to warn me about the Gray Talon and I didn't get it. I let you down. I'm sorry."

Finn didn't reply. Dusque wished she knew what he was thinking—if he was trying to think of a gentle way to reprimand her, or if he might tell her that it didn't matter. She was pretty sure he was disappointed, though. When he finally spoke, she wasn't reassured.

"Let's not talk about that," he said shortly. "We've

got a ways to go yet and I don't want to dwell on that. It's best forgotten."

Dusque would have liked him to explain her mistake in specific terms, so she could learn from it and not repeat it, but it seemed she had no choice but to let it go. *For now,* she amended silently. She would ask him about it later, when they had more time and were out of danger.

The weather continued to hold as they walked on. There were only a few purple-streaked clouds to compete with the brilliant stars, and neither Dusque nor Finn felt the need to illuminate their halo lamps. Gradually the steep hills gave way to gentler, rolling hills. The ferns and mountain flowers, conifers and evergreens melted into the large fields of lavender grass, and the spiky biba trees started to reappear. Dusque knew they were nearing the Imperial base.

A loud tearing sound startled them. Weary and ill equipped for another battle, Dusque and Finn looked around for a place to hide. A small rocky outcropping was all they could find. Dropping to the ground behind it, they drew their weapons and steeled themselves for whatever might be out there.

The roar grew louder, and a huge lizard, longer than several humans laid end to end, burst out of the brush. It snarled and shook its head violently from side to side, something clenched in its teeth. Dusque recognized the lizard as a bol pack runner. It looked malnourished and sickly, and at first she thought that they were safe, because it had obviously caught something . . . until she realized that what it had in its maw was a juvenile bol.

It thrashed the baby around a few more times and then threw it to the ground. The wounded juvenile emitted a weak call and tried to drag itself away. The adult charged at it, spearing it with one of its two curved horns. Raising the now dead juvenile in the air, the adult flicked its head to one side and tossed the carcass into a heap of plants.

"Are they cannibals?" Finn whispered to Dusque, as the adult bol stood there huffing.

"No, not even during the worst periods of famine," she replied. "That female is not going to eat her baby. She's using it for bait. Watch."

The bol huffed once more, then thudded off a short distance, just past the rise in the hill. The air was heavy with the scent of blood. Soon enough, another creature came out of the brush, drawn by the smell.

It was a lone huurton. It approached slowly, cautiously, but then put on a burst of speed and ran up to the fresh kill. Noisily, it ripped hunks of flesh free with its sharp canines. The adult bol came crashing out of her hiding spot, grabbed the huurton by the back, and shook it in almost the exact fashion that she had her infant. The huurton bleated in agony as it was tossed from one side to the other. The powerful incisors of the bol cut through the thick, woolly hide in a matter of moments. Finally, the huurton went limp in the bol's huge jaws. The lizard flipped the lifeless body to the ground and began to devour it.

Finn and Dusque watched the feeding for a while without saying a word. Eventually, Finn turned to Dusque and asked, "Why did she do that?"

"Because she was dying and her infant was, too," she explained.

"So she killed her infant?" he asked with a trace of disgust.

"Obviously the feeding has been scarce around here lately. The adult bol looked thin and her infant was emaciated. She couldn't feed her baby; that much is certain. Rather than let it face a miserable death by starvation, she killed it."

"But she deliberately used it as bait!"

"Even stronger than her desire to save her offspring from suffering is her instinct to survive. It makes sense for the preservation of the species. She did what she had to, sacrificed what she had to in order to save herself." She stopped briefly, suddenly thinking of the Rebels she had encountered— which reminded her that they still had a mission to complete.

"Come on," she told him. "While she's feeding, we should be able to slip past her."

They maneuvered around the feeding bol without alerting her to their presence. Dusque noticed that Finn remained quiet for some time after they had left the scene of feeding carnage behind.

"It still bothers you, doesn't it?" she asked, breaking the heavy silence between them.

"She killed her own offspring," he replied. "I can't think of a more horrendous betrayal."

"But that's where you're wrong," she said gently. "It was an act of survival. For it to be betrayal, there would have to have been malice involved. Malice and planning," she added.

Dusque's comments only seemed to darken his mood. She wished she knew what was bothering him so much; she wanted to help, but he seemed to want to be left to his thoughts. They walked for some distance without saying another word. It wasn't much longer before a distant glow appeared, close to the horizon. They were almost back to the Imperial base.

Finn slowed to a halt and turned to Dusque. "Make sure your weapons are ready," he said shortly.

"Why?" she asked. "We had no difficulty when we entered the base. Why should it be any different now?"

"We thought we were alone by the waterfall, too, didn't we?"

Dusque fell silent at that. Apparently, her failure at the waterfall had changed his opinion of her abilities. She couldn't bear that thought, and realizing how much his opinion had come to mean to her scared her even more than the evidence of her insecurity.

"What I mean to say is that some time has passed since we passed through there," he explained in a kinder tone. "Something you need to remember is not to count on anything to remain static. Get comfortable with a situation and you can get complacent. In this business, that is the fastest route to dying. Don't trust anything." He said nothing more, but turned to busy himself with his weapon.

Dusque thought about his words as she verified the charge on her heavy blaster. Now that they were so close to success, she wondered if this was just his safety mechanism. She had missed his cue about the Gray Talon—there was no denying that. But how had he seen them so quickly? She knew how to listen and look for cues in the wilderness, but the Gray Talon leader hadn't been clear of the waterfall when he'd surprised them with his threat. How had Finn known so quickly who was there?

She shook her head. It didn't matter how he did it. He was better trained than she was. If he'd stayed alive this long, he must be good at his business. Finn was right when he said there were no second chances. Thinking about it, she realized that it made sense that the last leg of a mission would be the most vulnerable time—simply because one would be elated with victory. Elation led to cockiness, which could lead to mistakes, failure, and death. She decided that was why he was riding her so hard: to make sure she stayed alive.

Once she verified that her blaster had a fresh power pack, she had to conceal it on her person. Both she and Finn had abandoned their cloaks at the waterfall along with the short-circuited scanner. She slipped her blaster into the waistband of her trousers and pulled her tunic down to cover the telltale bulge. Finn slid his weapons into the upper portion of his boots and untucked his trousers to hide them.

"I'm all set," she told him. Suddenly she was struck by another realization. Ever since they had recovered the holocron, Finn had slowly resumed the mantle of leadership. And she had acquiesced easily—mostly because he had made a few pointed remarks that had eroded some of her confidence.

He was hurt pretty badly, she reminded herself. Like a wounded animal, he would have been stripped to his basic self in the moment of absolute agony—and the fact that his main concern, even in the midst of his pain, had been her safety and the success of their mission comforted her. She decided she could take the sudden intensity he was projecting, at least until they were safely away. Then, maybe, she would give him an earful.

"Time to go," he told her, and led the way past the outer walls of the base to enter the compound proper.

Because it was so late, there was only one guard in front of the command building. The dark Imperial flags rippled in the slight breeze. Dusque didn't see anyone else around.

"Looks all right," she offered cautiously.

"Looks like it," Finn agreed, but he didn't sound convinced.

"Can you see the ship from here?" she asked.

Finn craned his neck. "Hard to say."

Dusque took a closer look for herself. Even in the low lights of the base, she could see that another ship had arrived. Its markings and wing structure were unmistakable: an Imperial landing craft. She let out a slow, quiet breath.

"They're here," she whispered.

"Yes," Finn answered darkly.

"Maybe they're just changing troops or something," she suggested hopefully.

Finn shot her a foul expression, and even she knew her words sounded lame. She was terrified that, inexperienced as she was, she might have made a critical error that had betrayed the Rebel Alliance. Maybe the Empire had gotten around to issuing a warrant for her because of her friendship with Tendau, or maybe something she had said or hadn't said to Commander Fuce earlier had tipped them off. Whatever the mistake, she didn't want Finn or the Alliance to have to pay for it. She handed Finn her pack and started to walk toward the craft.

Finn grabbed her by her arm and yanked her back into the shadows. "What are you doing?" He shoved the bag back into her hands.

"I'm doing what I have to so that I can live with myself," she replied.

"What are you talking about?"

She looked him deeply in the eyes and confessed, "I must have done something, or else it's simply because of who I am, but they've caught up to us. If I turn myself in, that will give you a brief window when you can escape. I can't let you or the Rebel Alliance down. Too much depends on this."

"The only way I'm leaving is with you," he told her. He unslung his pack and crouched down. He tugged Dusque by the arm until she dropped down, too. He tossed a few sundry items onto the ground before pulling out three round objects. Thermal detonators.

"What did you have in mind?" she asked him.

He flashed her a wicked grin. "A few carefully placed explosions should provide enough cover for both of us to escape," he told her. "I'll simply manually reprogram the timer mechanism to give us a few more minutes and alternate them so they go off at staggered times. That'll keep them running."

As he quickly adjusted the timers on the switches, Dusque kept an eye out for any activity. The post remained quiet.

"Okay," he told her. "Take this one and flip the switch when you get near the cantina. I'm going to lay one down by the data terminal near the medcenter, and the last one close to the Imperial craft. Now go!"

Dusque crouched low and scurried over to the cantina. Before releasing the trigger, though, she ducked her head in the door. The cantina was as deserted as the base appeared to be. She tossed the detonator inside and ran back to where she had been standing with Finn. She could see him returning from the Imperial ship, running fast. He crouched down next to her.

"Now we wait for the fireworks," he said, sounding satisfied.

After a long moment, the detonator in the medcenter went off. An alarm sounded from somewhere, and suddenly troops streamed out of what Dusque had wrongly assumed was an empty building. She noted bleakly that there were far more troopers here now than had been here when they had arrived. Her suspicions were sadly confirmed. They had been found out.

A moment later, the detonator in the cantina exploded, sending debris flying into the air. Finn threw his arms over Dusque to shield her from the initial wreckage that was raining down on them. When he saw that some of the stormtroopers had split up to investigate the new explosion, he jumped to his feet and yanked Dusque up.

"Now's our chance!" he shouted. She could barely hear him over the sirens and the secondary explosion caused by more of the medical equipment igniting.

Finn gripped a blaster in one hand and held on to her hand with the other. He ran as fast as his injured leg would allow him, tugging on Dusque as he went. She, too, had pulled out her blaster and was looking about wildly, frightened and confused. They were almost to the shuttle when a stormtrooper who was investigating the new explosion near the medcenter saw them.

"They're over here!" Even Dusque could hear his transmission.

They both opened fire as more stormtroopers started to turn at the sound of the laser blasts. Dusque was grateful for the scope on the blaster that allowed her to aim through the smoke and haze that filled the compound. She fired at anything that moved, even as Finn pulled her behind the Imperial landing craft for cover.

Somehow, in all the smoke and confusion, a stormtrooper slipped along the other side of the craft. Neither Finn nor Dusque saw him. The shuttle had been sealed, and Finn set to work with an electronic lock breaker to open the hatch while Dusque laid down cover fire. The stormtrooper caught her by surprise.

"Drop your weapons!" he shouted.

Whirling around to face him, Dusque could see that he had her in his sights. There was no chance she could swing her arm around fast enough to take him out. But she could block his view of Finn, so that Finn, at least, might get to safety.

"All right," she shouted, letting the blaster slip from her fingers. She slowly raised her hands, hoping to buy Finn a few more precious seconds.

"Move over here," the stormtrooper ordered. But just as Dusque was about to comply, two things happened.

Finn shouted, "Got it!" and the detonator under the Imperial ship exploded, knocking Dusque off her feet and incinerating the stormtrooper. Dazed, Dusque felt Finn yank her by her shirt toward the shuttle.

"I got it," she mumbled. "Just fire this thing up."

After a brief, questioning look at her, he dashed inside. While the shuttle rumbled to life, Dusque crawled up the hatch stairs and tumbled on board. She staggered to her feet and slammed the door-control panel. The stairs retracted and the hatch sealed up.

"Go, go, go!" she cried to Finn.

He punched the controls and the shuttle took off at a frightening angle. From the viewport, Dusque could see that the small outpost was in flames. The image grew smaller and smaller as they left Dantooine's atmosphere. Most important, Dusque didn't see anyone in pursuit. They were safe.

She made her way into the cockpit and slumped down into the free chair. She looked at Finn and almost laughed aloud.

"We did it," she said. "We really did it." And she laid her pack, the holocron still nestled inside, on top of the controls for Finn to see.

He turned to her and said, "You're right. We're done."

She wondered why he sounded so sad.

FOURTEEN

As Finn piloted the ship, Dusque stared into the silence of space. They had managed to escape the planet not only with the holocron, but alive. She let her head drop back against the seat and closed her eyes. A contented smile spread across her face.

"You okay?" Finn asked her.

She turned toward him and opened her eyes. "Yes," she answered. "Yes, I'm fine." She tried to include him in her smile, but he remained stoic. She frowned slightly, wondering why he was so serious. Then her gaze trailed down to his wounded leg and she saw that it was bleeding.

"C'mon," she told him. "Let's go in back so I can treat that more properly."

"It'll be fine," he said dismissively. "Don't worry."

"It'll be even better after I take care of it. We're safe in hyperspace. No one's following."

Finn looked at her and then, to her relief, relented. "All right. I just have to check one thing. Head aft and I'll meet you there. Okay?"

"Don't take too long," Dusque told him. She wondered why men could sometimes be so difficult and fight the only logical choice in front of them.

She got up and walked back to the main cabin. Only a few items had been knocked loose by their abrupt departure, and none of them was too damaged. She picked up some storage containers and returned them to their original locations. She was looking for the more comprehensive medkit she knew was on board. She found it in a cabinet.

Bringing it over to a small table, she sat on the bench behind it. The seat wrapped around the edge of the ship for about three meters. She didn't understand why on such a small ship, the designers felt the need to place items like this on board. Perhaps, she thought, they recognized how absolutely unnatural space travel was, and so they added such touches to ground travelers and make things seem more familiar somehow. At any rate, it was coming in handy now.

She opened up the kit and started laying out some of the supplies. She was about to call for Finn when she heard him shuffling through the cabin. By his gait, she could tell that his leg was stiffening up; if they didn't treat it soon, there would probably be some scarring. She got up to help him the rest of the way, but he waved her back.

"I'm not that bad off," he told her, a ghost of a grin on his face. "At least," he paused, looking at the supplies and then at Dusque, "I'm not that bad *yet*. You haven't started, however."

Dusque swatted at him playfully, glad that he was becoming more like the man she was getting to know. She was sure that after he was treated properly, his good spirits would return.

"Have a seat," she said, indicating the bench. He lowered himself down gingerly and extended his injured leg. Dusque pulled over one of the empty containers, set it near him, and, using it as a small stool, cut away his pant leg well above the injury. Finn grimaced.

"Sorry," she said, as she tossed the piece of cloth off to the side. With the wound more clearly exposed, Dusque could see that the damage was a little worse than she had thought. The bacta patch had probably kept the injury from becoming infected, but it hadn't done much more than that.

"We shouldn't have had you walk on it," she said, after inspecting the wound more closely.

"There wasn't a choice, was there?"

Shaking her head, she grabbed for a bulb of antiseptic wash. As she irrigated the wound and the surrounding area, Finn winced. He leaned his head back, and in a similar pose to the one Dusque had struck in the cockpit, he closed his eyes. But there was no smile on his tightly clamped mouth.

"That's what it really comes down to, doesn't it?" he gritted.

Dusque was so involved in cleaning out his injury that she was only partially listening.

"It's the choices we make in our lives. And once

we make them, we have to live with the consequences of our decisions," he continued softly.

Dusque looked up and saw that he was staring at her with his jet-black eyes. She paused, holding up a sterilizer for the burn, and finally let some of his words sink in.

"That's not always true," she said. "Sometimes decisions can be modified; the results can be changed when someone else comes into the equation."

She focused her attention back on his leg. "Like this, for example. You were wounded, but because we have the supplies, we can change the outcome. This wound doesn't have to leave any marks or lasting damage behind. We can effect a change."

She applied an antibiotic, but was concerned when the salve didn't penetrate as deeply as she felt it needed to. She searched through the more extensive medkit, pulled out a small canister, and started to apply the contents to Finn's wound.

"What's that?" he asked.

"It's chromostring," she explained. "It'll allow a deeper penetration of some of the medications without nerve damage."

"You know this stuff pretty well," he remarked.

She glanced up at him and smiled. "Well, believe it or not, sometimes collecting samples and specimens can get a little dangerous." She was rewarded by a smile from Finn.

As she rummaged through the kit, she continued with her previous train of thought. "While you're right that we do make choices and have to live with them, sometimes we're presented with the opportunity to make new ones. Like me, for example. I thought I had my life in order—"

"And I ripped you out of it," Finn finished for her.

"And you gave me a set of new choices," she corrected.

"Did I?" he asked. Dusque could swear she heard bitterness in his voice.

But her search in the medkit was distracting her. "Blast," she swore softly.

"What is it?" Finn asked.

"There's no tissue regenerator in here," she said disgustedly. "I'll have to make do with a couple of larger bacta patches. When we get back to Corellia, we're going to have to get this treated immediately." She rummaged through the kit once more, in case she had missed it.

"I thought for certain there would be one in here," she complained. She finished placing the last of the patches on his leg. "All done. Not quite good as new yet, but it will be." She smiled at him.

He reached over and caught her chin with his hand. "Sometimes it's just not possible to foresee everything," he said in an almost-whisper.

Although the cabin was temperature controlled, Dusque shivered. She placed both of her slim hands on his face. She could feel the rough texture of his skin, a new growth of beard starting to form. She delicately brushed away a lock of his unruly hair so that she could see his eyes more clearly. She realized that with such dark irises, there was no way to see his pupils; it made his eyes seem bottomless. She had never met a man like him before, she thought.

Lost in the depths of his eyes, Dusque wasn't sure who kissed whom.

After what seemed an eternity, Finn broke away from her.

"Finn—" Dusque began.

A ringing tone from the cockpit interrupted her, and Finn looked relieved. "I—uh—it's time to drop out of hyperspace," he stammered.

Bewildered, Dusque didn't know what to say. "I think I'll stay back here for a bit. Call me if you need me."

"All right," he said with a sad smile.

For a long time Dusque sat alone, wondering what had just happened between them. Thinking about what Finn had said about choices and consequences, she realized he was right. That was what it came down to: deciding who and what you were going to be, and being able to live with those decisions.

She thought back on the last few days and realized that her life had been transformed. She had thought she'd left behind so much, but in retrospect the only thing she had abandoned was an empty shell. Not a real life, but the shadow of one. As she sat and swiveled from side to side in the chair, she realized that she didn't even feel tired anymore. She felt invigorated and pleased with herself. The only concern she had was Finn.

She had always been so good at keeping people at

a distance, from her family to the colleagues in her sterile work environment. The only one who had found a crack in her armor had been Tendau. With his death, that crack seemed to have become a split that Finn had slipped into. She couldn't deny that she had strong feelings for him. That was something she had never expected.

She had to talk to him—that was all there was to it. When she felt the ship drop out of hyperspace, she figured that now seemed as good a time as any for that conversation. She got up and went forward to the cockpit.

What she saw made her stop dead in her tracks.

"Finn?" she whispered.

He was huddled over the control console, his back toward her. Then, as she moved closer, she saw the holocron. It was sitting in a receptacle on the panel, and a readout nearby showed a bar scale. Horrified, she realized that he was downloading the data from the holocron and transmitting it.

"What are you doing?" she shouted, running the rest of the way to him. Before he could say or do anything, she knocked the holocron out of the computer port. Out of the corner of her eye, she saw him hit a switch—and with a dark certainty she knew what he had done. She slammed her fist down on the control panel, uncertain if she had stopped the entire transmission.

"What were you thinking?" she yelled at him. "Don't you remember what Leia said? Under no circumstances were we to try to transmit any data from the holocron. If we thought we were in trouble, we were to destroy it!"

He looked at her with an unreadable expression. She ran over to the holocron and scooped it up. Looking about, she located the tiny chamber in the sidewall of the cockpit, tossed the holocron into it, and slammed the door shut. Before Finn could raise a hand to stop her, she jettisoned the holocron into space. Then she placed both her hands against the hull, swallowed hard, and tried to regain her composure.

"Why would you risk it?" She moved closer to him and touched his arm. "Why, Finn?"

A flash caught her eye and she noticed a blip on the radar. "Those are probably Imperials following us. They could have intercepted the transmission! We might have done all this for nothing!"

He shook his head. "It's not Imperials."

"It's right there on the radar," she argued. "And we don't have time for this, if an Imperial agent is on our tail."

Finn held his ground. "There's no way that can be an Imperial agent."

Dusque was startled by his flat monotone. "How do you know?" she whispered.

"I know there are no agents of the Empire following us because—" He paused and drew in a deep breath. "I am the Imperial agent."

For a moment, Dusque felt as she had on the stone bridge inside the cave. She didn't know which way was up or down, and everything seemed slightly unreal. She swallowed again, suddenly feeling hot and claustrophobic.

"What?" she whispered and her voice sounded like it was light-years away.

He turned and faced her fully. "I'm the agent," he repeated.

"That can't be," Dusque cried. "It can't be. You saved me when Tendau was executed, when the Imperials shot us down—"

"Stop and think for a moment," he snapped at her. "You're a scientist—use that analytical brain of yours."

Dusque actually flinched at the tone of his voice.

"Don't you think it was just a little too coincidental that after our first meeting, when you said you didn't want to lose anything more to the Empire and you turned me down, the Hammerhead was so conveniently arrested? And who just happened to be there to drag you away after you saw him murdered?"

Dusque blinked rapidly as her eyes filled with unshed tears. "You killed him?" she whispered.

"I arranged it," he admitted coldly.

"But I did see him talking with some Bothans in Moenia, and when I asked him about it, he denied it," she said.

"Did it happen before or after I put the thought into your head that he might be a spy? My guess," he added, "is that it happened after."

And Dusque realized she had been more suspicious of everything after her first meeting with Finn.

She had jumped to conclusions about Tendau and now knew he had died for nothing; the whole thing had been no more than a ruse to draw her out. She stared at Finn, unable to accept what she was hearing and even more horrified that he looked so angry. *She* was the only one who had a right to be angry, she thought.

"And now you're furious that I didn't somehow figure this all out? Didn't somehow guess that the man I was falling in love with was a mask? That he didn't exist at all? Congratulate yourself," she told him bitterly, "because you are very good at your job."

His shoulders sagged a little under the weight of her accusing stare.

"Don't you see?" he entreated her, and he looked again like the man she thought she knew. "Why do you think I asked you about your loyalty? When I asked you where your loyalties were, I had hoped that you were going to turn out to have only been searching for revenge. I had hoped your loyalty to the Empire ran as deeply as mine. After some of what you told me, I thought it did."

"Don't mistake fear for loyalty," she said through gritted teeth. "And don't try to fool yourself that you're loyal to them; you're afraid as much as I was."

She stood staring at him and she still could not believe what she was hearing. But, unbidden, some of the things he had said and done came back to haunt her.

"It doesn't make sense," she said, shaking her head. "If what you say is true and you are loyal to the Empire, why were we attacked on the way to Corellia? That was a little too close to have been planned."

"It *was* close," he admitted. "If I had been piloting the ship alone, I would've had a chance to signal where I was and the location of the Rebel base. But I didn't get to in time."

Dusque thought back to when the Mon Calamari's ship had started to plummet and she had heard an explosion. It had come from inside the cockpit; from a weapon that Finn had explained to her wasn't able to pierce a ship's hull.

"You killed the pilot," she whispered, dumbstruck.

Finn nodded. "I was able to get them to break off the attack, but we crashed before I could do more."

"And once we got to the base," she finished slowly, "you never had a moment alone."

"I just figured I would wait until we had retrieved the holocron. Then I could turn everything over to the Empire."

"So you just used me," she said bitterly, "to get everything that you wanted. The only thing I don't understand is why you didn't just turn me in back at the base. Why create all that damage when your superiors were probably there? I don't understand."

Finn was silent.

"Why?" she demanded. "You were, after all, done with me."

His face abruptly twisted in anguish. "I couldn't."

"Why not?" she asked him quietly.

"Because it was you," he shouted. "There you were," he admitted more calmly, "ready to march toward your death all to save me and the Rebels, and I just couldn't let you go. I couldn't let them have you."

Dusque could see that he was trembling slightly. There was no reason for him to lie to her now; there was no point.

"It's not too late," he told her. "We can both return to the Emperor. I can tell them some of the other Rebels arrived as backup and they were the ones responsible for the chaos at the base. If we return together with the information in this computer"—he tapped the console—"we'll both be safe. And we can be together," he pleaded. "Please."

Dusque was in turmoil. And she was so torn, because she knew exactly how he felt. She knew what it was like to live in the shadow of the Empire. But the man in front of her had helped her step out of that shadow. And if he could do that for her, she thought that maybe, just maybe, she could do the same for him.

"I can't go back," she told him and stepped closer. "Not ever. But you don't have to, either. Remember what you said about choices and consequences? Right here and now, you can choose to change your life. I know the Rebel Alliance—Leia and the others—will forgive you and take you in. It is that ability to forgive, that soul, that separates the

Rebels from the Empire." She moved closer still as she saw he was chewing his lip.

"And I haven't forgotten how you told me to go on without you at the waterfall, or how you shielded me from the blasts at the outpost. You can tell yourself whatever you like," she said, moving to stand directly in front of him, "but that was your true self. I know that in here—" She laid her hand on his chest. "—you are a good man. It will be all right. Trust me." He had never looked more vulnerable to her than he did in that moment.

He pulled her into his arms and embraced her fiercely. She stroked the back of his head and said again, "It will be all right."

"I'm sorry," he whispered in her ear. "I'm so sorry."

She pulled slightly away from him, wanting to see his face. When her gray eyes locked with his, she heard a strange sound and felt something odd. Still looking perplexed, Dusque took a step back and felt Finn's arms drop away. He turned from her, and she lowered her gaze to his right hand. There, covered in blood, was the hunting knife he kept sheathed in his sleeve. She had forgotten about it.

Stunned, she reached for him. "Finn, what have you done?"

At that moment, her legs buckled out from under her. She crashed onto her knees and dumbly looked down at the crimson flower blooming across her shirtfront. She touched it and pulled her hand away to see that it was covered in blood. She looked at Finn in bewilderment. She fell backward into the side of the hull and tried to focus on Finn.

"Why?" Her voice sounded weak and distant.

"I'm sorry," was all he could say. "I told you that sooner or later everyone betrays those they love to the Empire. It's inevitable."

He dropped to her side. Hazily, Dusque wondered if he was going to finish her off, although she believed she was dead already.

"I can't be with you," he confessed. "I fear the Empire too much."

His words echoed strangely in her ears, so similar to the ones she had said to him when they first met. It was as though they were completing a strange dance that had finally come full circle. Only this time, she was the one without fear.

Finn swallowed hard as he looked at her. He reached down, and Dusque couldn't tell if he still held the knife or not. Before he could touch her, the shuttle jostled ominously.

"We're being boarded," Dusque heard him say. She could only lie there and watch as he rose and ran to the rear of the vessel. She heard a hatch open and seal, and then the ship rocked again.

She felt her lids grow heavy. She tried once to stand, and a detached part of her mind was genuinely amazed that she couldn't even lift her hand any longer. She lay there in a heap.

The shuttle was jostled again, and the movement

caused Dusque to open her eyes just a crack. Although her vision was blurring, she could see several figures enter the cabin. None, she noticed, wore Imperial garb. One of them, a blond human male, looked familiar to Dusque, although she couldn't get her mind to focus on any one topic enough to try to figure out who he was.

He dropped to her side as his two companions went to the back of the ship. He stared at her, a worried look in his sky-blue eyes.

"I know you, don't I?" Dusque asked weakly.

"My name is Luke Skywalker. You saw me on Corellia." His voice was young and gentle. While he spoke to her, he pulled out a device and tried to treat the wound in Dusque's chest.

"The escape pod's been jettisoned," one of the others told him.

With the last bit of strength she had, Dusque placed her hand on Luke's arm and struggled to sit up. "You've got to stop him," she whispered, "before he gets back to his base. Finn is a . . ." She fell back weakly before she could say the word *traitor*.

"Blast," he said. "This anticoagulant isn't clotting her fast enough." He ordered one of the Rebel soldiers to retrieve something from their ship.

"Not important," Dusque mumbled. "You've got to stop him. Not important . . ." Her voice trailed off and her lids started to close.

"Yes, you are," she heard the young man with the ancient eyes whisper in her ear, and she won-

dered if that would be the last thing she ever heard.
Before she faded away, she realized it was a worthy
eulogy.

"You *are* important," he said.

FIFTEEN

The heavy mists blanketed the Emperor's Retreat like a shroud. Standing a solitary watch was a rigid figure. Dressed in dark clothes, Finn listened to the lonely cry of the peko peko. For some reason, the sound reminded him of a woman wailing. Even though it was raining lightly, he didn't seek shelter, as though he wasn't worthy of any protection from the elements. Or perhaps, it was because he didn't seem to feel anything anymore.

"Commander Darktrin," a deep voice called.

Finn turned about and marched off the stone balcony into a lushly carpeted hallway. The gold-trimmed crimson rug was meant to look sumptuous, but now it reminded Finn of a river of blood—and no matter where he turned, he had to walk through it. Standing in the center of the hall was Darth Vader, Dark Lord of the Sith. His black armor gleamed like polished ebony, although it seemed that rather than reflect light, it took it all in to some secret place like a black hole. The only sound besides the rain was his mechanical breathing.

Finn had only been in Vader's presence a few times in his service to the Empire. Three of those occasions had been to witness the deaths of men who had failed in their duty to the Dark Lord. Because Finn had been instructed to retrieve and return with the Jedi holocron, he suspected he knew what was about to happen. Strangely, he didn't feel afraid; he just felt numb. It was as though when he had stabbed Dusque in the heart, he had cut out his own, as well.

"Yes, Lord Vader?" he asked respectfully.

"Your transmission from the Rebel shuttle was incomplete," Darth Vader began without preamble.

Finn lowered his head. "I understand, my lord. I failed in my task to the Emperor."

"Yes," Vader agreed heavily.

"I welcome any punishment you deem fit," Finn said, raising his head to stare into the skull-like breath mask that forever hid the Sith Lord's face from view.

Finn stood for some time in Vader's presence. Not a word was uttered. The only sound remained the heavy intake and exhalation of Vader's breathing. Unconsciously, Finn found himself breathing in time with him. He did not turn away from Vader's unblinking stare.

"While it was incomplete," Vader eventually continued, as he started walking down the hallway, "several names did come through." He paused and waited for Finn to walk by his side. "So, in a broader sense, the mission was not a total failure," Vader continued.

"What will you do?" Finn asked.

"Several different agents will be dispatched soon enough to remove the Rebel threat from our midst," the Dark Lord explained. "Since you have been gone, we have had an increase in recruits. Some show great promise, while others . . ." He left the statement unfinished.

"And the others, my lord?" Finn inquired, not out of any real interest but because he felt it was required of him.

"And when the others die in their attempts, it will be no great loss," the Dark Lord finished without any emotion.

"While I have decided to let you live," Vader continued, "I have not yet decided what punishment is fitting for your failure."

"I understand, my lord."

"I am somewhat at a loss to understand," Vader continued, "why you were not able to transfer the holocron over to my agents at the Dantooine outpost."

"My lord, I did not realize the woman had placed those charges around the base. I was caught as off guard as the other agents were."

"Ah," Vader breathed. "The woman you killed aboard the shuttle."

"Yes," Finn said, almost tripping over the words. "She turned out not to be what I had anticipated."

"Still, you put an end to any threat she might

have posed to the Empire. That is partly why I don't retire you now. And the other," he rasped, "is because is I still sense great potential in you."

They walked in silence again. Eventually, Vader stopped and looked at him. "And what of the Rebel base on Corellia? In your report, you make mention of it, and yet I don't see the coordinates listed anywhere."

Finn stared at Vader for a long time before he spoke. "The reason is simple enough, my lord," he eventually said. "When I was taken to the secret location, the Rebels were in the process of breaking it down and emptying the buildings. Former Princess Leia Organa mentioned that they were about to relocate offworld and would send a transmission when we contacted them after our departure for Dantooine.

"Because the woman on board began to suspect my identity, I had to eliminate her before I could find out where they had relocated," he finished.

Vader nodded. "I see," he hissed. "Very well," he said after a brief pause, "we are done for now, Commander."

Finn saluted and turned to go, but his curiosity had gotten the better of him. Thinking he had nothing to lose, he turned back and cleared his throat. "My lord?" he asked.

"What is it, Commander?" Even though he spoke through a breath mask, there was no mistaking the chill in his tone.

"You said that you sensed potential in me. What did you mean by that?"

Vader walked back to Finn and looked down at him. "You have always been a faithful servant to us," he began, "but since your return, you seem cleansed."

"My lord?"

"I sense anger in you where there was none before. And that fire will burn and purify you over time. I am willing to give you that time. For now." And with that, he turned and departed.

Finn didn't know what to make of the Sith Lord's pronouncement. He wandered aimlessly and found himself back on the balcony, watching the clouded sky darken as night drew near.

He's right, Finn thought. *I am* angry. *Vader thinks I'm angry with the Rebels, but I know the truth. I'm angry with me.*

The clouds continued to thicken, denying Finn a view of the stars. He leaned his hands against the cold stone railing and stared at the night. He squeezed his eyes shut, but all he could see behind his lids was Dusque's face. She haunted his every waking moment.

He realized that it was probably some members of the Rebel Alliance who had boarded their shuttle after he'd left. If they had reached her in time, Dusque might have survived. They would have had to return to Corellia with her, however. Her injury was too severe for a medkit to heal. The only gift he had left to give her was safety. So he had lied to

Vader and the others about the location of their base. His heart was his last gift.

The gray skies only served to remind him of Dusque's eyes, and he realized he had no way of learning if she was alive. He placed a callused hand against his heart, and the single tear he shed became meaningless and insignificant in the rain.

Dusque leaned against the railing and looked out at the Corellian sky. Talus was visible, as well as a few other celestial bodies she recognized. But she wasn't really looking at them. The dark sky reminded her of Finn's eyes, and how she could almost lose herself in them. Even though he was gone, she remembered every line of his face. What troubled her most was the look he had worn when he had stabbed her in the chest. She couldn't decipher it, and that haunted her. Absently she scratched at the mostly healed scar near her breastbone and didn't notice that a door had opened behind her.

"What are you doing standing out there in the cold? You shouldn't even be on your feet yet."

Dusque turned at the sound to see that Princess Leia had entered her chamber. The woman was always in motion, Dusque thought, and she wondered when she ever found time to rest. Dressed in white, her long hair tied back, she seemed more mythical than real at times.

Dusque shifted completely around but made no

move to step inside. Her sandy hair blew around her in the breeze like a living thing. "If it hadn't have been for you—"she nodded to Luke, who was right behind Leia, "—I wouldn't be standing at all." And she grinned ruefully at him.

He's blushing, she thought.

"I'm glad I was there in time," he said sincerely.

"Yes," Leia said. "I don't think you would have survived without him."

"No," Dusque agreed, and rubbed at her scar again. "Why were you following?" she asked, wanting to change the subject.

"I had a feeling," Luke told her.

"His feelings have a way of turning out to be right," Leia explained. "But when he told me there was something not right about one of you, I'm afraid that I thought it was you. I didn't know you then," she added, and Dusque got the sense that she was apologizing.

"It's all right," Dusque said easily. "Finn fooled me, too. Here I was, thinking that I was going to face the enemy, and he was with me all along, like some false shadow. I'm sorry I didn't learn the truth before he got his hands on the holocron. What do you think happened to him?"

"Since our scouts haven't seen or heard anything, I can only assume that either he died in space or was executed for not fulfilling his mission. Otherwise," Leia reasoned, "he would have exposed us and our base, and we wouldn't be having this conversation."

"What'll happen now?" Dusque asked, uncertain if Leia's hypothesis made her feel better or worse.

"Well," Leia said with authority, "we were able to get all the information from the shuttle. As best as our technicians can tell, it appears that Finn downloaded the data from the holocron, but wasn't able to transmit all of it to the Empire."

"Do you know what names he managed to send out?" Dusque asked.

"No," Leia replied seriously. "The technicians can tell how many packets of information were sent out, but they can't say which."

Dusque shook her head. "So what will you do now?"

"I will be sending out agents to every name that we retrieved, not only to activate them but to warn them, as well. Since we have no way of knowing who might be in danger, we'll have to find them all." Leia sighed. "It won't be any small task, either. These people are spread throughout the galaxy."

"I'm sorry I wasn't able to destroy the holocron sooner," Dusque told her.

"Don't be," Leia consoled. "You did all that you could."

"Dusque," Luke said, and looked at her earnestly, "you did the right thing. And I'm glad you're all right."

"Thank you," she replied.

He turned to the Princess. "Leia, we'll talk later about this?"

"Yes," the Princess replied. And with that, the ex-farm-boy from Tatooine left.

Leia faced Dusque, and her brown eyes softened. "I should go and let you get some rest." She laid a gentle hand on Dusque's shoulder. "You do still need it. And I'm sure one of our surgical droids can remove that scar."

Dusque moved one hand up to trace the long, knotted lump of scar tissue. "No," she said eventually. "I want to keep it. It'll remind me where my heart is." And she grew silent.

"You will always have a place here, with us," Leia told her.

Dusque looked at Leia. "Thank you." She held out her hand and Leia clasped it warmly, covering it with both of hers.

"No," she corrected Dusque gently, "Thank you. I could not be more proud of your actions if you were my own sister."

Dusque lowered her gaze, suddenly moved. Leia released her hand and started to leave. As she reached the door, she turned and was once again a commander in chief. "Now get back into bed. That's an order."

Dusque smiled. She thought again how tactful Leia was, always seeming to know the right thing to say at the right time. The ex-Senator must have been a very effective politician in her time.

Dusque walked back out onto the balcony. One thing that hadn't changed was that she still felt more comfortable under the stars than under a roof. She was glad there was a certain amount of constancy still left in her life.

"Ah, Finn," she said aloud. There was no hiding the bitterness in her voice. "I look at the sky and I see you." For a moment, she couldn't speak, couldn't even think about the pain he had caused her.

Although she wouldn't admit it to anyone, she was filled with hatred. Much of it was directed at Finn. She hated him for being weak, for betraying her and the Rebel Alliance, for not loving her enough to leave behind his allegiance to the Emperor. But most of all, she hated herself for still loving him.

"It's because of you that I'm here. That much I owe you," she admitted. She thought about what Leia had said about Finn being dead, but couldn't quite bring herself to believe it. It was the only explanation that made sense; otherwise the Imperial forces would have already come down on their heads. And yet, she doubted.

The wind picked up, but Dusque didn't notice the cold. She stared out at the stars, her hair blowing about her face in a great cloud. Besides hatred, she was filled with a great conviction.

"You're out there, somewhere," she whispered

into the night. "When we meet again, we will both know who we are: a traitor and a Rebel soldier. May the Force help us both."

STAR WARS
KNIGHTS
OF THE
OLD REPUBLIC™

It is four thousand years before the Galactic Empire and hundreds of Jedi Knights have fallen in battle against the ruthless Sith. You are the last hope of the Jedi Order. Can you master the awesome power of the Force on your quest to save the Republic? Or will you fall to the lure of the dark side? Hero or villain, savior or conqueror… you alone will determine the fate of the entire galaxy!

- A brand new *Star Wars* role-playing experience with unique characters, creatures, vehicles and planets.

- Learn to use the Force with over 40 different powers - even build your own lightsaber!

- Choose from nine customizable characters including Twi'leks, droids and Wookiees and then bring up to 3 characters along in your party.

- Travel to seven enormous worlds including Tatooine, the Wookiee homeworld of Kashyyyk and the Sith world of Korriban.

- Build your party and upgrade equipment in your own starship, the *Ebon Hawk*.

AVAILABLE FOR PC AND XBOX
AT YOUR FAVORITE SOFTWARE RETAILER

For more information or to order a copy of *Star Wars*: Knights of the Old Republic,
visit www.swkotor.com

BioWare CORP™

STAR WARS
GALAXIES™

AN
EMPIRE DIVIDED™

EXPERIENCE THE GREATEST *STAR WARS*®
SAGA EVER TOLD. YOURS.

Immerse yourself in *Star Wars* like never before.
Declare your allegiance: Rebel, Imperial or remain neutral,
and explore exotic worlds, interact with thousands of
other players online, and fight battles large and small.
Define your own role and be whomever you want to be:
bounty hunter, merchant, smuggler, weaponsmith, hairdresser,
bartender. Make your choices and prepare to take
your rightful place in the *Star Wars* universe.
IT IS YOUR DESTINY.

- Choose from eight customizable species: Humans, Wookiees, Trandoshans, Twi'leks, Bothans, Zabraks, Rodians and Mon Calamari.

- Explore 10 massive worlds, from Tatooine to Naboo. Each environment is meticulously recreated to portray the *Star Wars* galaxy in the greatest possible detail.

- Build everything, from your own weapons and droids to houses, factories and shops.

- Cross paths and interact with famous *Star Wars* characters, including Luke Skywalker, Darth Vader, Han Solo and many, many more.

AVAILABLE NOW
AT YOUR FAVORITE SOFTWARE RETAILER

WWW.STARWARSGALAXIES.COM   WWW.STARWARS.COM
"Internet Connection Required to Play the Game." and "Valid Credit Card or Paid Game Card
(if available) and Additional Recurring Fees Required to Play the Game."

Game Experience May Change During Online Play